GHOSTS
& ASHES

Broken Moon Series

PRAISE FOR
THE STAR HOST
F.T. LUKENS

"Lukens writes a satisfying balance of action and romance in a science fiction setting that will feel familiar to fans of the genre.... Add this title to young adult sci-fi collections, and expect readers to eagerly anticipate the next book in the series."

—*School Library Journal*

"I continued my science fiction kick with a YA novel I have been eyeing for quite some time. The Star Host by F.T. Lukens hooked me from the blurb. It still hasn't let me go, and I finished reading it hours ago. I want more… like right, the heck now. I need more Asher and Ren in my life. You need more Asher and Ren in your lives."

—*Prism Book Alliance*

"The short version is that this book is amazing, and I am hard-pressed to be more coherent than ASKLJFDAH and OMGFLAIL."

—*D.E Atwood, author,* If We Shadows

Copyright © 2017 F.T. Lukens
All Rights Reserved
ISBN 13: 978-1-945053-18-4 (trade)
ISBN 13: 978-1-945053-31-3 (ebook)
Published by Duet, an imprint of Interlude Press
http://duetbooks.com
This is a work of fiction. Names, characters, and places are either a product
of the author's imagination or are used fictitiously. Any resemblance
to real persons, either living or dead, is entirely coincidental.
All trademarks and registered trademarks are the
property of their respective owners.
Book design and Cover illustrations by CB Messer

10 9 8 7 6 5 4 3 2 1

interlude press • new york

To the heroes of sci-fi—past, present, and future

*When your bow is broken and your last arrow spent,
then shoot, shoot with your whole heart.*

—Zen saying

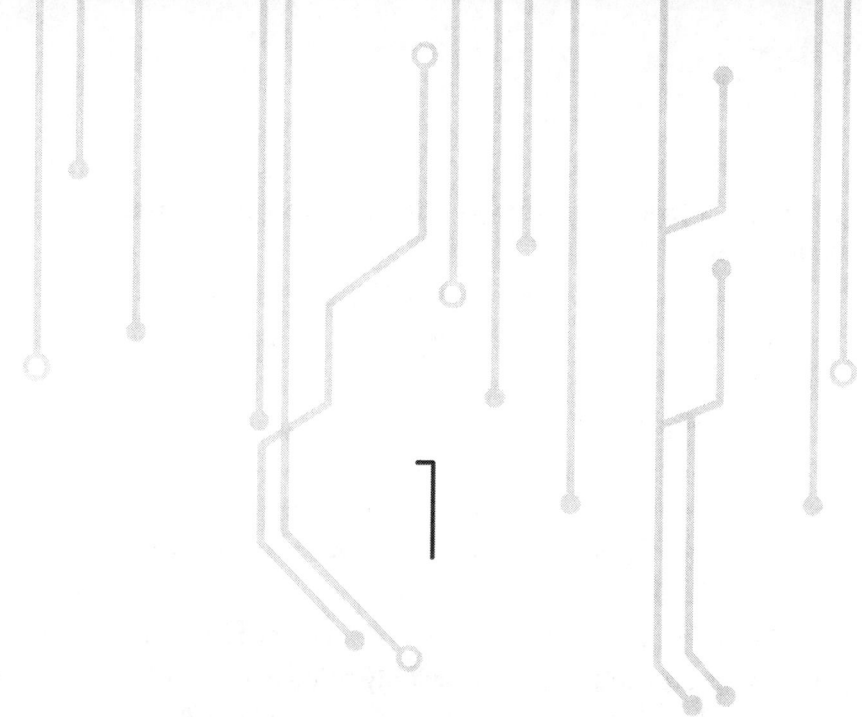

1

IN ALL THE DAYS REN spent dreaming about leaving his home planet and venturing to the stars, his imagination had never conjured a scenario like this.

"What do you think?" Penelope asked, holding up two shirts. "The blue or the black?" Her fingers curled over the stiff collars, and the fabric wrinkled under her grip. Her lips pulling tight over her teeth, she smiled, but it didn't reach her eyes.

"The black," Jakob said, from his position on Ren's bunk. He lounged on his elbows with his booted feet dangling over the edge. "It's subdued."

"But the blue matches Ren's eyes," Penelope said. Then she bit her lip, realizing her misstep. "Or… well… the black then."

Ren's small room on the *Star Stream* was crowded with the three of them in there, but he couldn't begrudge the company of his friends. They thought they were helping.

Ren leaned against the wall, dressed in his sleep clothes with his dark hair hanging in his face. He was half-awake; his senses were fogged, and he was processing slower than usual. The rumble of the ship vibrated through the soles of his bare feet and settled in his middle, where it soothed the pinpricks of panic that were starting to well within him.

He took the shirt Penelope handed him. "Thank you."

"Now, how about trousers?" She opened the small chest of drawers in Ren's room and rooted about.

Jakob yawned. "Weeds, Pen, I think Ren can dress himself."

"Yes," she said. She pulled out a tan pair and shook them. "But we want to make sure he is at his best for this meeting."

Ren raised an eyebrow. "General VanMeerten isn't going to care about my clothes."

"No," Jakob agreed. "She's going to be more interested in the circles under your eyes and that you're awfully pale for a duster."

"We've been in space for months. Of course I'm pale." Ren didn't mention the nightmares, the anxiety attacks, or the call of the ship—all of which contributed to his appearance and his mental state.

Jakob sat up and crossed his arms. "I know. Speaking of, are you going to ask today?"

The shirt fluttered from Ren's slack fingers. His mouth went dry. His pulse ticked up.

"Tact, Jakob," Penelope said, picking up the shirt and smoothing it. She folded it and placed it on Ren's pillow, next to the trousers and a pair of socks.

Ren licked his lips and focused his gaze on the floor. "I don't know. I don't think… It was hard enough to…" Ren trailed off.

Frowning, Jakob nodded. "Right." He took a breath. "Sorry," he added, his tone softer.

Ren lifted his head and managed to give Jakob a conciliatory half-smile.

"I think we should leave Ren to getting dressed. Asher will be here soon, I'm sure."

Ren's heart clenched; the smile dropped from his face.

Jakob stood and stretched his hands over his head. He yawned again, acting as tired as Ren felt. "Sounds good to me. I need a nap."

Penelope rolled her eyes. "Come on then. See you later, Ren."

"Good luck, buddy," Jakob said, clapping his hand hard on Ren's shoulder. "Try to keep the power under wraps."

"Tact," Penelope said again, as they left the room. She closed the door softly behind them.

Ren took a few calming breaths before crossing the small space and fingering the fabric of the shirt. It slid through his fingers, slick and cool, and finer than anything Ren had ever owned before. His new clothes were gifts—thank-yous from Asher's mother for bringing him home from the prison cell.

Ren shook his head and squinched his eyes shut to banish the memories before they could interlace and overwhelm him.

He padded to his connected bathroom and washed as fine tremors snaked up his body and into his hands. He dressed, sat on the edge of his bed, and tapped his foot against the deck plate. He stood again; his potential energy demanding to be kinetic.

Ren paced. He stalked the length of his cell—no, his room—it was his room on the *Star Stream*. He had to remember that. He couldn't become mired in memories, not now, not this time.

He shook his head and pressed his palms against his ears to try to silence his swirling thoughts, but they mounted, escalating into a cacophony. Panic choked him, and his inhale sounded reedy. His body was a live wire, a string pulled taut. His muscles were tense, and he shook out his hands to release the excess energy.

He hated these meetings. He hated *waiting* for these meetings.

Standing in front of General VanMeerten, the senior Phoenix Corps member who decided his fate, was nerve wracking, even when Ren was well. But now that he wasn't well, the daily meetings were worse—so much worse.

He grabbed his brown hair, tugged on the long strands, and focused on the pain to drown out the fear. He needed to be grounded in his body, not tangled in the ship. He needed an anchor. He needed Asher, but….

Ren pressed his fingers against his eyelids while visions and memories flashed through the black. He took another breath, shorter, gasping. Dread was a crushing weight on his chest. Bile crawled up his throat. Terror twisted his insides. His breathing was too rapid; he was on the edge of hyperventilating. The scope of his vision darkened on its edges. His heart pounded.

Ren's legs gave out, and he fell heavily to the deck plate; his knees banged on the metal. He hunched, wheezing, feeling as if he was drowning on land. He pressed his sweaty hands to the floor, took comfort in the thrum of the ship, and allowed his senses to fuzz out.

⊣⊢

The blaring of alarms wrenched Ren out of the panic attack. It was quickly followed by the sound of someone pounding at his door and calling his name. The voice was frantic, hoarse, and painfully familiar.

Cheek pressed to the floor, heart beating hard in his ears, Ren came back to himself. Drenched in sweat, he panted as he rolled to his back and stared at the ceiling. He took a moment to remember where he was; the fog of panic was thick in his head. In the glow of emergency lights and the red flash of claxons, he saw taped above him the stupid picture of a spaceship Jakob had drawn. The reminder jolted Ren to the present.

He was on the *Star Stream*. He was safe. He was *safe*. Well, relatively so, if the alarms were any indication.

Ren's chest was tight and his throat was raw, as if he'd been screaming. Maybe he had been. His grasp of reality was tenuous recently. Taking stock, Ren noted the air was cold in his lungs and on his skin—it tasted stale. That wasn't right.

Oh, yes, the alarms. Something was wrong with the ship. He could fix it. Untangling his consciousness, Ren pulled his attention to the situation at hand.

Damp shirt twisted around his body, he sat up and pressed his palm to the metal of the hull by the comm. He entered the systems and found the problem instinctively. Life support was failing, the air recyclers had stopped, oxygen levels were falling rapidly, and the temperature had dropped to freezing.

Ren fixed the glitch and restored power to the systems that had been blocked. The high-pitched whine of the ship's warning system was replaced by the rapid cadence of a fist striking the door.

"Ren! Ren! Can you hear me?"

Asher.

There was a time when Asher's voice, his presence, his touch, could snap Ren back to his corporeal self. A remnant of that remained, but it was a memory, an echo.

The deck plate was cold against the soles of Ren's bare feet when he stood, and his skin prickled with goosebumps. How had it become so cold so quickly? How long had he been out? What had he done to the ship?

With a thought, Ren sent a blast of heat through the air vents to all the crew areas as an apology.

He crossed the room to open the door. The lock disengaged without Ren touching it. Asher stood on the other side. His fist was raised in mid-movement, and Ren was certain only Asher's military training kept him from accidentally punching Ren in the nose.

"I'm all right," Ren said.

Asher dropped his hand. "That's debatable." His breath puffed out in a cloud.

Ren nodded and pushed his hair from his eyes. It fell right back. "Is everyone okay?"

Asher leaned against the doorjamb and crossed his arms. His muscles bulged. His cheeks had flushed from the cold; twin lines of pink showed along his cheekbones. He looked tired when he raised his eyebrows. Ren saw smudges of blue under his eyes. He frowned. "I assume so. The alarms stopped. That means everything is fixed. Right?"

Ren shrugged. "I don't think the crew is going to die gasping if that's what you mean."

Gasping.

Ren took a step back, and rubbed his chest. *Gasping.* The word triggered a sense memory from the attack, of Ren not being able to breathe, of not being able to get air.

"Ren," Asher said, expression going soft. "Are *you* okay?" He reached out but stopped, curling his fingers in toward his palm.

Lost in the implications, Ren stared at the aborted movement. He nodded. "I felt like I was drowning."

"Ah, that… makes a morbid kind of sense."

"I'm sorry." Ren pulled at the collar of his shirt because he found the fabric suffocating, and then he shivered as sweat dried on the back of his neck and left him cold. His skin tingled. "I couldn't breathe and I guess I made it so the rest of you couldn't either. I'm sorry. I'll try harder. Did anyone see?"

"It wasn't on the vid screens this time."

Okay, that was… okay. A small victory, at least.

The comm by Ren's door crackled to life.

"Shipwide," Rowan's voice cut through the static. "Everyone okay?"

Ren listened intently as a chorus of voices rang out over the comm system. Penelope and Jakob were fine in the common room. Lucas shouted through from his bunk. Ollie and Millicent answered from the cargo bay.

Asher pressed the small button next to Ren's door. "Ren and Ash checking in. All is well."

"That's questionable," Rowan said. "But all right. As you were, everyone. Except you, Ren. Let's try not to break any other valuable parts of the ship today."

Ren stretched out with a shaking hand and hit the comm. "Noted, Captain."

"Rowan out."

Asher fidgeted in the doorway. He reached out again, but paused, retreated, and clasped his hands behind him. He straightened and pulled his shoulders back.

Asher cleared his throat. "Your top button is undone."

Ren's shirt had pulled from his trousers. His hair was a mess. He knew he had dark circles under his eyes from lack of sleep. And Asher worried over a button, as if that was the one detail stopping General VanMeerten from taking Ren from the *Star Stream* and locking him away.

"Thanks." Ren raised shaking hands and fumbled with the buttonhole.

After a moment, Asher stepped closer. "Here. Let me."

Ren dropped his hands. If they waited for his fingers to stop trembling, they'd be late to the meeting. At the thought, his breath caught.

Asher's fingers were strong and firm but cold when they grazed the skin of Ren's neck. He smoothed a wrinkle over Ren's collarbone.

"There."

"Am I presentable now?" Ren's voice was a croak.

Asher assessed him. "We have time for you to freshen up."

So, Ren looked like absolute hell. Asher was gracious enough not to say it outright this time.

Despite the early hour, Asher wore his uniform. The crisp black fabric did wonders for his muscular frame. The symbol of the Phoenix Corps blazed on the outside of his upper arm—a stylized red bird rising from flames with wings outstretched. Ren stared at it. Though it was an image that had intrigued Ren when he was a child sneaking into his mother's things, and later had awed Ren when Asher wore it, he had begun to resent it. It invaded every aspect of his life, and sometimes he wished he'd never laid eyes on it.

Ren went back into his room and into the en-suite bathroom. Asher sat on Ren's bunk.

"Have you slept recently?"

Ren grasped the sink with both hands. "No," he admitted. "Nightmares."

"Yes, we know."

Ren cleaned his gritted teeth and ignored the mirror, which reflected a person with bloodshot eyes shadowed by dark circles. He checked them and was relieved to see their familiar brown color and not the blue he'd seen far too often. He tried to fix his hair, which was much longer than it had ever been; its ends curled under his ears and at the nape of his neck. He gave up, and a lock of hair fell into his face. His wayward hair might hide how tired he looked, but he doubted it. VanMeerten watched him like a hawk at each report. Nothing slid past her sharp gaze.

"Was it a nightmare this time?"

Ren washed his face with a cloth. "No. Panic attack."

"I'm sorry," Asher said.

Ren peered around the bathroom doorframe. "If I didn't have to stand in front of a vid screen every day and prove I'm not a threat to the Drift Alliance maybe it wouldn't have happened."

"Not this again," Asher muttered. He placed his hands on the bed and tipped his head back and looked at the ceiling. Spying Jakob's spaceship drawing, he snorted. "I don't want to have this discussion."

"Then don't."

Asher sighed. He rolled his shoulder. "I won't be drawn into an argument."

"It's not an argument."

"It is an argument. It's one we have had daily for the past three months. It's the reason we're not..." Asher trailed off. He looked away, staring at the doorframe.

Ren swallowed the lump in his throat. Asher's profile was as beautiful as the day he'd met him in the dungeon back on Erden. Then, he had been dirty and scruffy, and Ren had thought him handsome. Now, he was clean-shaven, and Ren had an unhindered view of the line of his strong jaw, the slope of his nose, and the beautiful green of his eyes. He was ethereal. He looked like an angel who had stepped out of myth. But he was a man, a soldier, and, on occasion, he was Ren's friend. A few short months ago, they had been on the brink of more. But it was difficult to be more when Asher was his handler and Ren was desperately trying not to be a threat to his friends. He was failing. His panic attack and the subsequent attempt to suffocate the crew was evidence—the latest in a mounting pile.

Ren's heart ached. "You're right. It is an argument and it is a reason."

Asher's gaze flicked back to Ren, and Ren read the naked hurt. "We need to go."

"I need another minute."

Asher pursed his lips, but didn't argue.

Ren sat on the bed; the mattress dipped from his weight. Avoiding distraction, he maintained a careful distance from Asher. His body sagged.

Ren put his elbows on his knees and scrubbed his hands across his face. He focused on his breathing, the inhale and exhale of air, the expansion and contraction of his lungs. He concentrated on the feel of the material of his shirt against his skin, the weight of his body, the deck plate beneath his feet. He flexed his muscles; his body was sore and stiff from a series of restless nights. Pressing the tips of two fingers against his neck, Ren counted the beats of his pulse until they slowed and he was certain he had slotted completely back into his body.

The cataloguing of sensation had become a ritual, a way for Ren to know where he was, who he was. He needed it, especially when he woke up so often now emerging from vivid dreams, muddled from images and emotions, and partially tangled within the ship. Reality was fluid. Ren was both man and star, human and not, and some mornings, like this one, it was difficult for Ren to discern what he needed to be. Before, Asher's presence, his voice, his touch could bring Ren back, could pull him from the thrall of the machines. But he couldn't continue to rely on Asher anymore. "I'm ready now."

"Are you sure?"

"Yes." Ren bit his lip.

Asher stood. "Good. Let's go."

Ren followed. "Jakob wants me to ask about going home, returning to Erden."

Shaking his head, Asher guided Ren down the hallway. "That's not a good idea."

"Why?"

"Because you need to keep your head down and your mouth shut," Asher stopped and grabbed Ren's arm. "I know you're an idiot duster, but I also know you're smart enough to understand that any attention from General VanMeerten is bad attention. Pressing to go dirtside after she's only just allowed you to leave the drift is pushing it."

Ren shrugged off the touch. The teasing barb, that had once been a term of affection, carried an edge it didn't have before.

"I'm asking." Ren clenched his jaw. "I have the right to go home. She can't keep me here."

"She can and she will. Or do you want to end up in the prison near Perilous Space? That's your only other option."

"Are you threatening me?"

"No, I'm—" Asher blew out an annoyed breath. He shook his head. "Fine. Don't listen." He turned on his heel.

Ren fumed. They walked the rest of the way to the bridge in silence. Trailing his fingers along the shiny surface of the bulkhead, he found peace in the systems of the ship, the vibrations of the engines, the sparks of the circuits. He could find freedom within these walls, if he let go. He wouldn't need permission then, to leave, to flee, to go home.

He banished the thoughts. They were too tempting.

At the steps to the bridge, Ren remembered in time to duck his head as he entered. Rowan, the captain and Asher's sister, greeted them with a tight smile. Millicent was already there. She was a fellow star host, a guest aboard the ship, also subjected to the scrutiny of the Corps.

Ren took his position. He stood in front of the vid screen with his head bowed and his gaze focused on the floor. Rowan stood to his right with her long blond hair in a braid and her pulse gun strapped to her side. Asher moved to Ren's left and caged Ren between them—trapped.

His pulse ticked up; his heart beat was a steady drumming in his ears.

The vid screen flickered to life and General VanMeerten appeared. She wore her gray hair pulled back in a severe bun and turned her head to show the scar that ran from her earlobe to the point of her chin. She looked down her nose at the group and peered at Ren as though he was mud on the bottom of her boot. Though she sat in a chair, her image loomed above them, and the artificial light from her office glinted along the row of medals on her chest.

Ren shrank in her presence. She didn't scare him, but she had the power to put him in a cell on the edge of Perilous Space and throw away the key. Even Asher's mother, an official of the Drift Alliance, couldn't protect him—not if VanMeerten deemed him a threat. He hated her, hated everything she stood for, and bitterness burned in Ren's gut.

"You look ill," she said without preamble.

Rowan shifted slightly, closer to Ren's side. "He's been under the weather recently," she lied easily. "Space sick. An inner ear imbalance. That happens to dusters."

"I'm aware. You forget I'm dirt-born, myself."

"Then you know how artificial gravity can affect the delicate equilibrium of the human body, especially when you're not used to it."

Her black eyes glittered. "Are you lecturing me, Ms. Morgan?"

"Captain," Rowan corrected. "And I wouldn't dream of it."

"Good." VanMeerten looked at Millicent. "And you?"

"I'm fine," she said, suitably meek.

"Not ill, like this one?"

Ren bristled, but bit his tongue.

"No, ma'am. But I've been eating and sleeping well."

She'd picked the absolute wrong thing to say.

VanMeerten's gaze darted to Ren. Her eyes narrowed as she assessed him. "You're not sleeping?"

Ren opened his mouth, but Asher cut him off. "He's not sleeping well. We're working on it. Stress, you know, from the ordeal."

She curled her lip. "It is my understanding one of the first signs of decompensation is the loss of the ability to sleep."

"But isn't oversleeping also a symptom?" Rowan said sweetly.

VanMeerten huffed. "And are you eating? I can't tell. You were scrawny when I met you and you still are."

Ren curled his hands into fists. His body shook.

"You can't expect a person who is space sick to be able to eat regular meals. As my brother said, we're working on it."

"I shouldn't have allowed this trip along the space route. He's a danger when healthy, and even more so if he's deteriorating."

Ren's heart sank. He bowed his head, bit his lip, and kept his posture bent and humble. He was penitent in image while his body thrummed. The same flood of warmth and energy filled him as when his star engaged in his chest, and he closed his eyes. He didn't want her to see the blue burning in his irises.

"Allow?" Rowan challenged. "Allow? May I remind you that I am the captain of this ship and I choose where my crew goes. We were grounded on Mykonos for ten weeks. Ten! While your bureaucracy deliberated over details before finally releasing us for this run."

VanMeerten narrowed her eyes. "No one hindered your departure except yourself. You could've left the star hosts and your brother behind."

"Not on your life." Rowan crossed her arms. "I lost my brother once. Never again. And if you think—"

"I want to be alerted at the first moment of any trouble regarding that one's sleeping patterns," she said, cutting Rowan off mid-word and addressing Asher. "No excuses. I'll not risk the lives of the people of the Drift Alliance because a star host can't get a good night's rest. Drug him if you have to."

Ren flinched, and his star swirled in his middle. Anger pricked up the length of his spine and settled in the tense line of his shoulders.

"Yes, we'll do what we can," Asher assured.

"Good. Anything else to report?" Her gaze flicked over the group, and they remained silent, though Rowan tugged on her braid and Millicent scratched at a spot on her skin. "Fine. We'll talk tomorrow. Until then."

The vid screen powered down.

Ren opened his eyes and stood in silence. He realized he hadn't asked Jakob's question, and guilt churned in his gut, mixed with the humiliation and the fear, and it was all too overwhelming. He turned and left the bridge.

Asher was a step behind and followed him until Ren stood in front of his own door.

"What do you want?" he asked. His cheeks were hot with embarrassment and he was tired, so tired. Exhaustion settled over him like a fog, dulling his senses, removing the barrier between him and the ship. His equilibrium unbalanced, he staggered and leaned against the wall. He wanted to lie in his bed, merge with the ship, and leave his mortal self behind for a while, to find the freedom that he missed within the circuits and wires and systems of the *Star Stream*.

"I want to talk with you."

"Haven't we talked enough?"

Asher sighed. He took Ren's hand and squeezed his fingers. "Ren, we haven't said anything significant to each other in weeks." He furrowed his brow and stared at their hands. "I understand you're upset. Things have been different. I have a job to do and… it's harder for us to be friends. I understand that, but I promised to protect you. And I'm doing it the only way I know how."

"I don't want your protection. I don't need your protection. I want you to be my friend, my…" Ren trailed off.

"I know you're not happy."

"You don't know the half of it."

"Then tell me." Asher moved closer. His body was a pillar of strength Ren had to resist falling into. "You didn't have a problem telling me off when we were trapped in a dungeon together. You didn't have a problem with making me listen to you on the *Nomad* and on Mykonos. What's the problem now?"

Ren's tongue was heavy. "If I tell you, can you promise me you won't report it back to the Phoenix Corps? That it will stay between us?"

Asher exhaled. "Ren." He paused. Then he nodded. "Yeah, it'll stay between us. This time." His voice was thick, almost uncertain. "I promise."

Ren swayed closer, rested his forehead on Asher's shoulder. "I know you keep your promises."

Asher cupped the back of Ren's neck. "I do."

"I needed to hear that."

"Come on, you can barely stand."

Ren allowed Asher to tug him into the room and push him to the bed. Ren stretched out on the sheets. He kicked off his boots. Asher lay next to him. Their shoulders touched, and that reminded Ren of the times in the dungeon on Erden, when they slept next to the lattice between their cells. It reminded Ren of the tense trip on the *Nomad* when they didn't know if Rowan would pay the credits they owed or if they were going to be turned in when they arrived at the Nineveh Drift. But then Asher had been Ren's rock, his anchor, his foundation.

The past few weeks without him had been torture, but for the moment, Ren was grounded. He held no illusions that the awkwardness wouldn't return, but now it was only them, as it had been in the dark nights in the cell when they'd trade secrets.

"I don't want to hurt anyone, but I don't know if I can stop it. It's harder now since I... since... the incident on the bridge when I couldn't let go."

Asher stiffened. He was obviously thinking about when Ren had been stuck inside the *Star Stream*, when Ren's humanity had burned away and the cold logic of the machines had taken over. Ren had gone beyond where anyone could reach him, and it was only Asher's quick thinking that had stopped him from killing dozens of people.

"When the power overtook you. Is that what happens at night?"

"I dream," Ren said, softly. "I dream of Erden. I dream of people I knew. The dreams are so vivid, so terrible, and I can't stop, even if I try."

"They trigger your power. Like before, when you were upset or threatened, like the panic this morning. Your power activated."

"Yes," Ren said.

"And the ship responds. You couldn't breathe, so life support kicked off."

Ren swallowed. "Yes."

"The dreams are getting worse, aren't they?"

Ren focused on the heat of Asher's body along the line of his side, the touch of Asher's pinky finger against his, the cradle of the mattress against his body. He allowed his eyes to flutter shut and didn't answer.

"Because you're not dead exhausted at night now? Or is it something else?"

Ren shrugged. The drowsy lull of sleep slipped over him.

"It's because we're not as close, isn't it? You don't know if you can trust me because of my position with the Corps. Because you feel trapped by the people you thought would save you. Because you don't believe I'm on your side any longer."

No one could say Asher wasn't perceptive. He was. It was what made him such a good soldier and a good friend. But Ren didn't want to talk about any of it. He was blunted, right then, with the blurred edges of slumber overtaking him.

"Remember, right after, when we stayed in that hotel." Asher shifted slightly on the bunk mattress. "And I took you to that garden? We walked around the paths and held hands."

"You kissed me next to the carnivorous shrub."

Asher chuckled. "You liked it."

"I did." Ren smiled.

"We got sprayed by the sprinklers. My shirt was soaked."

"Yeah," he said. "I liked the smell of the wet dirt and mulch. Your nose was scrunched the whole time."

"It reminded me of…" Asher trailed off.

Ren heard the words anyway. It reminded Asher of Erden, of his cell, of his captivity.

"It reminded me of home." Ren said. His smile faded.

"I miss us," Asher said softly.

The words were an arrow in Ren's gut. "Ash," Ren said. "I'm tired."

Asher patted his hand. "I know. Go to sleep, Ren."

A shiver of fear slipped up Ren's spine, and he gripped Asher's hand, laced their fingers. "Please stay?"

"Yes."

"Thank you."

"Rest, Ren. I'll be here to keep you safe."

Ren believed him, and, unafraid, eased into a doze.

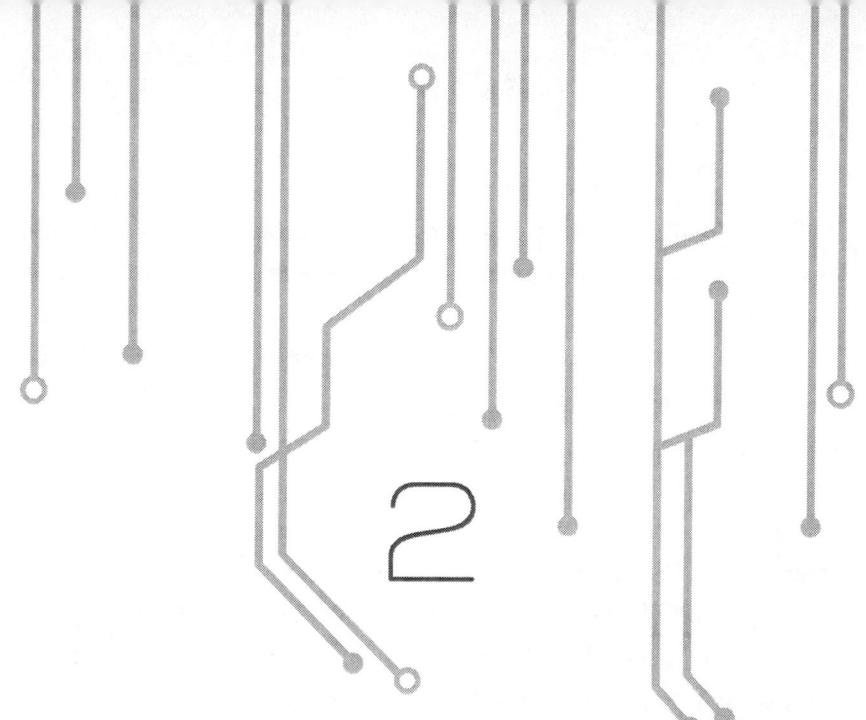

When Ren woke, the entire day had passed. Asher was gone, but a note sat tented by Ren's head.

> *I'm sorry, I couldn't stay. I was needed elsewhere.*
> *I'll see you at the next check-in.*
>
> - A

Ren crumpled the paper. He threw his legs over the side of the bed. He pushed his body erect and stumbled into the en-suite bathroom. He washed his face; the cold water shocked him into wakefulness.

Needing to see something different from the four walls, he slipped on his boots and left his room. Because their relationship was broken, Asher was no longer his anchor, and Ren relied on the others.

He heard voices in the common room and stepped through the doorway. The conversation stopped dead. He waved his hand at the occupants, Jakob and Penelope, before shuffling to the counter to pour a cup of day-old coffee.

"Hey, Ren," Jakob said, standing up from the sagging couch and crossing the room. He clapped his hand on Ren's shoulder. "It's been an exciting day."

Ren twisted his lips as he added sweetener to the steaming liquid and stirred it with a spoon. He preferred tea, but found the caffeine from the coffee helpful. Asher had shown him how to make coffee less bitter, which now seemed ironic.

"Is that your way of tactfully getting me to talk about this morning? Because you failed."

Jakob scoffed. "I've been practicing my tact. Haven't I, Pen?"

Penelope smiled, but the action did not reach her brown eyes. She brushed a long lock of curly dark hair from her cheek and tucked it behind her ear.

"Sorry, Jakob. I'm going to have to agree with Ren on this one."

"Weeds," Jakob said, giving Ren a shake. "I have to work harder then."

"Probably," Ren said, moving out from under Jakob's touch to sit at the table. He hunched over his drink and sipped it. It burned his tongue. Ren took comfort from the sting.

"Well, now that the ice is broken… do you want to talk about it?"

"Not really."

Ren pretended he didn't notice the concerned glance Jakob and Penelope shared.

"Are you sure?" Penelope said. "Talking may help?"

Irritation crawled through Ren's middle. He knew they were only trying to support him. They were his friends and undoubtedly they were scared because Ren had almost killed everyone that morning through oxygen deprivation and hypothermia and because of the other times Ren had accessed systems in the throes of a nightmare. But Penelope's tone rubbed him the wrong way, like sandpaper against his nerves.

"The picture helped," Ren said, recognizing that he had to give them something.

Jakob smiled as he sat down across from Ren. "It did?"

"Yeah, it reminded me I was on the ship."

After the first time, when Ren had dreamed he was locked in the cell on Erden with Abiathar's voice in his head and his sleeping, unconscious self had tried to open all the doors on the *Star Stream* including the airlocks, Jakob had drawn him the picture. Ren had laughed at the misshapen spaceship speeding along a map of stars leaving a rainbow trail in its wake. Stick-figure representations of the crew members dotted all sides of the border. Asher had a silver shoulder and a scribble of blond hair and a ridiculous frown. There had been several incidents after that.

No one was laughing anymore.

"That's great!" Pen said, sitting up straighter. "Would you like me to draw you one as well? Oh, I know, Lucas is a great artist. You've seen the maps. He could do it. Would that help?"

They both regarded Ren so seriously, so earnestly, that Ren couldn't be angry. "Sure," he said.

Penelope's smile went from forced to relieved. "I'll ask him. Maybe one of his maps would help? It could remind you we're in space?"

"And that it would be a bad idea to try to open the doors," Jakob added. "Because of the terrifying vacuum that is right outside and the fact we would all die."

"Noted," Ren said, dryly.

Jakob ruffled Ren's hair, and Ren scowled as he tried to pat it back down.

"Please, stop."

"What? It can't look any worse," Jakob said with a grin.

Ren rolled his eyes. He gulped down his coffee, unable to stand the forced levity of Jakob and Pen's combined presence. They tried too hard. Penelope wore her notoriously soft heart on her sleeve, and Jakob was acting like the boy he'd been in their home village on Erden. Jakob had always been haughty, brash, and impulsive, but likeable, and he'd inspired the admiration of the other youths. He had never teased Ren, because Ren wasn't worth the effort; he wasn't even on Jakob's periphery.

Jakob was far from that boy now: His exterior was hardened, his shoulders were weary, his mind had become calculating, his point of view had been widened by what he had experienced. But he pretended for Ren's sake.

Ren didn't have the heart to tell him to stop. "Don't you have something to do?" Ren stood and put his mug in the sink. "A task from our beloved Captain? Other than bothering me?"

Jakob's smile grew. "Nope, other than enjoy the ride. You were right, Ren, space is boring when you haven't been forcibly conscripted into the service of an insane despot."

"Glad you're having a nice time," Ren said; his sarcasm was both thick and sharp.

"Actually," Penelope said, interrupting, "we really should take stock of our supplies before we head to bed, Jakob. We're pulling into port soon and we should check to see if we're short of anything."

"Well, then, I do have something to do other than give you a hard time."

"Thank the stars for that."

Jakob playfully pushed Ren's shoulder, but then his expression turned serious.

"Did you ask?"

Ren's coffee turned sour in his stomach.

"Jakob…" Ren trailed off. He didn't know what to say. Jakob wanted to go back to Erden, to look for their friend, Sorcha, to look for his family. But Asher was right. The Corps wouldn't grant permission, not now. Ren had a sneaking suspicion the constraints were partly because if Ren were planetside, he'd be out of the Corps' jurisdiction and off their radar. They couldn't afford to lose track of him and couldn't be caught dirt-side following him. They didn't belong on planets unless invited.

"No, I know. I shouldn't have asked. Not with—" Jacob wiggled his fingers "—everything you've had to deal with already this morning."

Ren couldn't have felt more awful. "I'll ask. I'll ask tomorrow. The worst she can do is say no."

Jakob had a glimmer of hope in his blue eyes. "Thank you," he said.

Ren squirmed, unable to handle any more emotion. He turned for the door.

"Don't you want to eat?" Pen asked before Ren could slip away. "I have leftovers from dinner."

"I'm not hungry and I should probably check on the ship. Make sure I didn't break anything important this time."

"I could make you a sandwich to take with you."

"No, I'm good. Thank you."

"Are you sure?"

"I'm fine, Pen," Ren snapped. At her stricken expression, Ren moderated his tone. "I'm sorry. I'm fine, really. I should go."

She gave him a fragile smile. "Okay."

Feeling worse for being annoyed with Pen than he did for almost killing them all, Ren ducked his head and left the common room.

There was nothing wrong with the ship. Ren used the possibility as an excuse, which was a tactic he used often to escape uncomfortable interactions. He could feel the pulse of the *Star Stream* in his veins, could hear the heartbeat of the systems echo his own. The ship was an extension of him. His star knew every circuit, every wire, every inch of the vessel intimately.

Touching the wall, he closed his eyes and merged with the vid feeds. He watched his own body from a camera as he walked. The experience was surreal, but more real to him than looking out of his own eyes. He was a combination of machine and man and he didn't know what that made him—if he was human or a different entity entirely—but he did know he was safe in the systems.

He only wanted to be safe.

And he wanted his friends to be safe. But that, apparently, was a harder task than he had anticipated.

Ren pulled out of the ship and wandered to the cargo bay where he knew Millicent would be. She liked the open area and she liked that Ollie worked out down there. She wasn't fooling anyone—well, maybe Ollie. Not that Ren could give relationship advice, since his was fairly nonexistent, if it had ever existed at all.

He detected Millicent's own star's signature. She radiated a calm Ren could only hope to achieve. In the beginning, the thought was that Ren would teach her control, but they all soon learned it would be the other way around. Millicent had a soft-spoken way about her and impeccable restraint. She wasn't as powerful as Ren, though she could take over the entirety of Mykonos Drift, and she could nuance her power in a way that Ren was still trying to master.

She had been able to push Ren out of the drift's systems when they first met, and it wasn't all because she had been under Abiathar's control.

She, too, had found her niche in the crew of the *Star Stream*. Rowan and Pen treated her like a long-lost sister. Lucas and Ollie wanted to protect her.

Ren wasn't jealous. Or—he shouldn't be jealous—but he was. He'd rather be regarded as a harmless kitten than a threat. It was a strange dichotomy, and Ren was working on reconciling it.

"Ren," Millicent said, as he descended the steps to the floor of the cargo bay. "How are you feeling?"

"Fine," he said.

"You're lying."

She sat cross-legged on a rug with her back stiff. Her dark hair hung in long, straight strands; the tips curled on the floor. She stared, large eyes unblinking, pretty mouth pulled into a frown. Penelope's mixer sat in front of her. She put the tip of her finger on the casing. Ren shuddered at the pulse of Millicent's star, and the mixer came to life, only to short out a few moments later.

Ren sat on the floor across from her. "You should take lessons on tact from Jakob. He at least tried to cushion it when he called me out."

She didn't smile. "I'm not Jakob. The others may not be able to feel it, but I can."

Ren raised an eyebrow. "Feel what?"

"Feel that you're drifting. You're everywhere in this ship, and that means you're not in there," she said, pushing her finger into Ren's chest.

He rubbed the spot where her fingernail had dug in. "I'm fine."

"You're not anchored."

"Well, my anchor turned out to be a cog. It's a little difficult to want to be around someone who has more allegiance to his boss than his friend."

She blinked, her expression unreadable. "He's protecting you."

Ren frowned. "There doesn't seem to be much difference between being protected and being prisoner." That wasn't entirely fair, but Ren wasn't in the mood to be fair.

"That's not true. You need to talk to him."

Ren glanced away. "I know, but I… can't. We're… trying, but things are different now."

"You'd risk venting us all into space instead of talking to a person who holds affection for you?"

"I didn't say it made sense," Ren grumbled.

"He needs to understand that you don't need protecting."

"Did you miss the part where I have a powerful military organization wanting to lock me up? Lock us both up?"

Millicent slowly turned her head to the side. She may be calm, but sometimes the way she moved made Ren think of a puppet. It was eerily reminiscent of when he'd met her, when she was under the influence of Abiathar's voice and her eyes had glowed in her vacant body.

"We're stars. We're more powerful than any person or any group. Protection from Asher means nothing."

"I'd think twice about saying that to anyone other than me. It sounds a little scary and threatening. The crew might not understand what you mean."

"Do you understand?"

Ren's frown deepened. He cleared his throat. "What are you up to?" Changing the subject, he gestured at the machine.

Millicent slowly tilted her head to the other side. "Playing with Penelope's mixer. I haven't been successful."

"Is it broken?"

"I don't think so? Unless I broke it."

Ren hid a smile. Millicent and he were opposites. When Abiathar used her powers to take over the drift, it had drained her; Ren's powers only seemed to grow. He had tapped into the vastness of space and unleashed a torrent of potential, while her star withered. As they had discovered, their bodies reacted differently to the innate power. Millicent had control, and Ren was going to burn up from the inside. Abiathar could influence others with his voice. Nadie could see the future. Who knew what others could do?

Ren held out his hand and concentrated. The tingle of power emanated from his chest and trickled down to his fingertips; his vision went blue as he pushed out and explored the simplistic innards of the mixer. There was a slight glitch, which he fixed, but otherwise nothing was broken and the power source was fully charged. He found the switch, flicked it on, and the beater whirred to life. He turned it off and disengaged.

Millicent pulled her lower lip between her teeth. "How can you do that without touching it?"

"I don't know. I see it and I know what to do. I can't really explain it."

She shook her head so her long hair swept across the floor. "I understand why you have a hard time controlling it. We should work on control. Sit with me."

They'd done this before, when Ren had started to go haywire, after the first time he had entered the ship in his dreams. He mirrored her pose, and she guided him through breathing exercises.

"I think everyone has gone to bed," she said softly. "Except Lucas, who is on the bridge. *Wearing goggles.*"

"Yeah, I don't get that either."

She snorted.

Ren lifted the corner of his mouth. He closed his eyes and followed her lead, inhaling and exhaling. With each breath, his star centered. The warmth glowed in the middle of his chest and pulsed with his heartbeat. The ship enveloped him in tranquility. The soothing hum of its systems and the energy from circuits flowed through the ship like a life force. The exercises were meant to make him more concentrated in his own body, in his corporeal self, but Ren found the opposite.

He reached for calm, but it was elusive, especially when his emotions were in such turmoil. Serenity was slippery, like a fish pulled from the lake on Erden. The systems pulled on his being, and he couldn't resist, and his thoughts turned toward the dark and dire—the confines of his cell on Erden, the loss of his brother, the desperate days of wandering across the countryside.

He gave in to the *Star Stream*; he fled from the tumultuous mortal coil into the freedom and safety of the ship. He floated amid the systems, and found the ship's time much later than he thought. He'd lost time during his walk from the common area to the cargo bay, and the fact disconcerted him. Everyone was indeed asleep, except Lucas and Asher.

Through the comm system, he could hear Asher talking. Curious, Ren followed the stream of information.

"The subjects continue to remain stable."

Ren flinched from the clinical terms. Subjects. Then he bristled. He was a star host, and Asher would do well to remember that.

"The female is in control of her power. There have been no incidents. The male…"

Here, Asher trailed off. He put down the tablet he dictated into and rubbed a hand over his eyes. He pushed the tablet away and turned to the bed.

"Oh, Ren," he muttered. "What is going on with you?" He plopped onto the bunk and hit his pillow twice. "I don't know how to help you."

Asher seemed reluctant, confused, and *sad*. He didn't gleefully recount that Ren had nearly killed them that morning—while in the throes of panic, but no less dangerous for that. Asher didn't report the incident or Ren's confession. And when Asher sighed and kicked off his shoes, then pulled his shirt over his head, Ren spied the marred flesh of his shoulder, the shredded Corps tattoo, the reminder that Asher had suffered at the hands of the Corps himself. Yet, he had faith.

Ren's heart lurched.

Asher wore a tough front most of the time, but still waters ran deep. Ren ached to be with him, ached to wrap his arms around Asher and hold on, keep him safe, bolster him.

He couldn't.

Ren blinked his eyes open, fully present in his body. He sat across from Millicent, and his heart thumped, his pulse raced, and he could feel the moisture gather in the corners of his eyes.

"Ren?" Millicent asked. "Are you okay?"

He breathed. "I'm… fine. I think?"

"Where did you go?"

"Comm system," he said. He flexed his fingers and absently touched the cool deck plate. "Asher is awake."

Millicent frowned. "I didn't know. I couldn't feel it."

"I could." Ren wiped at his eyes. "I'm so confused. I don't know what to feel anymore. I'm… adrift."

Millicent gave him a commiserating glance. "Maybe you shouldn't worry about how you feel right now. Focus on being present in yourself, in your star and in your body. You're putting yourself in danger if you can't control it."

"I'm putting everyone in danger." Ren hunched and crossed his arms. "For so long all I wanted to do was be out here in space, among the stars, and now I think it would've been better if I had never left Erden, if I had stayed and hid and let Asher leave on his own."

Millicent blinked her large eyes and pursed her lips. "Then *he* would have won. And your friends would be in danger—or dead."

And Ren couldn't argue with that. He ducked his head and traced the scratches that adorned the deck plate of the cargo bay.

"You need rest," she said.

Ren nodded. Despite sleeping all day, he hadn't recovered from the past few weeks of insomnia and interrupted sleep. He had to look better for tomorrow when he would check in with VanMeerten.

He needed to give Asher reasons not to doubt him, not to have to choose between him and the Corps, because Ren was fairly certain he'd lose.

"Goodnight, Millicent."

She smiled, small and private. "Goodnight, Ren. Sweet dreams."

"Let's hope."

With that, Ren left the cargo bay and slipped like a ghost through the hallways to his room.

Ren was lost. He was in the forest, that much he knew. He could see the sinking sun through the trees and the canopy of leaves. He listened for the sound of anyone or anything, but it was silent: no birds, no wind, no animals scampering in the underbrush, no life. As he trudged along the winding path, the trees loomed, blocking the meager light, casting shadows that danced and threatened. Their spindly branches reached out, grabbed at his jacket, dug their claws into the fabric, and held him. Ren pulled away from the terrifying embrace, as the forest creaked, the tree bark moaned, and terror seized Ren's heart.

He ran. Legs pumping, Ren burst through the bracken and stumbled onto a familiar beach. The sun disappeared over the horizon with an unnatural quickness, and the stars and broken moon cast sparkles on the water. Ren's feet sank in the sand, and, when he tried to move, he was stuck fast. The air was syrupy, sticky and dense. He struggled to inhale and his hands shook as he clutched at his shirt.

Ren looked behind him and the forest swayed, menacing and unreal. But Ren recognized this beach; he recognized the lake and the sky. A memory stirred, and then a name.

"Liam!" he yelled.

He was on Erden. This was his and Liam's lake. He remembered. He remembered lying in the sand before the floaters came, carted him away, and scared Liam into hiding, beyond Ren's reach.

"Liam!" he yelled again; his voice caught on his brother's name.

He managed to pull his foot from his boot, leaving it in the quicksand. He moved toward the water, and from one wave to the next, the water turned from clear blue to red.

Crimson foam and red froth slapped on the shore and smelled of metal and fear. Ren tasted it in the back of his throat.

"Liam!"

"Ren," the voice came from next to him, over his shoulder. The breath was hot against his ear.

"Liam?" He spun and caught sight of a fleeting shadow. But there was nothing behind him, and Ren knew he was chasing a ghost.

He ran anyway, moving slowly, his limbs heavy. Even his blinking was slowed by the viscous atmosphere. Sound returned in the soft slap of the waves on the shore and the torture of Liam's voice taunting him.

"Why did you leave me?" Liam's voice echoed, accusatory and broken.

"I didn't!" Ren shouted, desperate. "I was taken. They took me away. I didn't want to leave!"

"You left me. You left me."

Ren spun in a circle and the wash of colors of the forest and the lake blended in his vision. He smelled the tang of the blood-water.

"I will find you," Ren said. He swallowed the lump in his throat. "I will find you. I promise. I will bring you home."

"You can't."

"I will!"

The voice faded, and with it the presence of whomever had been with him. Ren became frantic, pleading. "Liam?" He dropped to his knees and scrabbled along the beach; his hands sank into the wet sand. "Liam!"

"Ren," the voice was next to him now, but deeper, softer, not Liam's. Ren sobbed.

"Ren, wake up."

Ren rocketed out of sleep. There were no alarms, no indication he had entered the workings of the ship, but he had been dreaming.

Asher's arms were strong around him, and Ren fought. He pushed until he was no longer trapped and fell to the deck plate. His body hurt, sore from the dream, sore from slapping against the metal. He flailed his limbs and noted they moved at their normal speed, unhindered. He breathed and it was no longer a labor. Gaze wild, he looked around the room and saw the gleaming walls of the ship. Looking up, he saw Jakob's picture and a new star chart.

"Ren?" Asher crouched, and his voice was soft, as if he was gentling a wild animal.

Ren held up a hand. "Don't touch me," he gasped. "Don't. Stay away. I can't… I can't… I don't want to hurt you."

Asher nodded. He curled his fists against his thighs. "Okay. I won't touch you."

"Liam?"

"You were dreaming."

"I was on Erden. I was stuck in the forest. In the sand." Ren looked around, confused. The light was low and the shadows moved. They made Ren nervous, and, after a flick of his hand, the lights blazed.

Asher blinked, then stood. "Ren, it was a dream. You're on the *Star Stream*."

"I know," Ren snapped, pulling his body straight. He paced the length of his cell. His pulse thumped; adrenaline was a live current in his veins. He gazed around the small space, not seeing it. Expecting to see granules of sand, he studied his palms. There was nothing.

"I need to go back."

"Where?"

"Home. I need to go back home."

Asher put his hands on his hips and gazed at the ceiling. "Ren, we've talked about that. It's not possible right now. Not until you're stable."

"This is how you can help me."

Asher went pale. "What?"

"You want to help me. This is how you can help me. You want me to be the person you knew? I need to go back."

"How? Were you… listening to me? Spying on me?"

Ren froze. He ran a hand through his hair. It was sticky with sweat, and he pushed it from his face.

"I heard you over the comm. I was in the ship."

"Purposefully?"

"Kind of? That's not the point."

"It kind of is the point, Ren. You spied on me."

"That doesn't matter. If you do care about me, you'll help me."

"And if I don't?"

Ren hadn't considered that. He narrowed his eyes and slowed his manic pacing. "I'll do what I have to, anything I have to."

Asher pointed at him. "You are out of control," he said, enunciating every word. "Do you understand that? Do you get the position I'm in here? I'm trying to protect you!"

"You are trying to keep me captive!" The words erupted from Ren's mouth. As his power flickered, the lights dimmed, and the comm crackled. "I don't need you to protect me. I am a *star*, more powerful than anyone on this ship."

Asher stepped back. His green eyes narrowed, and his mouth clamped into a firm line. He clenched his jaw, and, with his shoulders pulled back, he was every inch a soldier.

Ren hated it.

"Your behavior is erratic. You can't sleep. You don't eat. You dream and you put everyone on this ship at risk. You are falling apart, and everyone can see it but you."

"You think I can't see it? You think I don't feel it? I know, all right? I know." Ren peered at his hands. He pulled his fingers toward his palm, then straightened them and spread them out as far as they could go. "I know all of that. I know and I'm trying. But you don't understand."

"And I suppose Millicent does."

Ren snapped his head up. "What the stars does that mean?"

Asher crossed his arms. He studied the door to the hallway intently, as if it held the secrets to the universe. "It doesn't mean anything."

Ren frowned. His body trembled. "I want to go back to my village. I want to try to find my family. I want to find Liam. I need to know if everyone really is gone."

Asher met Ren's pleading gaze with a hard, cold one of his own. "You can't."

"Ash—"

"Not while VanMeerten is looking for any excuse to throw you in a cell. You need to stay under her radar and keep your power under control. Am I clear?"

Ren flushed, embarrassed, ashamed, and *angry*. "Crystal. And I think you should leave."

"Ren—"

"Get out." He bit out the words. "Or do I need permission for that, too?"

The remaining color of Asher's complexion fled save for two bright spots on his cheeks. He stood with his body in one long, taut line.

"Fine. Report in an hour. Try to be presentable."

Asher spun on his heel and stalked out of the room. He slammed the door behind him with enough force that Ren's night table rattled.

The star throbbed in Ren's middle, and he was livid down to his bones. He yelled, wordless, and a pulse of blue light flashed. The comm crackled, and his lights stuttered. For a moment, every system halted, frozen by Ren's frustration. It was only a moment, then everything whirred back to life.

He sank to his floor and buried his face in his hands.

―⊩―

After he calmed down, Ren washed, and, following Asher's instructions, attempted to look presentable. Foregoing breakfast, he walked to the bridge and jerkily moved to his spot next to Rowan.

She raked her gaze over him, and her mouth tightened. "You wouldn't have had anything to do with the slight pause in the ship's systems about an hour ago, would you?"

Ren glared. "I don't know what you're talking about."

"I figured." She tossed her braid over her shoulder. "I'm glad you managed to rest. But you're looking a little… defiant today. You may want to tuck that away before the feed goes live."

Ren didn't answer. He lifted his chin and he heard Rowan sigh next to him.

Millicent skipped up the stairs and, meek as always, stood next to Rowan. Her deference made Ren burn even more. Asher was the last to join them. He didn't look at Ren. He kept his gaze on the far wall and when he turned to face the vid screen, his movements were abrupt and sure, soaked in military routine.

Rowan glanced at them, but said nothing. The tension on the bridge was thick enough to cut with a saw. It would be apparent to VanMeerten and it would launch questions and give her enough reason to make the *Star Stream* turn around and go back to Mykonos Drift.

But Ren was finished playing a part. He was a star host. He was a being imbued with the power of the stars. He was more than this body. He would not apologize for his existence any longer.

The screen blinked into life. In her uniform as always, VanMeerten sat at her desk. Her hair was pulled back in a bun, and there was no indication she had moved since the last time Ren had seen her. She could very well be as nonhuman as Ren. He had no proof she wasn't.

"I trust you are all well," she said, tenting her fingers and peering down at them from the end of her pointed nose.

Unflinching, Ren met her gaze. He didn't speak, but she raised her eyebrow at him and her lips curled.

"Everything is very well," Rowan said. "As you can see, Ren has rested and is looking better. His power is under control, and Millicent is adjusting to crew life."

"He is over space sickness in one day? That's impressive. In my experience, it takes closer to a week."

"It was a mild case, and our medic is second to none."

"I see. Well, if there are no concerns, then I will check in again tomorrow."

On the screen, VanMeerten reached to close the connection, but before she could, Asher stepped forward. He blocked Ren's view of the general. All Ren could see was the strong line of Asher's back and the symbol of the rising Phoenix, wings outspread, flames wreathed around the bird's talons, on the top of his bicep.

"Actually, I have an incident to report."

Rowan cut her gaze to Asher. She seemed concerned, scared, and confused.

"Ash," she said. "What are you doing?"

"Telling the truth," he said.

Ren couldn't see VanMeerten's face, but he could imagine how she appeared as her features took on a predator-like expression. She was hungry for any reason to lock Ren away for the rest of his natural life—until she had use for him.

"Ren has nightmares," Asher continued. "He has nightmares and panic attacks and he puts us at risk. He has attempted to vent the ship on one occasion. On another, the oxygen began to fail."

"Ash!" Rowan barked.

The words lanced through Ren like a sword; the betrayal bit deep into his flesh. His mouth fell open. Asher kept his eyes fixed on the screen.

"Why have you not reported this sooner?"

"Because I was giving the subject the benefit of the doubt. I was attached to him, but I cannot remain quiet any longer. He obviously cannot handle the environment here and he is putting us all in danger."

Ren recoiled from the impersonal language. Asher spoke in the past tense. He "was" attached, as if he wasn't now. Ren had known the end was coming, but to hear it, to experience it, in front of the woman who wanted him locked away and in front of his friends was more than he could bear. Part of him wanted to shrivel up and die, but another part of him, the part intimately connected to the star, that part of him *raged*.

"I see. Captain Morgan, I believe this experiment of allowing the subjects into space has failed. Come back to Mykonos immediately."

Rowan placed her hands on her hips. "No. The Corps does not dictate my business. I have made a commitment to see this supply run through and I will not have my reputation sullied because of a snit fit between my brother and Ren."

"Do you not agree that the subject is a danger?"

"He's about as dangerous as anyone on this ship. I have a pulse gun and know how to use it. Ollie easily is the strongest. Pen could poison us. A teenage twig from a dust-hole planet is merely one of many threats."

"So you do believe him a threat? A weapon?"

Rowan opened her mouth to retort, but snapped it shut. VanMeerten had twisted her words. Rowan couldn't backtrack.

Ren, however, had heard enough. He was through with others deciding his fate. He was taking control of this situation—his status be damned. He pushed Asher out of his way and stood in front of VanMeerten.

"I want to go home," Ren said, his voice even, his tone sharp as steel.

VanMeerten raised an eyebrow. She braced her hands on her desk, fingers spread. "What?"

"I want to go home," Ren stated. "I don't know how much simpler I can say it."

"Ren," Asher whispered harshly, but Ren ignored him.

"You don't have a home. It was my understanding that your village was destroyed."

Ren controlled his flinch and stood his ground. He pulled his spine straight and didn't shrink from her gaze.

"Maybe, but I want to see for myself. You can't keep me from going."

She stood, hands gripping the edge of her desk, and loomed forward. "I can. And I will. Captain Morgan, I want you to turn your ship around immediately and bring this young man back to Mykonos."

"No," Ren said. "You will not, Captain."

"Are you testing me, star host?"

"I have a name," Ren said. He clenched his fists; anger rose hot and quick. Sparks flickered around his fingers. "I'm not a subject. I'm a person and I have a home." His vision turned blue around the edges. "And I want to go back to my planet and find my family. You have no right to deny me."

"I have every right. You are a threat, and it is my duty to protect—"

"I am not a threat!" The vid screen fluttered as static gathered at the corners. "I am a star host, and you cannot stop me. Your Phoenix Corps cannot stop me, and you *know* that."

"Ren," Asher said, his voice a low command. "You need to calm down. Your eyes are blue."

"Stay out of this, Ash, especially if all you are going to do is take her side." Ren pointed a shaking finger toward the vid screen. Asher crossed his arms and kept his expression flat, and Ren saw the connection between them turn to cinder. Good. He didn't need Asher. It was better he didn't have any emotional entanglements.

"I can see that this situation has gotten out of hand. I've allowed you too much freedom. I'm afraid I am going to have to call you back to Mykonos and, if you cannot control yourself, I will be forced to send you to the facility near the Perilous Space."

Ren turned back to VanMeerten and stalked forward. "Do I need to remind you I disabled an entire ship with a thought? That I can make your weapons inert with barely a whisper? I can infect Mykonos Drift like a virus in a mere breath, and then where will you be? How can you protect your people from a power like mine?"

Ren hit a nerve. He could see it in the twitch of VanMeerten's mouth, the worried wrinkle that appeared on her forehead, the almost imperceptible movement of her eyebrows.

"Okay, that's enough," Rowan said. She slammed her hand down on Ren's shoulder and yanked him back. "Obviously, Ren here is a little homesick and a lot more space sick than we thought. General, the crew of the *Star Stream* will gladly take him back to Erden under the watchful eye of your very own corporal here after we finish this supply run. If you grant us this request, of course. I am sure you understand that with the extra mouths to feed on the ship, I need all the income available to me, even with the Corps' generous stipend. I will personally see that Ren gets a good night's sleep, drugged if needed as per your suggestion." She gave Ren a shake as if he was a naughty puppy. "We'll check in tomorrow, and you can give us your decision regarding the trip back to his planet. Until then, Morgan out."

Asher lunged for the comm console and ended the transmission before the general could so much as blink.

Then Ren found himself pinned to the wall with Rowan's forearm like iron across his chest and her face tilted up to stare right into his.

"What the stars has gotten into you?" she demanded, seeming utterly furious; her cheeks were pink. "Are you addled? Threatening the Corps? After what you did yesterday morning? Stars, Ren. I should shove you out the aft airlock right now after that stunt. Seriously. Taunting a *general*? You are going to end up in Perilous Space!"

Ren could barely breathe. His head thunked against the wall. He didn't want to cry, he didn't, not in front of Asher and Rowan and Millicent, but the tears burned in his eyes. He tried to blink them away, but they spilled down his cheeks in rivulets.

"And you!" she said, swinging around to thrust a finger into Asher's chest, and thereby letting go so Ren could breathe again. "What the stars was that? I thought the plan was to protect Ren, not throw him to a black hole?"

"It needed to be said."

"What is going on with you two?"

Asher stuck out his chin. "It needed to be reported for our own safety. Rowan, do you honestly think the Corps wouldn't charge you with treason if they found out what's been going on without us telling them? They'd take away your license to captain. Stars, they'd take away this ship! Are you willing to risk everyone's home? Your livelihood?"

Rowan stared, astonished, mouth open. "What's wrong with you? A few months ago you would've died for this kid and now you're acting like you hardly know him."

Asher crossed his arms. "Things change."

Rowan threw up her hands. "That's great. Just great. You're both acting like your personalities were replaced when I wasn't looking, like you've been swapped out." She paused. "You haven't been, have you?"

"No," Ren said.

Asher rolled his eyes.

"Well, I don't know. Since I've met you I've seen things I didn't know were possible. What's body snatchers compared to transporting a ship across the cluster?" She tossed her long, golden braid over her shoulder. "What do we do now?"

"I need to go back to Erden," Ren said softly. "I'm sorry, Rowan." He was. He was so sorry. "I'm not myself. I don't feel like myself."

Her expression softened. "We'll figure it out, Ren. But you can't do that," she said, sweeping her arm toward the vid screen. "Understand? You have a target on your back a league wide, and if you want to live, if you want to have any kind of freedom, you have to be on your best behavior."

Ren bit his lip and nodded. He didn't want to say anything about his supposed freedom. This wasn't the moment. But he understood. Cogs, what had he done? "I understand."

She touched his arm. "Good. Now, go do something and get out of my sight. I'm irritated just looking at you."

With his eyes downcast, Ren nodded. He brushed passed Asher. Their shoulders touched, the tips of Ren's fingers whispered over the back of Asher's hand, and, for a split second, the components of Asher's shoulder flashed in Ren's mind. But the moment ended, and the feelings Ren had for Asher were mired in complications and regret.

Maybe it would be easier if Ren hadn't formed such a strong bond with Asher in the beginning. Maybe if they hadn't kissed; maybe if Ren hadn't allowed himself the affection he had for Asher; maybe if Ren hadn't fallen so quickly, so deeply, hadn't counted on Asher and cared for Asher; maybe the thick tension between them wouldn't seem so terrible.

In his heart, Ren wanted Asher's friendship back. He wanted to explore their relationship. He wanted to hold hands and kiss and be together. And once he'd been certain Asher wanted that too. Ren wasn't sure of that any longer. And stars, Ren couldn't get past the fact he had traded one prison for another. Instead of a despotic baron, the organization to which Asher held the most allegiance was his captor.

Now, when Ren saw Asher, all he could see was another person who wanted to control and use him—and who had betrayed him.

It made panic and fear crawl into his throat and sweat break out along his skin. It made his heart stutter, and not in the way it should. Everything was wrong.

And there was no way to fix it.

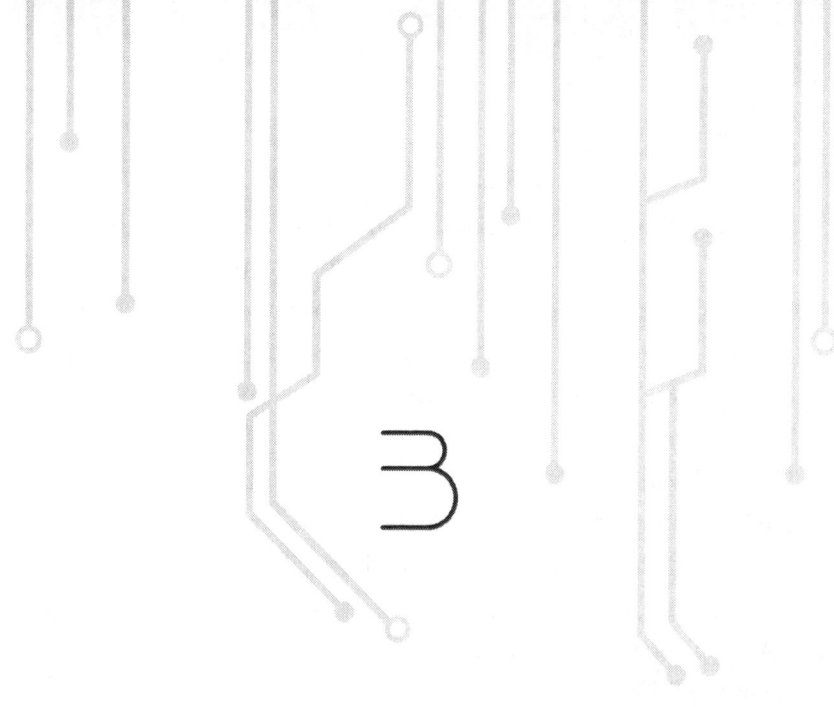

Another day in space. Another dream.

Ren woke on the floor with cold sweat rolling down the nape of his neck as he panted; his breath fogged the deck plate. He didn't know how he got there. He hadn't woken when he'd jarred to the floor, but his fingers were pressed flat against the metal and his arms were tense, as though he had dragged himself there. No ship alarms sounded, but his door swung open. There stood Jakob and Asher, both in their sleeping clothes and both absolutely panicked.

Ren turned his head and regarded them with a hazy slitted gaze. Jakob was ashen; his brown hair was mussed and in disarray. Asher crossed his arms over his chest and looked at Ren with his jaw clenched. Neither breached the threshold, and that told Ren more than anything.

"What did you see?"

"Everything," Asher said at the same time Jakob replied with, "Nothing."

Jakob lied.

Ren nodded with his overheated cheek pressed to the cool floor. He stayed sprawled there for a long moment as his senses came out of the fog of the nightmare like the sun breaking through a cloudy sky.

"Did I do anything else?"

Jakob shot a glance to Asher. He licked his lips. "Not this time," Jakob said, staring over Asher's shoulder. "No turning off the artificial gravity. No trying to vent the ship. Not even the creepy woman's voice over the comm telling stories. Just the… images on the vid screen."

Ren gasped and nodded. "That's good… that's better."

Asher's mouth twisted.

"Yeah. Incident number six was way better than incident number five when you tried to suffocate us."

Humor. Levity. Ren couldn't bring himself to appreciate it.

"Good. That's good. I'm glad."

"Are you okay?" Jakob asked.

"I'm fine."

"Liar," Jakob said softly. He mustered a smile in Ren's direction.

Asher merely frowned.

Ren waved them both away and pushed his aching body upright. He didn't go far, but chose to remain on the floor, leaning against the lip of his bunk, with his legs crossed.

When he looked up, Jakob was gone, and Asher had stepped into the room and closed the door behind him.

Ren sighed. Asher wanted to talk, and Ren's insides ached with a fierce loneliness he hadn't experienced since the first night in the cell of the Baron's citadel. He didn't want Asher's words or his pity. And he didn't want to relive the details of the nightmare, which had sent him twisting in his sheets and crawling across the floor. The sense memories clung to him, like cobwebs whose phantom threads, fluttery and strange and stubborn, brushed against his skin. The strands were infinite; they touched the deep places of Ren's consciousness and burrowed down to his marrow to pull out the things that terrified him most.

He didn't want to share the nightmare, but Asher's flat countenance and sure gaze couldn't hide his worry. It flashed in his eyes and ran in shaky tremors down the length of his crossed arms, as if he hugged himself to keep in his concerns and not as a defense to reflect whatever Ren had to throw at him.

Ren bent his knees, propped his arm up, and allowed his fingertips to dangle. Sweat flattened his hair against his temples. He regarded Asher coolly as Asher sat on the edge of Ren's bunk.

"Do you remember when we went dancing?"

Asher blinked at the non-sequitur. "On Mykonos?"

Rowan had taken them dancing in a place with loud music and rotating lights. The beat had vibrated through Ren's boots. "I had never been dancing like that before."

Asher raised an eyebrow. "You weren't bad. Well, not as bad as Jakob."

"I liked the slow dance." Asher had grabbed Ren in his arms and pulled him to the dance floor. They'd laughed and moved, and all Ren's worries had dissolved in happiness and the rhythm of the music. "I liked being with you. With the crew. I miss that."

"We're here now, Ren."

He shook his head. "No. You're not. It's different now."

"It doesn't have to be."

Ren looked away.

"Ren, you're not okay," he said flatly.

"No. I'm not, but I didn't feel like broadcasting it."

"It's a little late for that," Asher said softly. Ren's stomach twisted. Asher had all but confirmed his latest nightmare had played on the vid screens. The crew had seen what Ren couldn't remember, didn't want to remember. "You're getting worse. And they know it."

Ren twisted his lips. "I'm aware the crew already knows. Pen can't lie for anything."

"Not them. The Corps."

Ren rested his head on his knees. "You told her. You threw me to the wolves."

"I had to."

"Why? Do you want me to leave? Be locked away?"

"Stars, Ren. You know I don't want that."

"I don't know what you want, to be honest. I don't understand why you hold allegiance to them at all."

"Because I have to. I promised five years."

"You and your promises," Ren said bitterly. That was loyalty Ren couldn't understand, not after what the Corps had done to Asher, not after having left him for a year to rot in a cell on what they called a backwater planet. But Ren was beginning to realize there were things he would never understand and maybe wasn't meant to.

"And I promised I'd keep you safe. Any way I could. This is the only way. Don't you understand that?"

Ren felt the slight touch of Asher's fingertips across the back of his hand. His star sparked and sought out the mechanism in Asher's shoulder instinctually.

Asher shivered.

"There's a fine line between safety and captivity."

Asher tensed and frowned. "You think this is bad? Wait until you get yourself locked away in a real cell."

Ren laughed. His laughter bordered on hysterical and it bubbled, harsh and loud, from his throat. "You think I don't know? You think I want to spend my nights mired in dreams? You think I want any of this?"

Asher's jaw creaked. "I don't know. You're certainly acting like you don't care. What the hell was wrong with you yesterday in front of VanMeerten?"

"Me?" Ren asked, voice breaking. "You're the one who ratted me out as being unstable."

Avoiding Ren's gaze, Asher studied the walls. "It needed to be done. I had to."

Ren swallowed the hard lump in his throat. He narrowed his eyes, and the sense of being betrayed welled up fresh within him. It bled out from Ren's core, like a tide, push-pulling its way through him until he was filled with it, until it was a torrent right under his skin.

"I never thought you would become the person I would need to fear."

Asher whipped his head around and stared, his green eyes bright and furious, at Ren sitting on the floor. His skin turned red, and his mouth pulled into a taut, flat line. His voice quivered, though Ren didn't know if it was due to fury or shock or both. "You're afraid of me?"

Ren was hollow down to his bones. He didn't have it within him to placate Asher, to reassure him. He listed to the side and allowed his head to thump against the pristine wall. "Aren't you afraid of me?"

Asher didn't respond right away, and that was answer enough for Ren.

It seemed Asher didn't have the humor to respond with his usual, "of a stick like you?" or, "of a duster? Never."

All the levity that had marked their relationship had been sucked out and replaced with an uneasy truce, which included secrets, tense silences, and duplicity.

Ren rubbed his face. "I can't do this."

"I know."

"I don't trust you."

Asher's eyes turned sad. "I know," he said again softly.

Ren flexed his fingers and kept eyes down. "You were my anchor and now... I'm drifting."

"I know that, too. You have to... find someone else."

"Are you telling me to give up on us?" Ren dragged his gaze up to meet Asher's.

Asher wouldn't meet his eyes. He picked at his sleep trousers, worrying a thread between his thumb and forefinger. "Yes."

This moment had been inevitable. Ren had begun to dread it over the last few days and, now it was here, he was oddly relieved. He had imagined the feeling would be akin to a punch to the chest. Ren had envisioned that if he were standing, he would've gone weak-kneed and fallen to the deck plate, doubled over and clutching at his heart, barely able to breathe. But he was sitting, with his legs bent, his chin resting on his knees, his feet flat on the floor. It wasn't nearly as dramatic. In fact, the pain was more like a throb than a stab, and even that was pitiful compared to what Ren's thoughts had conjured.

"Oh," Ren breathed. He knotted his fingers in his shirt. All traces of his earlier anger fled, and he was left with a numbness that settled into his middle. "I guess that's it, then."

"I guess it is." Asher stood. "Ren," he started, looking down on Ren's hunched form, "I know it doesn't seem like it, but I'm doing everything I can. Even if I can't be your tether, I'm going to follow through on my promises. All of them."

And there was the dagger-sharp pain Ren had been waiting for. It came wrapped in familiar language and concern, in a combination of truth and lies and pity. It sliced through Ren, making his eyes sting and his hands tremble.

"Please go," he said, blinking.

Asher nodded. "Report in an hour," he said. "If you're up for it. I can cover for you, maybe, if you'd rather–"

"I'll be there," Ren said his voice was a whisper. He shook his head, cleared his throat, and willed himself to be stronger. "I'll be there. I don't want to arouse suspicion, especially after last time. So I'll be there."

"All right. Ren, I–"

"Please leave." Ren squeezed his eyes shut. He didn't want to hear any more.

Asher didn't hesitate, and Ren heard his slow footsteps as he crossed the room. He paused at the threshold, but, to Ren's relief, didn't say anything and left, softly closing the door behind him.

Ren stayed on the floor for a long moment. Then he opened his eyes, shook his hand from the fabric of his shirt, and pressed his fingertips to the floor. He slid into the ship, cast off his body, and stayed in the freedom of the systems as long as he could.

The defiance that had marked Ren's appearance in front of VanMeerten the day before had tempered into a feeling less fierce, less incendiary—a slow-burning stubbornness. He yearned to go home, to find Liam, to see his village, but those desires had shifted to the back of his mind after his conversation with Asher that morning. His immediate thoughts centered on other matters, such as staying sane without an anchor.

However, he lifted his chin and narrowed his eyes when the general appeared on screen.

For the first time since the check-ins had started, VanMeerten appeared *human*. A few flyaway strands of her iron-gray hair escaped her bun. She had a worry line between her eyebrows, and, while her medals still shined, there was a crease in her uniform.

It didn't seem like a victory. Ren didn't look much better, wearing his sleep clothes, barefoot, hair mussed. Their confrontation had taken a toll on both of them. Ren wondered what that meant.

"Good morning," Rowan said from her position between Ren and Millicent.

"Hello, Captain Morgan. I trust everyone is well."

Rowan was thrown by the politeness. "Sure?" she answered.

VanMeerten nodded. "Good." She lifted a manila folder from her desk and shuffled a few papers. "Corporal Morgan has reported that the male star host has been experiencing vivid nightmares bordering on hallucinations and has unconsciously caused failures in several different systems aboard your ship. He shows symptoms of mental decompensation. He is an active danger, though unintentionally, and could become a substantial threat if his connections with technology continue. Is this correct, Corporal?"

"Yes." Asher didn't hesitate.

Ren bristled; his body went tense. He bit his lower lip to keep from lashing out, from saying anything stupid to get him in more trouble.

"And your recommendation is to remove the subject from an artificial environment?"

"Yes. For a while. A break from technology may provide a necessary reset."

Ren stiffened. His eyes wide, he glared at the side of Asher's head. Was he recommending Ren be removed from the *Star Stream?* Did he want Ren to be locked away? Like in the iron cell at the citadel? The star in Ren's chest pulsed, and the warmth of it spread down his limbs.

"Captain Morgan," VanMeerten said, tenting her fingers and leveling her hard stare at Rowan. "Does your offer stand of taking the star hosts to their home planet?"

Ren's mouth dropped open, and he whipped his head around to stare at Rowan.

Rowan blinked. She cast a glance in Ren's direction; her eyebrows were pulled together. "Excuse me?" she asked, addressing the general.

"Can you take them back to Erden?" VanMeerten said, punctuating each word.

"Yes. Yes, after we finish our current trajectory, we'll plot a course and—"

"No. It must happen immediately."

Rowan placed her hands on her hips. "I think I've been clear about how I feel in regard to the Corps interfering in my business."

"I understand, Captain." VanMeerten said, putting down the papers. "I will have a regiment meet you at your destination."

"Wait," Rowan said. "What?"

"To take the male into custody."

"Explain."

"If Corporal Morgan's assessment is correct, then the threat is imminent. Either the star host goes back to the dirt to *reset*, as the corporal has endorsed, or we take him to the prison near Perilous Space and monitor his progress there."

Cold fear washed down Ren's body, and he shoved his hands into his pockets to hide their shaking. He knew that he had pressed last time, but he didn't think he'd done so much damage. He had touched a nerve, exposed VanMeerten's fear, and now he paid the price. Ren shrank back and pressed his shoulder blades against the wall.

Rowan's jaw worked. "That seems a bit of an overreaction."

VanMeerten smiled, predatory, with the scar on her cheek prominent. "You said yourself he was a danger."

"But—"

VanMeerten placed her hands on her desk and loomed. "Either the planet or the prison. It's your choice, Captain."

Rowan tapped her foot and tugged her braid, then crossed her arms over her chest. Using their eyes, mouths, and eyebrows, she and Asher shared an intense silent conversation, which Ren couldn't decipher. For a strained moment, Ren thought Rowan would choose her job over him, especially given the influence from Asher. "It's not much of a choice, is it?" she finally replied. "I'm not going to condemn Ren to another cell."

"Very well. Your decision is confirmed and will be documented."

"I'll have our pilot plot a course to Erden."

VanMeerten didn't acknowledge the statement. She cut the video feed. The screen went blank.

The tense atmosphere relaxed as if a taut string had been cut and the ends were fluttering to the ground. Ren sagged against the wall. Rowan bowed her head, and Asher rubbed a hand over his brow. They didn't speak. Ren silently thanked the stars for Rowan.

"She didn't ask about me," Millicent said, softly.

Rowan laughed, breathless. "No, no she didn't. I think that's a good thing."

Millicent's mouth turned down at the corner, but she shrugged and swayed off the bridge.

"We're going to have a talk," Rowan said to Asher. "About what the hell you're up to."

Asher shifted uncomfortably. "It got him back to his planet," he muttered, looking at the floor. "It's what he wanted." He turned on his heel and marched down the stairs.

In disbelief, Ren watched Asher leave.

"I don't know what is going on between you two, but I think Asher just manipulated a high-ranking military official to make sure you get to go back home."

Ren's mouth went dry.

"I think he manipulated me, too," Rowan said, smiling softly. "Brothers, huh?"

Ren took a long moment to answer. "Thank you, Captain." His body trembled, and he didn't have the strength to move from the wall. "Thank you."

"You're welcome, string bean. We'll figure it out." She tapped her fingertips against her mouth. "We'll have to. I need to talk to Lucas." She mustered a smile, but it didn't reach her eyes. On her way out, she ruffled Ren's hair. "We'll be okay."

Ren was certain she said it more for her own benefit than his. But it was a nice sentiment. They'd figure it out. In the meantime, he was going home. He was going *home*.

The thought was a bright spot amid the dark, and Ren clung to it.

Ren drifted from the bridge to his room to engineering and finally found himself in the cargo bay.

Millicent was not there but Ollie was. He glanced up from where he moved crates around; his brown eyes glinted under the naked light that hung above the expansive room. Ollie's muscles flexed under his brown skin as he dragged a heavy cargo box across the floor. The sound of scraping was loud and harsh, until he paused near where Millicent kept her rug.

Ollie beckoned to Ren. "Hey, Ren. Got this box in a trade. Might be of interest."

Ren didn't think it would be, but Ollie was the first person to interact with Ren since the conversation on the bridge. Ren needed companionship. Maybe it would take the focus off the thoughts in his head and the whispers of the ship around him.

Ren descended the stairs and stood by the crate.

Using a crowbar, Ollie popped off the lid; the wood clattered to the floor. A cloud of dust floated up, and Ren coughed and waved it out of his face.

"Did you know when you traded for it that it was full of junk?"

Ollie shrugged but didn't answer. He sifted through the parts and pieces of broken tech as Ren peered over his massive shoulder.

Ollie straightened and clapped his hands together to brush off the sawdust.

"Go on then," Ollie said, gesturing at the broken bits of circuitry.

"Go on what?"

"To practice. Figured you and Millie might want a few objects to mess with other than Pen's mixer."

Ren swayed closer to the mess.

"So you did know what it was."

Ollie's smile was small but it was there.

"If you got these back on Mykonos, why wait so long to share them?"

Ollie shrugged again; his mouth straightened into a flat line. "You want them or not? If you can fix them, we can turn them around and sell them for a profit."

Ren thought he should stop questioning motives and take the gesture for what it was: a gift of distraction, born out of concern and thoughtfulness.

Ren pulled out a few circuit boards. "Thanks, Ollie."

"No problem, Ren. Anything to help."

Ren clutched the circuitry to his chest. The metal and wire caught on the fabric of his shirt and bit into the skin of his hands. "No, really," he said, throat tight. "I appreciate it."

Ollie dropped a large hand on Ren's shoulder and squeezed. "You're welcome, Ren. I know things may seem like dirt right now, but ride it out and you'll be fine. You'll never be lost as long as you look to the stars."

Ren nodded. "Did you learn that in all your years of traversing the cluster?"

Ollie laughed. "No. I read it in a book of maps Lucas had. Doesn't mean it's not true though."

"I'm not so sure, Ollie. Looking at the stars only made me lonelier and more lost."

"Maybe you weren't looking at the right angle."

Ren toed at the corner of the box; his boot broke off a splinter.

Ollie crossed the bay to move another crate. "Back to work for me," he said, as he picked up his clipboard. "I need to prepare if we're going to pull off what Rowan wants. Apparently, her reputation is at stake." He grinned.

"Yeah, I'm… going to go work on these."

"Come back and get more when you're finished."

"All right."

Ollie waved over his shoulder as Ren ascended the stairs to the main part of the ship. He made his way to the common room, which was blessedly empty.

Settling on the end of the couch, Ren picked up the first of the boards and lost himself in work.

⊣⊢

Ren was still there when time for the midday meal rolled around. Penelope was the first to breeze in and she gave Ren a light tap on his outstretched leg as she passed to begin fixing lunch. Asher was next, and Ren pretended to be busy with the circuit board, even though he had fixed it and its partner in about twenty minutes. He fiddled with the circuits; his eyes glowed blue. Asher stared at him but Ren ignored it.

Penelope engaged Asher in light conversation. She whipped up a quick midday meal. When she finished, she alerted everyone via shipwide comm. As Ren fiddled, the crew members shuffled in and sat in their usual places around the large table. A plate of sandwiches made with meat spread sat in the middle beside a bowl of a congealed noodles with vegetables. It was obvious their fresh supplies had run out.

Ren's stomach turned at the thought of trying to eat anything. No one else seemed fazed.

"Not joining us, Ren?" Rowan asked as she bit into her sandwich.

Ren shook his head and kept his lips together in a firm line. Much to his relief, Rowan didn't press. Instead, she leveled her gaze at Jakob.

"Have you heard the news?" she asked.

Jakob looked over his shoulder and then at the group. "Me?" he asked, pointing to his chest.

Rowan nodded.

"What news? Ren, what's she talking about?"

Ren bit his lip.

"Asher, you tell them," Rowan said, saving Ren from having to participate. He was grateful for that and uncertain how to report that his captors had granted him a small reprieve.

Asher snapped his head and stopped pushing his food around on his plate. He straightened, tugged at the collar of his uniform, and brushed out imaginary wrinkles.

"General VanMeerten has granted the request." He pulled his shoulders back. Ren wanted to scoff at Asher's transformation from friend to lapdog soldier. "To take you back to Erden."

Jakob sat stunned. "We're going back?" he asked, dropping his spoon on his plate. "You're not joking? Are you? Because that would be cruel, Ash. Very cruel."

"It's not a joke. We're going to Erden."

Seeing the smile that broke over Jakob's face was like watching the morning sun crest the horizon and throw sparkles on the lake. He bent his head, smiled at his plate, then glanced up and fidgeted. He picked up his bread and set it down. His cheeks flushed, and he laughed while rubbing a hand over his eyes.

Ren had never seen Jakob so excited he did not know what to do with his limbs. It was endearing.

"Did you hear, Ren? We're going home." The tone of awe was also new.

Ren nodded and forced a smile. "We are."

"I... I... thank you," he said to Asher. "Thank you. I don't know how you convinced her, but thank you."

"Don't thank me. Thank Ren for threatening the Phoenix Corps and nearly getting himself thrown into the prison near Perilous Space."

Jakob's joy tempered. "You did what?" he asked quietly. "Ren, what?"

"I reminded VanMeerten what I'm capable of," Ren said, lifting one shoulder in an awkward shrug. He set the circuits aside and threaded his fingers.

Jakob pointed his finger at Ren. "I said ask, not threaten. Are you addled? Stars, Ren, all they need is a reason."

Ren crossed his arms. "I thought you'd be happy."

"I am happy. But you didn't need to poke a beehive."

"What's a beehive?" Lucas asked, coming into the room. He gave Penelope a kiss, then took his seat at the table.

"Seriously?" Jakob asked.

Lucas plopped a large serving of the noodles on his plate. They splattered and oozed into an unappetizing puddle. "What? Is it a duster thing?"

"Yes, it's a duster thing." Jakob rolled his eyes and shared a look with Ren that conveyed his disbelief.

"Oh, I saw that," Lucas said. "I grew up in space, okay? I don't understand the flora and fauna of your dirt."

"I'm not even going to respond. There's so much wrong with that," Jakob said.

Ren smiled, but he stayed on his perch on the couch. No one seemed to notice that he was not joining in, or if they did, they didn't comment.

"Mill," Jakob said, "can you believe it? We're going home."

Millicent blinked her large eyes. "Home?" she asked.

"Yeah, to Erden. Ren… convinced them. Isn't that great?"

"Oh, yes. I was there. I heard." She took a bite of her bread. "But Erden isn't my home."

Everyone froze. Jakob cocked his head and tapped his fork against his plate in a nervous rhythm. He shot a look to Ren. Ren frowned, as confused as everyone else. Millicent didn't talk much of her past before they'd met her on Mykonos. All Ren knew was she had grown up with the knowledge of what she was.

Asher leaned forward. "What do you mean? You were in the cell next to mine."

"Yes," she said. She took a bite from her sandwich and dabbed her mouth with a napkin. She folded it. "I was in the cell next to yours, but I was brought there." Millicent didn't seem to notice how the crew hung on every word. She didn't notice that Rowan stared and Asher clutched his fork so tightly it was beginning to bend. "I'm from the planet Crei."

"How are we just learning about this?" Rowan demanded.

Millicent's hazel eyes were wide and her face was pale. "No one has asked."

"Then how in the hell did you end up on Erden with Asher?"

She sighed. "Because that is where Abiathar took me after he found me and offered me the chance to leave my planet and travel if I helped him. He promised me a prominent place among the drifts if I would use my gift in his service."

After a moment of thick silence, of disbelief, Ren's stomach dropped.

"You enlisted?" Jakob shouted. "You agreed to help that cog?"

"It wasn't like that," she said, voice never wavering. "He said he'd take me away from the factories and the smoke and the pollution and bring me to the stars. How could I say no?"

Jakob's jaw dropped. "Ren, are you hearing this?"

"Yes," he said. "But it doesn't matter."

Jakob jumped to his feet, sending his chair skidding behind him. "Doesn't matter? Our village was destroyed. Our families are gone. Sorcha is gone. And she played a part." He pointed a shaking finger at Millicent.

Ren placed his hands in his lap and tried to sort through his thoughts and feelings. He took a breath. "I know, Jakob. I'm sorry."

It was the wrong thing to say. Jakob slammed his fist on the table; his plate clattered, and the water in his cup sloshed. He heaved a few breaths, and his body shook; the rest of the group stared in awkward and sympathetic silence.

"I need air," Jakob choked on the words. He stalked out.

No one moved except Millicent, who took a bite of her sandwich unperturbed.

Rowan cleared her throat. "I think the bigger issue here is: What the stars was that insane old man doing on Crei in the first place?"

"Looking for star hosts," Lucas said. "And finding them, obviously." He jerked his chin toward Millicent, and his goggles slid crooked.

Millicent continued to eat her lunch.

"Or," Asher said, "the threat against the drifts is bigger than we thought."

"I'm sorry," Pen said softly, "But please explain. I don't understand."

Asher dropped his bent fork. With his elbows on the table, he tented his fingers and leaned forward. "What if it's more than one crazy despotic Baron on a backward planet? What if it's two planets, or three, conspiring against the drifts? What if it's Erden and Crei and Stahl and more? What if Baron Vos was only the first?"

"That's a lot of ifs, Ash," Rowan said. "And it's not what we need to concentrate on right now. Because of this decision by the Corps, we're not going to be able to finish our cargo run."

"What are we going to do?" Pen asked.

"I've already asked Ollie to arrange the cargo as needed for an in-transit pick-up. And I've asked Lucas to find a friendly along our route." She leveled her gaze at Lucas.

He fidgeted, pushed his goggles onto the crown of his head from where they had slipped down to his brow. The strap caught in his red hair and left a strand standing on end.

"Yeah, about that."

"Yes?"

"We really only have one choice." He squirmed. "It's Hatfield."

The protests were loud, and Ren shrank back, startled at the vehemence not only from Ollie and Asher, but from Penelope as well.

"Do you not remember what happened last time?" Ollie spat. "They tried to pull us into an ancient feud they had with another trading family. We were shot at."

"By *both* families," Penelope added.

"In a *crossfire*."

"I was dressing pulse gun grazes for weeks."

Lucas threw up his hands. "Well, what am I supposed to do? I can't make a cargo ship appear from nowhere. And they are nearby, within a day if they stuck to their submitted schedule and route."

Ren zoned out as they argued. Maybe Lucas couldn't make a cargo ship appear, but Ren could transport the *Star Stream* across the cluster. He'd done it before. It would take concentration and tapping into the well of his power, but he could do it. It would help Rowan, too, and she had given up so much for him. He could repay her.

"I could do it," he said, interrupting.

The group turned to look at him. Asher's gaze swept over Ren.

"Do what?"

"Transport us. To the drift. I've done it before."

Asher's response was quick. "No."

"Absolutely not," Rowan agreed.

Ren jutted out his chin. "I could do it. I'm powerful enough."

Asher planted his palms on the table next to his plate, and his chest heaved. "You've done it once under extreme duress. And even then you didn't know when you did it, how you did it, and where you transported us. It wiped you out for *days*. And do you honestly think you're in control enough to do it? If you think for one moment I will allow you to endanger the crew or yourself then you have absolutely gone as crazy as the Corps believes."

In a long moment of silence Ren's insides twisted in confusion and frustration.

"I think what Asher is trying to say," Penelope said, "is let's try meeting with the Hatfields first, and if that fails, we'll try… star-powered transporting."

Ren nodded. "Fine."

"Good, then it's settled," Rowan said, with the finality of a captain. "We'll meet with the Hatfields tomorrow, transfer the cargo, and head to Erden." She took a bite of her food. "It'll be easy. I'm certain of it."

No one else was convinced.

4

In fact, it wasn't easy.

Maybe Lucas was the best pilot in the cluster, if everyone on the *Star Stream* was to be believed, but maneuvering to seal with another ship was difficult even for him. And Ren was forbidden to assist, as was Millicent. Asher was wary their powers may give them away and cause more stress in an already stressful situation.

So Ren waited impotently on the walk above the cargo bay while Ollie and Asher readied the crates. The twin thunks of towing cables hitting the hull triggered the memory of the *Star Stream* under attack by Abiathar. Ren clutched the railing and willed his fear to stay in check while he endured every scrape of metal against metal and every jolt and shudder as the ships bumped into position. It was difficult. He'd been connected to the ship since the moment they'd departed Mykonos and he could feel the distress of metal in his throat and the groan of the systems in his bones.

Ren's power itched inside of him, right in the middle of his chest, and he clenched down on it and drew it in instead of allowing it to flow out.

"You look like you're in pain." Millicent's voice startled him, and he gritted his teeth as she drifted toward him. "Your face is scrunched."

"I'm doing what Asher asked." Ren's grip tightened on the railing. Sweat beaded along his hairline.

"You've been in the systems too long. Pulling back will be almost impossible."

"I can do it."

"I don't understand why you need to." She placed her hand on Ren's forearm, where the muscles strained beneath the fabric of his long-sleeved shirt. "You're only hurting yourself when you could be helping."

"According to Asher, this is helping."

Millicent blinked. "He doesn't understand that holding back is more dangerous than letting go. He isn't one of us."

That was... true. Asher didn't understand the nuances of power or its terrible sweetness.

"He's trying to protect you again, but he can't protect you from what you are," Millicent continued.

Ren closed his eyes and relaxed just a bit; his shoulders dropped from near his ears. Spurred by Millicent's power, his star traveled down the length of his body, searching for a destination. Ren was only the conduit. The *Star Stream*'s systems were home and welcomed him with open circuits as his power poured into them. He found solace in the video feeds and, even with his eyes closed, he could see the whole cargo bay and observe as Asher and Ollie talked. He could see his own tall, willowy body and shaggy brown hair, and noted that his face was relaxed as if he were asleep. Compared to Millicent's small frame and pale skin, Ren looked alien.

"There you go," Millicent said. "See? That feels better, doesn't it?"

Ren nodded. Yes, this was good. Millicent was right. She was always in control, and Ren should learn from her, learn to wield his gift to help others instead of being in constant fear of it.

The ship vibrated under Ren's feet, and instantly he was at the aft airlock and in the comm system. He listened as the Hatfield crew talked with Lucas and, after a wrenching sound, confirmed they were in position. Ren eased along the docking apparatus and coaxed it out of the *Star Stream*'s outer pocket until it met with the extension from the *Family Honor*. He monitored the seal and the pressurization of the resulting tunnel, ensuring everything was safe.

Though there was no video in the access tunnel, there was audio, and, through the connection, Ren snuck into the systems of the *Family Honor*. He scrolled through the crew manifest—fifteen hands, all family if the names were any indication, led by Captain Anse. He browsed their video feeds and found their cargo area, noting the four crew members who stood near their airlock, waiting for the go-ahead to venture across. Three were men, dressed in clothes Ren thought were more duster than spacer, all with shocking red hair. A woman was the point, and her posture reminded Ren of Rowan as she stood with her arms crossed and her back straight. She wore a tool belt and had goggles on her straight red hair and a pulse gun strapped to her leg. In fact, they all had weapons. They each carried at least one gun, and two of the men had electric staffs that reminded Ren of the prods back on Erden.

Tuning into their comms, whose static rendered them almost useless, he heard most of their conversation.

"Are you sure about this, Rosie?"

"Yes. Rowan Morgan is no pirate. She's not going to do us wrong."

"What if they're cross about last time?"

"Then they wouldn't have contacted us."

"Wonder what was so coggin' important that they have to relinquish their cargo in the middle of a run?"

Rosie shook her head and shifted. "Didn't say much. An emergency with one of their crew."

Ren crackled.

"Be on your guard, though," she continued. "I may trust Rowan, but who knows what is going to be on the other side of this walk."

"And if it goes south?"

"Protect yourself. Kill who you have to. Take the cargo."

"Maybe we should do that anyway." Ren zeroed in on the speaker—a tall man with freckles across his nose, a tattoo on his neck, and half an ear. "Forget the niceties."

Rosie smirked. "I wouldn't say no to that."

The group laughed.

Ren snapped back into his body. He staggered backward, released the railing, and almost fell on his backside. While he'd drifted, Millicent had wandered away, and Rowan had joined Asher and Ollie on the bay floor. She had her weapon, but the other two were unarmed.

They were *unarmed*.

Ren jolted upright, gathered his shaky legs under himself, and stumbled down the metal steps.

"Don't let them come aboard," Ren shouted as he tripped his way to the trio. "They're armed. They want the cargo. Why don't you have weapons?"

"Ren? Are you okay?" Ollie asked, grabbing Ren's arm as he barreled into their group. "What are you talking about?"

"The Hatfields are armed to the teeth. They were talking about killing you and taking the cargo."

Rowan's eyebrows shot up, but Asher's expression turned dark.

"How do you know that?" he asked.

Ren shook off Ollie's grip. "I *heard* them."

"By using your power after I specifically said to stay out of the way and out of trouble. I told you that you were not to do anything to add stress to this situation."

Ren clenched his teeth and narrowed his eyes. He was not going to be scolded like a naughty child for trying to protect his friends. "Are you seriously lecturing me when I'm trying to warn you? The Hatfields are dangerous."

"We know, Ren," Rowan said, voice quiet but harsh. "We aren't going into this blind."

"But, they said—"

Asher sighed, cutting him off. "Look, there is trade etiquette going on here your little duster self doesn't understand, which is why *I didn't want you here*. Not to mention your erratic behavior the last few weeks. We don't need you spouting accusations at people we're trying to do business with."

"Hey, guys," Lucas's voice came over the shipwide comm. "They're approaching. Be ready to open the airlock."

Rowan nodded toward Ollie, who left the group after a worried glance cast Ren's way.

"Go sit down on the stairs, Ren," Rowan said, and it was an order, not a suggestion.

Ren took a step back. "But—"

"Go. Or are you disobeying a direct order from your captain?"

Ren slunk away, head down, shoulders hunched. His stomach churned. He knew what he'd heard, but what if he had misunderstood? Rowan was confident. Ollie was intimidating by merely standing there; his bulky form was heads taller than most men. And Asher had military experience. He wouldn't allow Rowan to walk into a dangerous situation.

Ren sighed as he settled on the stairs. Ren spotted Jakob and Penelope on the overhead walkway, overlooking the proceedings. Jakob had a pulse gun in the crook of his arm, and Penelope had a small gun peeking from her tool belt. Ren winced when he realized the rest of the crew had had a plan all along.

One they hadn't shared with him.

Ollie opened the airlock, and the seal hissed as the group from the Hatfield ship walked into the bay. They paused on the other side of the threshold. Rosie was in front as the three men fanned out behind her.

Ren focused on the man who had joked about foregoing niceties and taking their cargo. The man observed Ollie, sizing him up, as Ollie resealed the door. His eyes twitched, and his mouth set in a frown. And he held his body in a way which suggested a familiarity with these types of situations. He was dangerous. Ren saw it in the missing piece of his ear, the tattoo of a wildcat on his neck, the nicked body armor, and the ease of his steps. Ren's chest burned.

"Rosie Hatfield," Rowan said, with a forced smile. "Welcome aboard."

"Thank you, Rowan Morgan." Her smiled wasn't overly friendly; the corners of her mouth barely lifted. "Long time, no see."

"I trust your father was able to confirm the information with the recipient." Rowan wasn't one for small talk, but was always to the point, especially when it pertained to business.

Rosie took stock of the hold. Her gaze stopped on Ren before raking across Jakob and Penelope.

"Yes. We'll give you ten percent of the take."

Rowan arched an eyebrow. "Ten percent? That's ridiculous. My crew brokered the deal. My ship has taken it over halfway. Ten percent is robbery." The atmosphere grew tense. Asher shifted. Ollie moved to stand behind Rowan.

Rosie controlled her expression to look bored, but her gaze flicked to the suspended walk and back. "And?"

"Sixty percent," Rowan countered, hands on her hips.

"Now who is being ridiculous? Twenty."

"Forty."

"Twenty-five."

"Thirty."

Rosie rolled her eyes, then checked over her shoulder and held a silent conversation with the guy with the tattoo.

Were negotiations *niceties*? Ren sat up straighter and watched the exchange, on alert.

Rosie turned back. "Fine."

She held out her hand, and Rowan took it. The handshake sealed the deal.

"Pleasure doing business."

"Likewise." Rose jerked her head toward the crates laid out in front of Asher. "My brothers will be taking those." The three large men moved, but Rowan held up her hand.

"The thirty percent first, please."

Rosie frowned. Her fingers danced along the holster at her side. "Thirty upon delivery."

"No, thirty now. I wasn't born yesterday, Rosie. Credits now, then cargo."

Rosie twisted her lips, but she reached into her pocket and pulled out a chip. She held it between two of her fingers. "This chip has twenty-five percent on it. Take this now or thirty upon delivery."

Rowan tapped her foot. She brushed her blond braid over her shoulder. "Are you *crunching* me?"

Shrugging, Rosie spun the credit chip between her fingers. "This is what I got, Rowan. Take it or leave it."

Rowan placed her hands on her hips. "Save me from cutthroats," she muttered. "Fine, we'll take it. But I'll remember this."

Rosie's smile grew, but it wasn't friendly. "I'm sure you will."

She tossed Rowan the chip, and Rowan handed it to Asher, who checked it in the reader. He nodded.

Rosie gestured, and her family stepped forward to gather the crates. The brother approached Ollie. He laughed at an untold joke and pushed Ollie's shoulder, roughly. It was too friendly and too aggressive, with his mouth twisted into a smile or a snarl, Ren couldn't tell. He touched Ollie again, on the arm, and his grease-stained fingers wrapped over Ollie's bicep, his nails making indents in Ollie's brown flesh.

Ren's heart sped up.

Then the Hatfield brother's other hand fluttered near his side, and his fingers brushed over the grip of his pulse gun. Ren trembled with fear.

He shot to his feet. Static filled his head. His vision flickered blue. Ren's limbs jerked as he crossed the space. His muscles were taut, his eyes were ablaze, and he raised his hand, fingers splayed.

The star poured from his fingertips and burst from his body in a pulse of blue light. For one chilling second, everything went still. Time slowed to a crawl as the wave of power engulfed the room.

Their weapons were easy. He broke them with a thought, all of them—snapped the mechanisms in the pulse guns' triggers and burned the wires in the prods. He even shorted their comms, keeping them from contacting support. No. They weren't going to hurt this crew—his friends, his family.

Ren stalked forward with electricity sparking between his fingers. One of the intruders pulled his inert weapon and, with twisted pleasure, Ren disassembled it. The mechanisms fell like snow to the deck plate, where they pinged. The invading group scrambled back, yelling, *screaming*, and Ren smiled.

Let them be scared. Let them run. Let them be *terrified*. They were bullies—cutthroats as Rowan said. They were dangerous. They didn't belong on the ship.

Ren opened the airlock. The metal door banged open, and the Hatfields lunged for it. With his senses tangled in the systems, Ren could hear the conversation through the comms.

"What is he?" Rosie yelled. "What the stars is happening, Rowan?"

"Ren!" In the vid feeds, Ren saw Asher step into his path. The pressure of Asher's hands on Ren's shoulders was negligible. His voice stirred nothing.

"Stop him, Ash."

"Ren, listen to my voice. Listen to me. They're not trying to hurt us."

Ren tilted his head. "*Forget the niceties.*"

"That was a joke!" The voice cracked with fear. "I swear. It was a joke."

Ren was in the *Star Stream*. He was in the airlock and in the tunnel. He was in the *Family Honor*. He was spread between the two ships, in every system, in every nook, and he could do *anything*.

"We're leaving. Keep the cargo and the chip."

"No!" Asher held out a hand. "Stay put. Don't go in the tunnel."

"Snap him out of it, Ash!"

"Ren! Move out of the way, Pen. I can help!"

Rowan pointed a finger toward the walkway. "Stay where you are, Jakob."

"Ren, listen to my voice. Listen to me. Come on." Asher was close, filling Ren's blue vision. His grip was tight on Ren's body, though his touch was distant. "What happens when an unstoppable force meets an immovable object?"

Ren paused. The question didn't make sense. He couldn't answer it. Why was Asher assisting the people who wanted to hurt them? He'd kept them from entering the tunnel where Ren could've vented them, but no matter. They threatened Ren's family. He could threaten theirs.

"The *Family Honor* is sealed. Crew manifest shows fifteen hands." He couldn't vent them, not while they were connected to the *Star Stream*. He'd have to kill them another way. "Preparing to disable life support systems."

"Ash! Stop him!"

"I *can't!*"

Rowan's voice was a shriek. Asher pushed on Ren's corporeal body as paradoxes fell from his lips. The questions made Ren twitch and flinch and stalled him from continuing with his plans. They were annoying, like a vibration, a sticky cog in a machine. Ren pulled his attention from the ships and fixated on Asher.

His shoulder was tech, metal fused with bone. Ren pushed into it and rendered the apparatus inert, and the arm fell useless to Asher's side. Asher staggered back; his eyes were wide, and his hand clutched his unusable bicep.

"Ren," he whispered, confused, hurt, and afraid.

And then Ollie arrived in front of him.

"Sorry, friend," Ollie said. He pulled back his fist, and Ren didn't duck.

His head snapped around, and his vision flickered from blue to normal to spotted black. His jaw *ached*, and tears gathered in his eyes. Ren's knees went weak, and he fell to the floor like a rag doll.

"Can a man drown in the fountain of youth?"

Ren cradled his jaw in his hand. "Paradox," he slurred.

"He's fine," Ollie called. "Everything is fine."

Ren wasn't sure about that. His body was limp against the deck, and his face *hurt*. He closed his eyes and allowed the exhaustion and the force of Ollie's blow pull him into darkness.

Ren woke to an argument. He was on the couch in the common room, of that much he was certain: for one, it smelled a bit, and two, a spring dug into Ren's back just enough to be truly uncomfortable. He didn't move, however, because his head swam and his face throbbed. Feigning sleep seemed a good choice, especially since there was yelling.

Rowan's voice bounced off the metal walls, almost drowning out her steps as she paced. "Stars, Ash! When were you going to tell me that Ren has gone completely around the bend?"

"Rowan," Ash said, sounding pained. "Can we not go into that right now?"

"Are you coggin' kidding me? We can and we will. Did you not see him attack the Hatfields? And they were friendlies!"

"They were armed," Asher replied. He sounded weary and troubled.

"And," Ollie's voice came from the other side of the room, "that one guy did push me, and his hand touched his pulse gun. Ren was only protecting us."

"That doesn't matter. He went supernova *again*, and almost cost us the cargo, the credits, and my reputation, not to mention he *almost killed people!*"

There was a scrape of a chair sliding across the floor. "I know. All right? I know."

"Why the hell couldn't you pull him out of it? Why didn't your voice or the questions work? For stars' sake, why didn't you kiss him?"

Ren's throat went tight. "Because I'm not his anchor anymore. We're not… he's not… he doesn't trust me."

Rowan stopped. Ren pictured her sinking into her chair at the head of the table. "We need to take precautions. He doesn't sleep alone anymore in case he tries to access the ship in his nightmares. And no more using his power. If we need a fix, we have Millicent on board." Rowan paused. "Where the hell was she when this all happened anyway? Couldn't she have pushed Ren out? She's done that before."

"Probably hiding from Jakob. They're not friends at the moment."

"Cogs," Rowan breathed. "Am I running a ship full of actual children?"

"It's going to be all right, Cap," Ollie said. His boots were heavy as he crossed the room. "I'll move the hammock into Ren's bunk. Jakob and I will switch off. We're only a few days out from Erden. We'll manage."

"I hope so. I don't want anyone to get hurt, Ren included. He's a kid, and I know he's doing the best he can. It's… well, it's hard to reconcile the *thing* that can disable weapons and vent a ship with the duster asleep on the couch."

Ren's eyes stung. His insides twisted with guilt and anger and sorrow. He needed to leave the ship. He needed to get home, so he would stop putting everyone in danger.

Ollie left the room and his steps retreated down the hall, presumably to move the hammock.

Rowan spoke, voice low. "How's your arm?"

"Hurts," Asher replied.

"I figured that, moron. Can it be fixed?"

Asher sighed. "I think so. Ren could. Millicent maybe, too."

Ren bit his lip to keep from begging Asher to ask him and not Millicent. He'd fix it. He broke it, he *hurt* Asher, and he'd do anything to take that back. Just because Ren couldn't rely on Asher any longer didn't mean he wanted Asher to be in pain. He wanted Asher to have everything, everything Ren couldn't give him, and that was one of the reasons Ren had to leave.

"Be careful," Rowan said.

"I will."

"What are we going to do when he wakes up?"

There was a rustle and the creak of a chair. "We're going to move on. We're going to take him back to his planet and hope being away from the ship helps him."

"And if it doesn't?"

"Then we figure out another way for him to be safe. For us to be safe."

"Even if it means he goes to the Perilous Space prison?"

Ren's heart clenched as icy fingers of fear wrapped around it and squeezed. He stiffened and begged his body to keep from trembling and giving himself away.

"We'll do what we have to."

And just like that, Ren knew once he set foot on Erden, he would not be returning with the crew to the *Star Stream*.

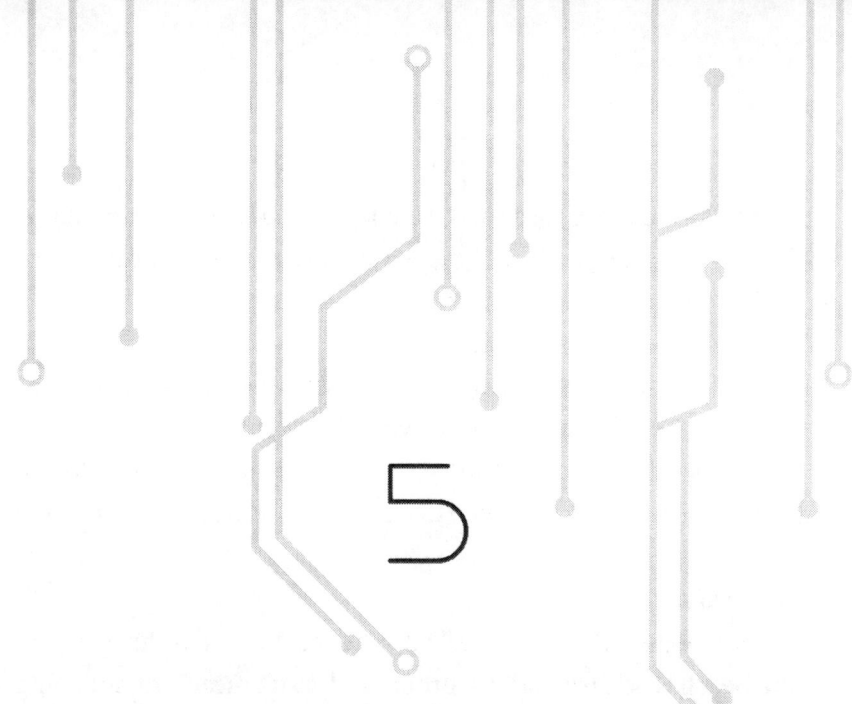

5

HE WAS BY THE LAKE. His toes sank into the warm sand; the water nipped at his skin. He leaned back on his elbows. The stars twinkled above him. He wasn't afraid. Ren inhaled the scent of the water and of the fresh green trees behind him.

"I'm not here, you know."

Ren sat up and craned his neck to look over his shoulder at his younger brother. Liam stood behind him with his hands in his pockets, dressed the same as the day Ren was taken from their home.

"Liam?"

Liam stepped forward, moving like a ghost with his feet barely skimming the ground. His skin and hair were paler than Ren remembered, his freckles were barely discernible in the light, and the red of his hair not as bright: It seemed washed out.

Liam peered out over the water.

"Why always here?"

"What?"

"You always dream you are at this dumb lake. You've been all over now—drifts and ships—and you come to this place. Why?"

Ren followed Liam's gaze and watched the lake. In the dark, it was endlessly black; the rhythm of the waves was a living, shifting thing, terrifying and comforting at once.

"Because it's home, I guess."

Liam shook his head. "Then dream about the house. Or the village."

"Because it's the last place I saw you."

Liam stared at Ren, and his gaze seemed to pierce Ren to the marrow. Ren hunched in, pulled his knees to his chest, and protected his core.

"I'm not here."

"I know, Liam," Ren snapped. "I don't expect you to be hanging out on the beach when we land on Erden. It doesn't mean I'm not going to look. I'm going to look for you and find you."

Liam frowned. He shoved his hands into his pockets and shook his head.

The water inched closer as the waves, increasing in intensity, slapped against the shore.

"You need to leave before she pulls you in."

Liam nodded toward the lake to point out how the icy water spilled over Ren's ankles and climbed up his skin to his knees.

Ren jumped to his feet, but the lake was sentient, and the water became fingers, gripping his legs, yanking him down. He fell to his knees, and the water surged to his waist, then his shoulders.

"Liam," Ren gasped. "Help."

"I'm not *here*." Liam said. He stepped away. His figure shimmered, and then he faded.

Ren struggled against the water, but it was viscous and stifling, squeezing around his chest, leeching up his neck, to his chin, to his mouth—

"Wake up!"

Ren sat up gasping. Jakob sat on the edge of his bunk. His hands were heavy on Ren's shoulders; his hair was mussed, and his eyes were wide.

"Did I... have I...?"

"No," Jakob shook his head. "No. You're okay." Jakob's reassurances and smile were brittle. His face was pale; his expression was a thin veneer of calm over panic.

"I was on Erden, and Liam was there at the lake and he kept saying he wasn't there. But he was and..." Ren pushed a hand into his hair and gripped it and breathed.

"It was a dream. Only a dream, Ren."

"I... I'm not sure. Jakob, I don't know what's happening to me." Ren grabbed Jakob's sleep shirt and twined his fingers in the fabric.

Jakob's cheeks were sleep-pink, and he had a crease across his face from the pillow. He sighed and patted Ren's hand. His touch eased the tension in Ren's grip.

"We'll get you home, Ren. And you'll be better. It's not much farther."

Ren nodded. He eased his fingers open, releasing Jakob. "Okay."

"We're going home, Ren. Aren't you happy?"

Ren didn't know what he was, but he wouldn't describe it as happy. He shrugged. "I don't know what we'll find."

Jakob nodded; the corners of his mouth were turned down. "I don't either. But we'll look for our families. We'll look for Sorcha. And we won't have to be on this ship any longer." Jakob offered a hesitant smile. Ren didn't speak as the feelings from the dream were clinging to his waking thoughts.

"Are you going back to sleep?" Jakob asked.

"No. No, I'll stay up for a while."

"Is it okay if I sleep in your bed? The hammock is uncomfortable." Jakob made a face.

Ren supposed it was meant to lighten the mood. It didn't, but Ren appreciated the effort. "Sure." He stood, his legs wobbly, and crossed the room. He hoisted himself into the hammock while Jakob scrambled into Ren's bunk and flopped across the mattress with a groan. It was only a few minutes until Jakob's breaths evened out in sleep.

Ren stayed in the hammock with his feet dangling over the side. They would land on Erden in a few hours.

Ever since the incident with the Hatfields, there was always a member of the crew with him, especially when he slept. The presence of another person made it difficult for Ren to sleep, to think, to do anything knowing someone was watching him. The room was cramped. Jakob talked in his sleep, and Ollie snored, but as much as Ren hated being treated as if he couldn't take care of himself, he knew it was necessary.

Ren's sleep schedule had been erratic at best the last few days. He lost track of ship's time, and if it wasn't for his shadows, usually in the form of Jakob and Ollie, Ren would've wandered the ship at all hours.

As it was now, he couldn't sleep. He gave up lying in the hammock and went into the en-suite bathroom. The bruise on his jaw from Ollie's punch was deep blue, and, at times, he could see Ollie stare at it. Ren needed to talk to him, to thank Ollie for pulling him from the ships.

Ren stumbled to the cargo bay to find him before he remembered Ollie probably wouldn't be there, but would be tucked safe in his own room.

Finding Millicent's rug, Ren folded down onto it and sat cross-legged.

Despite being ordered not to access his power, Ren pressed his fingertips to the hull, took a breath, and closed his eyes. The ship hummed around him, and he meandered through the systems. He peered through the sensors at the vastness of space. He sensed the signatures of a few other vessels along the route, and Ren catalogued their specs, their names, their registries. Once he had finished, he left the sensors, sat in the comms, and listened in on the other occupants of the ship.

Millicent was asleep, if the sound of her soft even breaths was any indication. Ollie snored in his room. Jakob muttered as he tossed and turned. Lucas and Pen shuffled a few times in their shared bed, whispered to each other, then went quiet.

Rowan was awake in her quarters muttering to herself over what must be financial reports.

Asher was also awake. On the bridge, he was flicking through news reports, reading, and studying. Ren focused on him through the video feeds.

Asher wore his sleep clothes, but he was wide awake, sipping coffee as he tapped away on his tablet. He wore a sling on his arm, and Ren sighed. He needed to fix that, too, both the shoulder and the relationship. Asher's brow furrowed, and Ren saw the tight lines around Asher's mouth, as if he were worried or in pain.

A lifetime ago Ren would have gone to Asher and sat with him. They would have joked, played a silly game, talked until the clock ticked into the morning hours and the rest of the crew woke.

Ren's chest ached. His interactions with Asher since the incident had been exercises in avoidance on both their parts. At some future time, they would need to talk, but Ren didn't know if he could handle what Asher had to say. Maybe it would be better once they arrived on Erden, and Ren was clear-headed. Until then, Ren would continue to make his presence scarce.

It was better that way.

⊣⊢

A few hours later, Rowan announced over the shipwide comm that the *Star Stream* was approaching the planet and would begin the descent into atmo. Ren went to the bridge and stood in the corner, watching as the green and blue sphere became bigger on the screen. Jakob stood next to him and elbowed Ren in the side.

"Beautiful, isn't it?"

"Yeah."

Jakob eyed him. "Perk up, Ren. We're going home. We're going to see our families and Sorcha, and everything will be okay. Aren't you excited?"

It was the same speech Jakob had given only a few hours before, but this time, it wasn't tempered by exhaustion. Jakob's excitement was effusive. Ren was surprised that his own grin didn't need too much forcing. "Yeah."

Lucas didn't have much experience with planet gravity, and the descent was less smooth than when he docked at a drift. But the ship survived, and soon they were resting in a space dock slip on the planet.

The group gathered at the aft door. Jakob vibrated with happiness and nerves; his smile broke over his face as the group gathered supplies. He stopped every few moments and tucked his face toward his arm. His excitement was palpable. Ren couldn't begrudge him his happiness, but unease slipped between Ren's ribs, prodded his insides.

"Everyone ready?" Rowan asked, standing near the door. She checked with Asher. He nodded, jaw clenched; his bag was looped over his uninjured shoulder.

Penelope clapped. "I can't believe I'm going to be on a planet— unrecycled air and dirt. I'm going to touch dirt!"

Jakob looked at Penelope as though she was insane. He turned to Ren. "Listen to her. She thinks this is a vacation."

"I'm only excited. I know this is serious."

Ren remembered the first time he'd been on a ship and later on a drift. How excited he'd been despite the circumstances. He nudged Jakob's shoulder. "Let her have her fun. No harm done."

Jakob frowned, but nodded.

"What's the plan, Cap?" Ollie asked. He wasn't as excited as Penelope or, if he was, he hid it better. Calm and composed, he stood next to his sister.

"We'll first travel to Ren and Jakob's village and see what's there and if there is anything we can do to help." Addressing Jakob and Ren, she said, "I can't promise anything. What we find will determine what happens next. My crew comes first and foremost. Understand?"

"We understand," Ren spoke. He squeezed Jakob's arm. "We won't hold you to anything, Rowan. We appreciate everything you've done for us already."

She smiled. "I know."

"Lucas, I think you should stay behind. Millicent, you, too. Pen, we'll need you if we find anyone in need of medical assistance. Ollie, your presence is always welcome."

Millicent nodded. "I don't want to go on the planet anyway. It's not my home."

Jakob bristled, and Ren shook his head.

"Um… I really don't either. The thought of all that fresh air is terrifying. I'll gladly stay on the ship." Lucas wrapped an arm around Penelope's waist and reeled her in for a quick kiss. "Be careful."

"I will."

"Asher should stay behind too," Ren blurted.

Asher stiffened. "What?"

"You heard me," Ren said. "You're injured and…" He trailed off and gestured uselessly.

"And who is responsible for that?" Asher shot back.

Guilt flooded Ren. "I'm sorry," he said. "I can fix it."

"If I wanted you to fix it, I would've asked."

Ren clenched his jaw. He narrowed his eyes as guilt gave way to anger. "Well, I do seem to remember you saying my home planet was a backwater dirt hole. I doubt you want to experience it again."

Asher tilted his head and swept his hot gaze over Ren. "Maybe you're right." He took a step forward. "I should stay where I'm actually wanted."

"Good choice."

They faced each other and stood chest to chest. Ren didn't know how they'd moved so close, but they stared levelly, unflinching.

Rowan shouldered between them.

"Enough. Asher is coming. He's the only one of us who has true military experience, and his knowledge of the planet may be useful."

"Jakob and I know the planet, and Ollie should be force enough."

"Are you questioning my orders, little one?"

Ren broke the staring contest and dropped his gaze. "No, Captain."

"Good. I don't care what's going on between you two, but let me make myself clear. If either of you does something stupid because of a spat, I will not hesitate to drag your asses back to this ship and lock you in your rooms. Now, Ren, hurt or not, Asher is an asset, so he's coming." She turned to her brother; her finger pointed hard in his chest. "No Corps uniform. Go change. We'll wait. And keep your disparaging comments about the planet to yourself. Clear?"

Asher glared at Ren. "Crystal," he said. He turned and left.

Jakob gripped Ren's shoulder; his fingers dug into the blade. He said into Ren's ear, "You're my friend, Ren. And I stand with you, no matter what. If we need to ditch this lot to do what we came here to do, we will."

Ren patted Jakob's hand. "Okay."

"Are you ready for what we might find?"

Ren took a shuddering breath. "I have to be."

"Yeah, I'm not either."

Jakob dropped his hand when Asher returned. He had changed into civilian clothes but there was no hiding the bearing of a soldier. Beneath the nondescript jacket and shirt and trousers, Asher's shoulders were broad, and his posture was straight. The air of confidence Ren had admired so many months ago emanated from him. He had a pulse gun strapped to his waist, a large knife attached to his outer thigh, and a bulging pack on his back.

"Ready?" Rowan asked.

Asher nodded.

She tugged her braid. "Good. Let's go."

She hit the switch, and the bay doors slowly opened to reveal the space dock. Ren could've cut the tension with a knife. When the doors stopped moving, the group stared out at an underwhelming scene.

"Oh," Pen said, stepping out. "It's not much different than a small drift. I was expecting it… to be more alien, honestly."

Jakob rolled his eyes. "Idiots," he said, brushing past the group with his boots thumping against the metal. "Follow me."

It wasn't the same dock Asher and Ren had departed from what seemed like centuries ago. This one, closer to the village, was where Ren had wished his mother would've allowed him to visit and find work. When Ren had lain on the beach at the lake and watched the ships fly through the sky, they had originated from this port. To the boy who dreamed of leaving Erden, this place would've been amazing. To Ren now, it was small, dingy, and poorly maintained. It confirmed every duster cliché he'd heard on the drifts.

Ashamed, Ren kept his head down as the crew, his *friends*, experienced such a lackluster introduction to his home planet.

Maneuvering through this space dock was about the same as it had been the last time Ren had been in one, but without the soldiers trying to capture him. Then, he'd been so exhausted his power had seeped out at every turn. This time, he wasn't as tired, but his power, though not sparking randomly, did wash out of his fingers and the soles of his feet.

He could feel everything. He could see it all, and his consciousness spread out into the flooring, then crawled up the wall and into the systems. He could hear the chatter between the dock and the ships descending into atmo. He could feel the environmental controls, the lighting, the vid feeds, and the force fields in different sections. Everything whispered to him, invaded him, and he welcomed it as he strode through the dock with his consciousness filling up with the tech until it was all that remained inside of him. He slowed his pace, lingering, and his star flickered as the crew disappeared around the corner and out to the planet surface.

Ren ignored the calls of the tech, ignored the errors and breaks, and followed. Once he stepped through the double doors into the open air of Erden, the connection to the systems faded with each step he took. It stretched until it snapped, and Ren was wholly corporeal. The static cleared, the voices dimmed, and Ren saw the planet clearly. Sunlight broke through the heavy layer of clouds and illuminated the bleak landscape. Trees stood spindly and barren against the gray sky. When Ren breathed, he smelled the crisp, fresh snow, which fell in large flakes. His ears burned from the cold, and the tip of his nose went numb.

He saw the group and joined them. With his consciousness uncluttered, Ren could think freely for the first time in ages. His thoughts centered on the journey ahead.

"What is this stuff?" Pen said, stepping carefully through the white powder that covered the landscape. It gathered wetly on the toes of her boots. "And why is it so cold?" She crossed her arms over her chest and shivered.

Ren scuffed his heel, revealing dirt under the thin white layer: snow. It had snowed. He'd been away so long he'd forgotten about the weather, the seasons. It had been early spring when he'd been captured, and, in his mind, the planet hadn't changed. To him it had always been early spring on Erden. But the fresh layer of ice and slush told him otherwise.

It was a shock to realize his home had continued on without him. The planet had moved; the seasons had changed. His family would have changed, too, just as he had.

His breath hung in puffs of condensation, and the tips of his fingers started to freeze. He was glad he wore a jacket, and he tucked his hands under his arms, which were crossed over his skinny chest.

"It's snow. And this isn't so bad," Jakob said. He tilted his face to the sky and took a deep breath. "It'll get much colder once the sun sets."

"We should get going," Ren mumbled. The clouds were pregnant with the promise of more snow, and half their group wasn't dressed for the cold—Ren included.

"Do you know the way?" Rowan asked, brushing flakes from her shoulders and hair. "And will we get there before this becomes any deeper?"

Jakob hefted the pack on his shoulders. "I know the way. It's only about an hour on foot. We'll be fine."

"Ren?"

Ren held out his palm, and snow landed on his skin, then melted. How could he have forgotten it would be winter?

"Ren?"

He turned his hand over, staring at it. The tips of his fingers were pink; his fingernails were white. The nail on his ring finger was torn and jagged, and a bead of dried blood sat at the corner. When had that happened?

"Ren!" Rowan snapped.

He jerked, dropped his hand, and lifted his head. "Yes?"

The group stared at him. They all looked ridiculous in their drifter clothes with snow gathering in their hair and around their collars. Rowan's nose was red already. Penelope's brow furrowed as she kicked at the ground. Ollie shivered. And Asher…

Asher's expression was haunted.

"Is Jakob right? We can walk there?"

"Oh," Ren said. He nodded. "Yes. It's not far."

"Then lead the way, you two. Or do you want to stand here and freeze to death?"

Jakob brushed past Ren and took the front position. "It's not *that* cold," he muttered.

Ren fell in behind him, and the group trudged forward. Ren kept his focus on putting one foot in front of the other, trying to find the familiar rhythm of walking on the planet's surface, but he couldn't shake the look on Asher's face.

⊣⊢

"I feel like I've gained a million pounds," Penelope said as they walked. "I didn't realize the gravity would be this different."

"I'm cold," Ollie responded. "How come no one mentioned it would be your cold season? And there might be… whatever this stuff is?"

"I'd forgotten," Ren said.

It was the first thing he'd said in almost an hour. No one had spoken much, though Ollie and Penelope had a hero's go at keeping up a conversation.

Rowan was tense. Her body was taut as a bowstring, and her hand was never too far from her pulse gun. Asher was alert too, but in a different way, as if one wrong move would catch him up in his memories of the planet and his own capture. Ren had forgotten that as well. Asher carried as much emotional baggage about being back here as Ren and Jakob did. He, too, was a victim of circumstance, of wrong-place, wrong-time.

Jakob's long strides and fast pace were too much for those not dirtborn, and several times he had to slow down, stop, and wait as the drifters' bodies adjusted. He wore his frustration like battle armor; his expression dared anyone to remark on the speed. No one did.

They weren't far from the village now. The snow had tapered off as they walked and the sun sank lazily into the horizon.

Ren recognized the landscape: the forest on either side, the trees with names carved in the bark—a ritual for betrothed couples. A boundary rock marked the entrance to the village lands. Ren brushed away the snow to reveal the language of his ancestors.

"What does it say?" Rowan asked, studying the symbols.

"It's a warning to anyone who wants to do harm to the village. And it is a spell for protection."

Her eyebrows shot up. "Really? Those squiggly lines are all superstition?"

Ren stood and his shoulder knocked into hers. "Doesn't matter. It doesn't work anyway." Leaving Rowan and her drifter arrogance behind, he caught up to the group,

Ren's apprehension and excitement grew as they drew closer to the village. The snow had begun to blow again, harder than before.

Everyone huddled in their coats except Jakob, who pushed the ankle-high snow out of the way with his determined stride. In front of them stood a small rise, and right over it would be the bowl that held the village.

Jakob plowed on, but Ren stopped at the bottom of the rise.

Asher ran into his back. "Ren?"

Ren swallowed hard. "It's over the crest of the hill."

"You okay?"

"I'm fine. I… don't know what we'll find."

"Hopefully shelter," Ollie said, rubbing his arms.

Ren ignored him.

Rowan's cold fingers encircled Ren's wrist. "We're with you."

"I know."

Jakob stopped at the top of the hill. His silhouette, backlit by the setting sun, was bathed in reds and golds. His shoulders slumped, and he dropped to his knees. The anguished cry he let out ripped through Ren. He ran forward, pushing Ollie and Rowan out of his way. He tripped once, slipping on the ice, so his hands skidded. The fall didn't stop him. He scrambled, boots kicking up snow, until he could sink next to Jakob's side.

Rubble spread out as far as he could see. A few buildings stood, but they listed under the weight of the snow. Ren wrapped his arms around Jakob's shoulders, and Jakob clutched at him, burying his face in Ren's neck. His body shook, and his hands clenched the fabric of Ren's jacket.

Jakob howled. Ren didn't know what to say. He didn't think there was anything he *could* say. He had no comfort to offer. Grief and pain surged in his middle, and his star sparked, but there was nowhere for it to go. There was no tech to draw from, no machine to flee into, to hide from the emotions raging inside him.

He didn't know the others stood beside them until Pen knelt behind him and wrapped her arms tight around them.

"I'm sorry," she said, her voice watery. "I'm so sorry."

"We need to move," Rowan said. "Let's go down there and see what we can find. I know it's tough, boys, but we're not safe standing in the open on this hill."

"On your feet," Ollie said, gripping Ren's upper arm and hauling him up. Asher and Penelope pulled Jakob to standing, but Ren gripped Jakob's hand tight. Jakob rubbed at his cheeks. His face was flushed, and his eyes were bright with tears.

Ren didn't cry. Tears had been wrung out of him months ago. But his body trembled, and his knees were weak as they walked down the other side of the hill and into the village. Ren and Jakob had grown up here. They knew every inch of road and path and maneuvered them easily despite the broken bricks and the detritus in their way.

"We should split up," Ren said, his voice thick and scratchy. "Cover more ground."

Ren didn't mention that Jakob had grown up on the other side of the village from him. They could take stock separately, instead of slowing one another down. They had led such different lives in the same place. Because of their class differences, Ren wasn't prepared to share his sorrow with the only person who could come close to understanding.

"Pen and Ollie go with Jakob. Asher and I will go with Ren. Meet in an hour by the big pile over there." Rowan jerked her chin to what was once the town square and the mound of rubble which had been the council meeting place.

Jakob moved like a ghost; his once-brisk steps were slow and reluctant. His face had gone pale. The flush of anger and pain had been replaced with a sickly look. He seemed hollowed out, as if what had made him Jakob had been scooped away. Ren squeezed his hand in a gesture of companionship and then let go.

Ren had always been a dreamer, but since he'd been captured, been chased across the cluster, and merged with machines, he'd become pragmatic. Jakob had always held on to hope that the soldiers had been lying when he was told the village had been destroyed. After all, they had lied about blowing Ren out of the sky.

But Ren had known there was little hope. He hadn't known what he would find when he walked over the hill, but it wouldn't be good. He'd held no illusions about what he would find, but he wouldn't have been able to live with himself if he hadn't confirmed what he'd been told.

Ren was reluctant to lead Rowan and Asher to his home on the outskirts of the village, where it was tucked away in a crescent-shaped copse. His determination to find out what happened to his family whipped away with the snow on the brisk wind.

He stopped in front of what was left and put his hands in his pockets, desperate for something to hold on to. The door of the house stood, and the frame was held up by the crumbling sides. That was all, though. The roof was mostly gone; the sides had caved in. Its contents had been tossed into the street and the small yard, where they peeked through the snow.

Ren tried the doorknob, and it was locked. He laughed, loud and half-hysterical, and Rowan and Asher pressed close to his sides.

"This was where I grew up." His voice sounded shredded, foreign to his own ears.

Asher and Rowan exchanged a glance but said nothing. Ren didn't blame them. He'd had no idea how to comfort Jakob, and they had no idea how to comfort him. Maybe there was no comfort to be had.

He walked around the doorframe and stepped through a hole in the standing wall. With every step he took, his feet crunched on rubble mixed with mud and ice. A tinkle of glass made Ren bend down and dig with frozen fingers until he found a vid-still of him and Liam—too young and too happy—in front of the lake. Slowly, Ren stood and shook the picture free of the wood frame and broken glass.

"Is that your brother?" Rowan asked.

Ren nodded. His throat went tight and, suddenly, Ren realized his tears hadn't dried up. He folded the picture and put it in his pocket. "I'd like to be alone for a bit," he said. "To look around." To mourn.

"Are you sure you'll be safe?" Asher asked. His voice was gentle, and Ren resisted recoiling from it.

He peered at the destruction. He questioned the structural integrity of the building, but it had held on thus far. Ren was fairly certain he'd be okay, for a little while at least.

"I'll be fine."

"We'll be right outside," Rowan said and winced. "I mean, around the corner. Over there," she amended, waving her hand. "Take your time."

Ren nodded, unmoved by her uncharacteristic awkwardness. He stood still as they ducked through an opening in the wall and disappeared. Turning his head to stare at the scorch marks on the wall, Ren ignored the last glance Asher cast his way. Once the sound of their footsteps faded, Ren walked through the remnants of his home.

The last time he'd been here, he and Liam were racing through their chores, hoping to get out to the lake before the sun sank too low. An age had passed since then.

He went into the room he and Liam had shared. He stared at the chest of clothes at the end of his bed and thought about stuffing his favorites into his pack. But he remembered Asher's mother had bought him new clothes, clothes made of finer material that fit better, and he had no use for homespun rags.

The bed that had been his was hidden beneath a fallen wall. Liam's bed was cluttered with a few cheap books he had bought from another village kid. Ren fingered the pages. The sheets had shriveled, and the ink had run. The words were barely discernible. Liam would be furious they were ruined. He should put them in a drawer away from the elements. He should find the scrap of blanket Liam treasured and slept with constantly. He'd want that back. He should find the rock Liam had claimed was a meteorite and gave to him one birthday because it was a piece of a star. He should clean everything up for when they returned. He should… he should…

Ren shook his head. He wasn't staying here.

He couldn't stay here.

He snatched a comic from the bed and stuffed it into his pocket with the picture. He backed out into the hallway. The clench on his heart was painful. He swallowed the sorrow and moved to the room his mother and stepfather had shared. It was mostly intact, but the roof threatened to bow under the gathering snow.

Ren fell to his knees, shoved his arm under the bed, and felt for the keepsake box his mother kept there. It would have things his mother held dear, and though he might not have any emotion tied to them, his mother did. That would be enough.

But he found nothing. Frowning, Ren ducked to look into the sliver of dark space, but didn't see the small tin box. That was odd. It wasn't worth anything. It wasn't worth taking by anyone other than his mother.

Unless… unless.

Hope was a dangerous thing, frightening, yet thrilling. Ren shot to his feet and tore open the closet door. A smattering of clothes hung there, but more were missing. He pushed the remnants to the side. The large pack his stepfather used on hunting trips was gone.

Ren ran to the kitchen. He righted a chair, climbed onto the counter, and reached to the top of the shelves. He pulled down the glass jar his mother used for her special sweet juice, and it shattered on the floor. He pushed aside the serving platter they used for birthday cakes and the pottery bowl his stepfather had bought his mother from the next town over. He stepped along the counter, perched dangerously, and swiped down everything from the cabinets; around him crockery rained, shattering and splintering along the floor.

Asher came running in and skidded to a stop as Ren flung open another door and pawed through the remnants.

"Ren? What are you doing? I thought the house was coming down."

"It's gone," Ren said. His tone didn't match the thrumming of his veins or the pounding of his heart. "It's gone. They escaped. They had to have escaped."

Asher frowned. "Ren, come down."

Ren hopped to the floor. His boots crushed the memories to dust. "Don't you understand? The keepsake box is gone and the emergency credits."

"So? The soldiers took them? Ren, they've ransacked the place."

"No." Ren shook his head. He resisted the urge to shake Asher. "They were hidden. And the box has no value to anyone other than my mother. There would be no point for a soldier to take it."

Placating, insufferable, Asher's raised his hands. "I know you want to believe they got away."

"They did!" Ren said, kicking over the nearest chair. It slid across the floor. "Don't act like you understand. You don't!"

"I know I don't, but I'm trying here. Okay? I am not going to support you in a delusion."

"Why? Why do you care?"

"Because I do!" Asher stepped around the table and gripped Ren's shoulder with his good arm. "I do because I care about you. I still care about you and I'm not going to stop just because you hate me."

"You only care if I'm a threat."

"That is not true, and you know it."

Ren clenched his jaw. He ignored that statement; he had to, or he might break in pieces. "And what makes you so sure it's a delusion? The keepsake box is gone. The emergency credits. My stepfather's travel bag. It all points to—"

"Rowan and I found a mass grave."

Ren wrenched out of Asher's grasp. Breathing heavily, he pushed his way past Asher and into the main room. With shaking hands, he unlocked the door and stepped out into the darkening day and the falling snow.

Rowan approached him. "Did Asher tell you?"

"Yes."

Gently, her voice low, she nudged him with her shoulder. "I'm sorry. I can't imagine what you're going through right now. Is there anything I can do? Are you going to be okay?"

No. No, he was not. "I'm fine."

She raised an eyebrow. "Ren, it's okay if you're not—"

"I need a minute."

Ren walked briskly to the path he knew so well. His body was flushed. Sweat gathered at his temples and the base of his hairline. It dried on his skin, and he shivered. Snow fell into his eyes and his hair. It gathered around the collar of his jacket and chilled him, but it didn't hinder his progress. His steps didn't falter.

He pushed through the low-hanging, snow-laded branches of the evergreens along the trail and ignored the bare, spindly twigs of the deciduous trees as they caught on the fabric of his clothes. The farther he went, the more anxious he became; emotions and memories overwhelmed him. Suddenly walking wasn't quick enough. His body hummed with energy, so he broke into a jog, which turned into a full-out run. He sprinted, his legs and arms pumped, and his breath came in fraught gasps, until he stumbled wildly onto the beach.

Kicking up sand and snow, Ren fell to his knees at the edge of the water. Chest heaving, Ren stared out over the lake, flat as glass with the shore of the other side barely visible in the gathering darkness. A thin layer of ice glinted in the fading light. Underneath, the water moved, swirled inky-black like in his dreams.

His dreams, where Liam was alive and real and talked with him. *I'm not here.*

Sitting there with the cold leeching into his legs through the thin fabrics of his trousers, Ren *knew*. Liam wasn't here. He wasn't at the lake. He wasn't in the village. He wasn't in the ground.

Hope was dangerous.

"This must be the lake you talked so much about," Asher said, coming to stand next to Ren at the water's edge.

Ren hadn't heard his footsteps and he jumped at his voice. He craned his neck and looked up. Asher stared at the lake.

"It's not quite like you described."

Ren frowned. "That's because it was barely spring when I left."

"Ah," Asher said. He toed at the ground. "It's nice."

"It's not."

Asher raised an eyebrow.

Ren continued. "It's almost always cold except in the heat of summer. The sand gets stuck everywhere. Things live in it, and they bump into your legs when you swim. And if you splash too much, the water gets too murky to see. It's gross and it's nothing like the clear fountains and warm pools on the drifts where you can swim and not be afraid of being pinched by a creature or getting tangled in lake grass." Ren pulled his knees close to his chest and wrapped his arms around his legs.

Asher sighed. "I wasn't comparing it to the water on the drifts."

Ren didn't say anything. The sun was gone, and the sky edged from twilight to full dark. The broken moon was visible through the breaks in the clouds, as were a few pinpricks of stars.

"Was this the spot where…" Asher trailed off. He swallowed; his expression was pained, as though he realized his question bordered on cruel.

"Where I last saw my brother? Not the exact spot, but…" Ren waved his hand dismissively. "But nearby."

"I'm sorry."

"For what?"

"I don't know. For everything. For all that's happened. For pushing you away. For the people of your village. For your home."

Ren stood. "My family is alive. They escaped. I *know* they did."

Placating, Asher raised his hand and took a step back. "Okay," he said. "Okay, Ren. Whatever you need to believe."

Ren didn't register the doubt behind Asher's words. Instead, he zeroed in on Asher's limp arm. He wasn't wearing a sling, maybe to hide the fact he had limited use in case they wound up in a fight. Asher's fingers twitched.

Again, shame overwhelmed Ren, but not for his humble planet, or his gross lake. This was deeper.

"Last time you were here," he said, clearing his throat, "you were attacked, injured, and captured. I've been selfish. I never thought about your feelings about coming back here, what that might trigger for you. I'm sorry."

"You've not been yourself."

"No, I haven't."

"And how do you feel now?" Asher's voice was hesitant; the question was weighted with meaning.

Ren tilted his head and watched the clouds drift. He blinked against a few wandering snowflakes.

"Ashamed. Guilty. Heartbroken. Hopeful." He met Asher's gaze. "Uncluttered."

"Is that good?"

"Yeah." Ren's voice came out in a whisper; his breath made a puff of cloud. He stood and brushed off the back of his trousers.

"We should get back," Asher said. "It's getting too dark to see."

"I know the way." Ren stepped into Asher's space. His pulse raced, and in the low light he saw Asher's bemused expression. Carefully, slowly, Ren ghosted his fingers over Asher's hand. "Let me fix it."

The space between them charged with electricity, and the spark raised the fine hairs on Ren's arms. He shivered, and it wasn't only from the cold.

Asher licked his lips. His green eyes were wide in the dying light, reflecting the broken moon and the ice on the water. "I don't..." He took a breath. "I don't know if it's a good idea."

"You don't trust me."

"Honestly? No, and you don't trust me either. But I trust my own judgment. You may not be the Ren I became friends when we were on this planet together, but that doesn't mean I don't care for you." Asher closed his eyes, as if in surrender. "Do it."

Ren threaded his fingers with Asher's lax hand, their skin frigid. He closed his eyes, and pushed out with his power. Asher's shoulder lit up in Ren's mind. He saw a blueprint of machine and bone, of tech surrounded by flesh and sinew. In the hold of his star, Ren had rendered the mechanism inert, crippling Asher, his friend, the person for whom he held the most affection. Remorse threatened to drown him. Ren pressed closer, needing to convey his contrition. His lips rasped over the stubbled skin of Asher's cheek in a whisper of a kiss. Asher's body was a wall of heat and comfort, and when Ren pressed his cold lips to Asher's jaw, he released his star.

Asher's gasp puffed against Ren's cheek. He shook his hand free of Ren's grip and reached up to splay against the back of Ren's neck, holding him still.

Other than that small gesture, Asher didn't move, merely held Ren as they breathed, as they shared a moment by Ren's childhood lake under the stars Ren used to dream about, with the gentle whispered hush of falling snow the only sound.

"Thank you," Asher said, quietly, after an eternity.

At the words, Ren's eyes filled. A lump lodged in his throat, and everything he had held back broke over him in a wave. He dropped his forehead to Asher's shoulder and sobbed.

Asher's grip tightened while Ren shuddered apart.

He didn't let go.

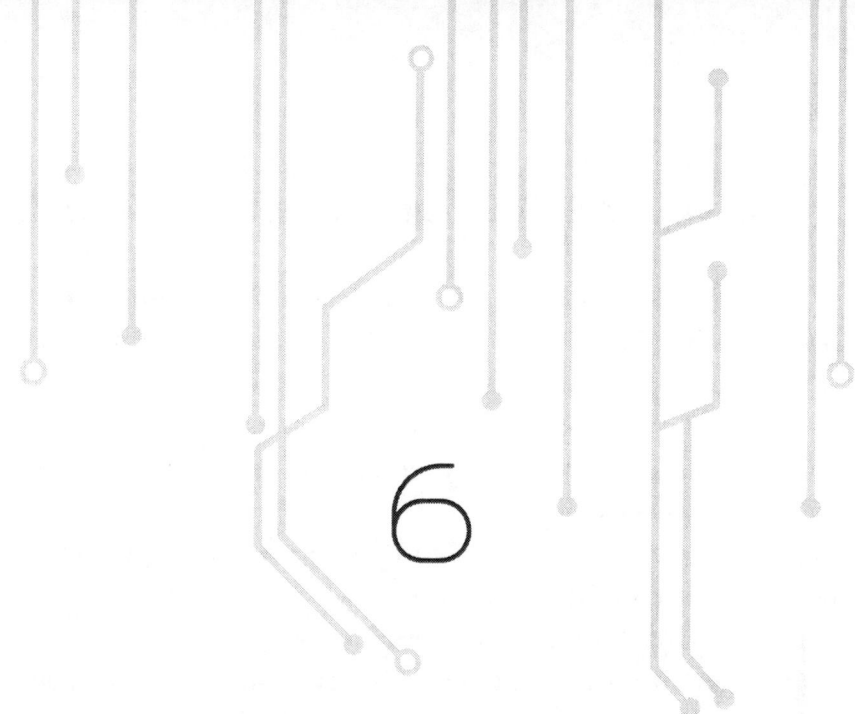

6

Trudging back through the forest was a solemn process. With little light, Asher relied on Ren to guide him, and that required Asher to rest his hand on Ren's shoulder. They didn't speak, not after Ren, shy, embarrassed, and rubbing at his eyes, had hiccupped and pulled back from Asher's embrace.

Healing Asher's shoulder and crying had been cathartic, and, though their relationship wasn't what they'd once had, they were closer than they had been since leaving Mykonos all those weeks ago.

Ren spied the flickering of flame up ahead, and they found Rowan holding a torch and wearing a sour expression.

"Where the stars have you been?"

"We're fine, thanks," Asher replied. He picked up one of the two packs at Rowan's feet and slung it over his shoulder.

Rowan huffed, opened her mouth—undoubtedly for a retort which included the word *idiot*—but paused. Her eyes widened as she saw Asher grasp the packs straps with both hands. She looked to Ren and back to Asher and her mouth pulled down at the corners.

"Your shoulder—"

"We'll talk later," Asher said, cutting her off. "We should find the others."

"This way," Ren said. At a brisk walk, he followed the path from his home into the village. He didn't wait for Asher; the closeness they had shared at the lake had evaporated in the face of Rowan's quiet appraisal.

Toward the village center, he found Ollie, bundled in a scavenged coat. The fabric stretched tight over his shoulders, and the buttons strained over Ollie's chest.

"Jakob's over there, down that road. His house is standing and will be good shelter for the night."

"Lead the way," Rowan said.

Ren jumped, not realizing how close Rowan stood at his shoulder. Ren turned slightly and found Rowan and Asher flanking him. Their breaths puffed in soft clouds; their cheeks were flushed with cold. Flakes of snow clung to Asher's golden eyelashes and framed the green of his eyes in the flickering shadows caused by Rowan's makeshift torch.

Ren spun back around and stared at Ollie's back as he led them toward Jakob's home.

Ren knew where it was. He remembered it from when he was a child, when he and Liam had passed it while they played or completed chores. To young Ren, it had appeared enormous, like a mansion or a castle.

Approaching it now, the house resembled a skeleton with its bone white columns broken and falling. The open front door was a maw. Scorch marks tattooed the shutters. The glass in the windows was broken. It had fared better than Ren's humble home, but the family's possessions were strewn all over the front porch and yard.

Ren peered around the entranceway and noted the solid construction and the extra spaces that Ren's home didn't have. He turned a corner and found Jakob and Penelope dragging mattresses from the upstairs bedrooms into a den. A fire roared in a fireplace. Broken furniture had been pushed to the back wall. A pile of blankets rose in a corner, and another pile of clothes sat by the fire, warming. The room gave off a cozy, but intimidating, vibe. Ren wanted to sink into the nest of cushions closest to the fire and warm his bones, but he shuffled to a stop. He'd never been in Jakob's social class, let alone in his home.

Jakob dropped the mattress he dragged and greeted Ren with a lukewarm smile. "Welcome to my home."

Ren shrugged out of his damp jacket and laid it by the fire to dry. "I've never been in your house. It's big."

"I think the word you're looking for is opulent."

"Sure," Ren said.

"Look, we made a fire. And we'll have a nice, warm place to sleep tonight." Penelope sat on a mattress and patted the space beside her. She smiled, and her brown eyes caught the firelight and seemed to glow. "Have a nice dinner from our packs and a good rest. Everything will look brighter in the morning."

"Obviously," Jakob muttered.

Ren bit his lip to stifle his snicker.

"No power?" Rowan entered the space with no stutter in her step or worry for propriety and looked around with her hands on her hips.

"We have candles," Penelope offered.

"We could have power if Ren is willing," Jakob said. He crossed his arms. "And then you would be able to enjoy the splendor of my family home."

"Ren is here to disconnect. I don't think having him power anything is a good idea." Ren agreed with Asher. He shrugged his shoulders at Jakob in apology. "Besides," Asher continued, "lighting this place up would be a beacon. We shouldn't draw attention, especially if we are going to stay here a few days."

"We're not," Rowan stated. "We'll head back to the ship in the morning."

Jakob dropped his arms. His mouth flapped open, and he took a step forward. "What? But we've only just arrived!"

"And staying would be for what purpose? Your families are gone. No one is here. There isn't a reason to hang around."

"You're joking. You have to be joking." Jakob looked to Ren, pleading. "We got here only a few hours ago, Ren."

"I know."

"Then make them let us stay."

Rowan twisted her mouth and grabbed her braid. "No one is going to make me do anything. Understood? I am the captain here, and no little dusters are going to order me around. I don't care if they have technopathic abilities or opulent houses."

Jakob turned red; the color burned in the apples of his cheeks. "Screw you. Screw all of you weeds." He kicked the pile of blankets, and Penelope lunged to keep them from tumbling into the fire. Jakob stalked off, slamming the door behind him.

"Good job, Cap," Ollie said. He joined his sister by the fire. "I think Ren showed more empathy when he tried to kill the Hatfields."

Ren winced.

Rowan rounded on Ollie, finger pointed. "Don't start. I've rearranged my, *our*, entire lives for these two. We've been pursued by an insane man, stormed a drift, and almost *shot out of the damn cluster*. We've done everything we can and now we're on some stars-forsaken ball of dirt looking for people who are probably *dead*."

"Rowan!" Penelope said, scandalized. "They could be alive."

Rowan cut her gaze to Asher.

Asher sighed. "We found a gravesite. It was large."

"Does Jakob know?" Ollie asked.

Asher shook his head.

Penelope stood. "One of us should tell him."

"I'll do it." Ren needed air. The pressure in the room was stifling.

Penelope wrung her hands. "Are you sure?"

"Yeah," he said, looking at Rowan. "It should come from me. I'll make sure to use all my empathy."

Rowan glared.

Ren left the room through the door Jakob had just slammed. The house was dark, but Ren followed the glow of a candle to another room.

Jakob sat on a bench in the curve of a large window. He had one leg tucked beneath him, and he stared out over their village. The candle sat next to him in an ornate holder; the flame flickered in time with Jakob's breaths. The window surface was fogged from the heat of Jakob's body while the snow continued to drift outside.

The carpet softened the sound of Ren's footsteps, but in the tomb-like silence of the room, and with the creak of wood beneath him, he couldn't have sneaked up on Jakob if he'd wanted. Jakob didn't turn around, but Ren's image reflected in the window and their gazes met before Ren looked away.

"Did the drifters send you to talk me down?"

"No, they didn't. I volunteered."

Ren pulled out a chair from a large, decorative-but-sturdy, table. A chandelier hung overhead, where its crystals flung tiny rainbows on the ceiling and the walls. A broken cabinet stood nearby which, by the look of the mess on the floor, had once been filled with fine dishes. Ren sat stiffly, imagining fancy, stilted dinners, complete with rich foods and wine. Then he dragged the chair to the window and joined Jakob in staring at the landscape.

"Well?" Jakob prodded. "Are you going talk to me about how it's better if we leave? How we're selfish for wanting to stay here and risk Rowan's reputation and their livelihood?"

"No."

"I'm not going back, not until I've found my father, not until I've found Sorcha. They can't make me. And if you want to join them and go do whatever it is the Phoenix Corps wants you to, then go. I'll be fine here."

"I'm not leaving you."

Jakob rubbed his forehead. His brown hair stuck up in the back. His skin looked pale, even in the warm, yellow light. He shivered, since the room was much colder than the den, and tucked his coat tighter around his body. He looked fragile, as if he might break into shards like the china at their feet.

"You're not?" He turned and swept his gaze up and down Ren's frame. "Are you in your right mind? Or are you addled?"

"I'm better." Ren swallowed, knowing everyone had realized he wasn't *correct* while on the *Star Stream*—everyone but him. "I'm not… fixed. But I'm better being away from the ship."

Jakob nodded. "Then what's the plan? Are we heading out on our own?"

"Yes. I think my mother and stepfather escaped. I think… my mother's keepsake box was gone and so were the emergency credits we hid in the kitchen."

"I think my father and sisters fled, too. Their rooms are destroyed but things are missing that only they would care about."

Ren had forgotten Jakob had sisters. He didn't talk much about them. They were younger, still in school. Ren didn't remember their names, but he did remember Jakob's account of being captured, how he'd run to draw soldiers away, to protect a group of younger children.

"Do you have any idea where they might have gone?"

"I don't know, but I intend to find them, even if I have to search the whole countryside. And no one is getting in my way. Clear enough?"

"Yeah, Jakob. I'm with you."

Jakob cleared his throat. "Liam?"

"He's not here."

"Right."

"We should get some rest. We'll sneak out in a few hours, when the others are asleep."

"Do you think they'll follow?"

Ren's gut twisted. "No. And if they do, they don't know the area like we do. They won't find us."

"Not even Asher?" Jakob raised his eyebrows. "He's your protector. He's your friend."

"He's my jailer." Ren needed to remember that. Even if their relationship was being repaired, Asher held allegiance to the Phoenix Corps. And the Corps wanted Ren locked away near Perilous Space.

They would never allow Ren to gallivant across the Erden landscape looking for his family. He was only here to reset, to detox from the thrall of the star. They didn't care about him. They only cared about what he could do for them or against them.

"He'll look for you."

Ren didn't believe that. "Come on." Ren stood. "We don't want to raise suspicion by being gone too long."

Jakob nodded and glanced back to the window. He pressed his fingers to cold glass, leaving smudge marks. "We'll find them."

"Yeah, we will."

Ren didn't mention the graves. There was no point in undermining Jakob's belief, his hope. Jakob did stupid things when he was desperate. Jakob couldn't find anyone if he was dead.

After a hurried dinner of dried meat from their packs and water from the canteens, Ren curled up in a nest of blankets on top of one of the mattresses. The softness was murder on his back. He didn't take off his boots and kept his feet off the end of the mattress and on the floor, but it was hard not to fall into a deep sleep with the crackling of the fire, the gentle hush of the snow outside, a full stomach, and warm, heavy covers. The mattress Ren had chosen was on the outskirts of the circle, and no one questioned it. Jakob hung back and checked the locks on the doors before he found his own spot at the edge of the group.

Asher was the last to settle. He stretched out on the couch. He toed off his boots and flung an arm over his eyes. Ren studied him, as Asher's body slowly relaxed into the cushions and his breaths evened out when he gave into sleep. Ren had seen this when they were in the dungeon together, when they were on *The Nomad* escaping Erden, when they stayed up too late in the common area of the *Star Stream*. Knowing he might not see it again, Ren committed the image of Asher to memory: the gold of his hair, the slope of his nose, the peaceful curl of his fingers, the slight bend of his knee.

Amid the ambient sounds, including Ollie's snores, Ren closed his eyes, sighed, and slipped into a light doze.

It seemed only a few minutes had passed before Ren was woken by a shake to his shoulder. Finger to his lips, Jakob stood over him. He had a pack over one shoulder and wore a heavy black coat and a hat pulled down over his ears. He handed Ren a similar coat, and Ren shrugged into the thick fabric. Once he had it zipped, Jakob passed him gloves and a hat.

The fire had burned low. Asher lay curled into himself under a blanket. Rowan and Penelope hadn't stirred, huddled together under blankets on the floor near Asher. Ollie's snores had ceased, and Ren found Ollie propped up on his elbows with his brown eyes reflecting the firelight.

Ren froze. Jakob noticed and his body stiffened.

A silent staring contest ensued. No one moved. Ollie's mouth turned down in a frown; his eyebrows raised. Ren gave him a shrug and tried to convey his apology with his expression. Ren didn't know what Ollie saw or if he understood the driving need for both Jakob and Ren to at least look farther.

A log cracked in the fireplace. Rowan stirred, rolling around in her comforter, before snorting and falling back into sleep.

Ollie nodded once at Ren and lay back down.

Ren didn't dare breathe. His muscles were tight and cramped, as he and Jakob crept out of the room and into the kitchen, down a hallway to a pantry, and then out a back door. Jakob closed it softly behind him and ensured it had locked.

The clouds had cleared; the broken moon was bright. It lit up the snow, and what Ren could see of the village looked like a painting, a tranquil scene of rustic life, and not the site of a horrible tragedy. The air was cold and crisp and burned Ren's lungs as he took a relieved breath that they had come this far.

Silently, Jakob and Ren moved away from the mansion. Jakob didn't look back, but kept his shoulders straight and his eyes forward. The only sound was the crunch of their boots in the snow, but even that was hushed.

They found the familiar path that led them out of the village and curved toward some outlying farms. Having learned from his and Asher's trek across the countryside, Ren hopped down into the ravine beside it and pulled Jakob down with him. Ren gestured for Jakob to follow, and together they ducked into the trees that lined the road.

The branches bowed under the weight of the snow and blocked the light of the moon and the stars. It was slower going, and they had to step more carefully than if they were on the trail, but their tracks would be harder to find and they blended in wearing their dark clothes.

They trudged through the wood, keeping the path in sight to their right. The village disappeared behind them. A farmhouse, large but rundown, appeared in front of them. As they neared, Ren made out broken windows and a door barely holding on to its hinges.

Abandoned.

They passed it and kept going. Hours went by. The sun rose; darkness gave way to a slow brightening of the sky. Ren stopped to watch as it crested over the horizon: dawn breaking magnificent, the landscape awash in pinks and golds.

Jakob bumped into him. "What are you stopped for?" His voice was muffled behind the collar of his coat.

"I forgot what sunrise looked like." As much as Ren loved space, the terrifying beauty of the stars dotted in the black, he couldn't deny the warm splendor of the planet waking up.

"Well, now you remember. Let's keep walking."

"Do you have any idea where we are going?" The chill had worked its way under Ren's coat a few hours ago. The small part of his face that was exposed was numb. His feet were lead weights; snow was caked to his boots and pant legs. "Or any idea of where we are other than east of the village."

"I know exactly where we are and I have an idea of where we're going." Jakob shouldered past.

"An idea? Care to share?"

Jakob stopped. He looked behind them and then met Ren's gaze. "You're going to be mad."

Ren raised an eyebrow.

Jakob sighed and pulled his hand from his pocket. Using his teeth, he pulled off his glove and reached into his coat. He removed a slip of folded paper and held it out.

Carefully, Ren took it and unfolded it. He read: "East to North. North to flee from the sun like Daphne. Then there's an X."

"I found it on the floor of my father's room. It took me a few hours to figure it out, but I think that's where my family is."

Ren furrowed his brow. "I don't understand."

"East to North. Do you remember the Roper family? They came into town on festival days to trade. There was the one daughter with the… really nice… assets."

"Vaguely," Ren answered.

Jakob took the note. "Anyway, the head of the family was named North. Their farm lies east of the village. So East to North Roper's farm. It's only a few miles ahead, Ren. We're almost there."

"And then what? What the stars does 'flee from the sun' mean? Who is Daphne?"

"That confused me, too, since I didn't remember anyone named Daphne, but once I realized he was talking about a story, I got it."

Ren tilted his head. "I have no idea."

"Oh, come on, Ren. I know you didn't stay in school as long as I did, but surely you know the story of Daphne."

It clicked. Flee from the sun. In the story, Daphne had fled from the sun god and her legs turned to roots and her arms splintered into branches. She became a tree to escape him. "The Laurels."

"And the X means to cross the Laurels."

"Why didn't you show Rowan? We wouldn't have had to sneak away! She would've taken us there instead of us trudging through the snow. Cogs, Jakob!"

Jakob shook his head. "Do you really believe that?"

"Yes!"

"Then you're more naïve than I thought. You honestly think she would risk more days on a hunch? On a piece of paper that may mean nothing at all?"

"But it does mean something!" Ren waved his hands. "It's obviously a code. You figured it out."

"It's a code to us dusters. Not to them. They would've dismissed it because they're drifters. They're not like us."

Ren's mouth fell open. "What the hell, Jakob?" he yelled. "Those drifters took us in! They've acted like our family. Penelope thinks the world of you. They've fed us, included us, *protected* us."

"They want to throw you in a prison!"

That brought Ren up short. "Asher and I are... working on it."

"And if they don't do that, they want to use you. You are nothing but a tool or a weapon to them."

"That's the *Corps*, not the crew." It was an important distinction to make, since sometimes Ren couldn't see the difference himself.

"It doesn't matter. Now you're free and you can use your power to help us. Think about it. You could be a hero to Erden."

Ren took a step back.

"Jakob," he said softly, "did you lure me away to *use* me?"

"What? No, that's not what I meant! I swear. I just..." Jakob kicked the snow. "I want everything to go back like it was, before the stupid soldiers showed up, before being captured. I know it can't. I know it will never be the same, but this is my chance, *our* chance, to find our families and have a normal life again. I need that, Ren. I'm not strong like you."

Ren looked up and blinked against the brightness. He didn't want to make a choice of leaving one family for another, but that is what he'd done.

Had he chosen the correct one? There was no going back now.

"Jakob," Ren said, looking east. "I don't think I'm destined for a normal life."

"Probably not." Jakob pushed past Ren. "But you can have one for a little while."

"And if you're wrong? If they're not across the Laurels, what will we do?"

Jakob didn't stop. "My father left me this note. He had faith I'd come back and find it. I have to have faith that they're there."

Ren sighed. Anger roiled in his gut. "Save me from idiot dusters." He shoved his hands into his pockets, steeled his resolve, and followed.

⊣⊢

They made it to the farm after a few hours.

Ren shivered despite the layers he wore; his limbs were freezing despite constant movement. To find the old house, he and Jakob had to abandon the safety of the trees and cut across flat land. The wind whipped viciously, blowing snow, obscuring their vision, and cutting through Ren like a blade, slicing him to the bone.

Out in the open, they were unprotected, visible to anyone nearby, even in the swirling snow storm: two dark blobs that staggered in the deepening snow. Maybe recent events had Ren paranoid, but he swore someone was watching them as they trudged toward the Roper farm. He thought he heard footsteps other than his own over the whistling wind. His skin crawled with the feeling of a gaze upon him. Ren tried his best to look around, but the stab of the cold on his cheeks and nose kept him hunched into his coat and scarf. He wouldn't have been able to spot them anyway. And that made him all the more guarded. His power flared in his middle and searched for any nearby tech.

There was an inkling, a tug on the edge of his perception, but when he stopped to concentrate, it flitted away. Someone was out there, and Ren and Jakob were sitting ducks.

However, by the time they stumbled up the walk to the front porch, Ren didn't care if someone was out there or not. He was determined to go inside and sit by a fire and warm the frozen nubs that were his toes.

"We'll stay the night here," Jakob yelled over the wind's howl.

"We have to. We'll both be icicles if we keep going."

"Good point."

The chill was no better on the porch. Ren stomped on the weathered wood, kicking off mounds of snow, while Jakob knocked on the door. With the protection from the overhang, Ren pulled the cloth from around his face and turned to scan the landscape.

He could see nothing but the blankness of snow. It didn't soothe his unease, but at least there was not an immediate threat.

Jakob knocked again, louder, insistent, but there was no answer.

The house didn't look as if it had been disturbed by the same forces that had destroyed his childhood home, but it didn't look inhabited either. The building appeared sturdy, as did the surrounding outbuildings—the barn, the chicken coop, the tool shed. It was all intact, and in the winter Ren wouldn't expect to see anyone walking around outside. However, he would expect to see the healthy glow of a fire, or heating elements, or even light coming from the window he peered into. He saw nothing, except his breath fogging on the glass.

"I don't think they're home."

"Astute observation, Ren." Jakob tried the door, and the knob turned. "It's unlocked."

They entered and looked around. A layer of dust clung to the flat surfaces, and the house was almost as cold inside as it was outside.

"They're gone," Jakob said. "They must have left with the others."

"Or they were run off," Ren said. He wandered into the main room and was relieved to find a stack of wood by the fireplace. "Let's get a fire started and eat and rest. We'll leave for the Laurels at first light."

Between the two of them, they had a roaring fire in no time. They searched the deserted house and found blankets and linens in the upper rooms and set them in front of the fire to warm while they continued to explore. In the kitchen, Ren drifted his fingers over the small pieces of tech that the family had left behind. His star pulsed under his skin and throbbed with the desire to be allowed out, to merge, and Ren gritted his teeth against a deluge. He allowed a trickle to seep from his fingertips, and it vibrated down his limbs and sought out the circuits and systems of the appliances. With the power came familiarity and comfort, and Ren controlled the flow easier with each passing moment. He didn't feel as if he were drowning in a current or being helplessly swept away. In fact, flexing his star was like stretching a muscle, a good ache, and, when he reined it back in, he had minimal trouble. There was no overwhelming need to fix everything or kill anyone, which he counted a plus.

Asher had been right about Ren's need to disconnect. Without the *Star Stream* in his head, Ren could think clearly. He was slotted in his body experiencing every hunger pang, every throb of his joints, and every stretch of his muscles. At the current moment, Ren wasn't certain being able to feel everything was the gift it was supposed to be.

Ren went back into the main room. He and Jakob ate a meal from their packs. Ren toed his boots off and peeled his trousers down his legs. His skin was red and stinging from the combination of wet cold and sudden heat. He set out his wet clothes near the hearth. He wrapped himself in a blanket and curled up in a plush chair. They didn't talk, and the darkness crept closer around them as the sun started its descent and the wind beat against the house. The wood creaked under the assault. The fire snapped and crackled. Ren pulled the blanket closer, tucking the corner under his bare feet, warding off the chill and the eerie atmosphere. He couldn't help but imagine that he was a character in one of his mother's stories, trespassing in a sacred place. With each passing moment, Ren was more certain he was in a room of ghosts.

Exhausted, warm, and fed, Ren let his eyes droop as he watched the sun slowly sink toward the horizon. He was half asleep when he heard it—a loud thump and then a rattle at the front window.

Ren snapped to instant wakefulness and sat up in the chair. Heart thumping hard and sitting still as stone, he strained to hear. Just when he had begun to think it was his imagination and had relaxed into the cushion, he heard it again.

"Jakob," he whispered, tone harsh, panicked. "Wake up."

Jakob stirred where he had slumped on a soft rug under a large quilt. He made a noise which was part snore and part shout.

"Be quiet," Ren said, shooting to his feet. "I hear something."

There was another loud noise, and then the door handle of the front door shook. It didn't give, because Jakob had locked the knob and the deadbolt. There was another noise, and the stomp of footsteps retreating.

Ren shook, body trembling, as he watched the front door. Agonizing minutes passed. Ren relaxed his shoulders. A thump reverberated on the other side of the house. Ren whipped around. The handle on the back door began to turn.

Jakob inched close to Ren. "Please tell me you locked the back door."

Ren gulped. "I didn't."

A gust of wind shook the house. The flames flickered, casting shadows along the walls.

"Maybe it's North Roper." Jakob attempted a hopeful tone, but his voice cracked.

"Or maybe it's someone responsible for what happened at our village."

The door pushed open, but stopped, caught on a rug by the door. A gust of wind blew inside, and goosebumps bloomed on Ren's arms. The person on the other side struggled with the door, and Ren glimpsed a pulse gun in a gloved hand.

"Hide!" Ren said, shoving Jakob's shoulder.

The door budged, and the rug gave way. Jakob dropped his blanket and took off, bare feet thumping across the wood floor.

Ren faced the intruder. He reached for his star; the power crackled at his fingertips like lightning in a storm. The hairs on his legs and arms rose. Blue bled into his vision, and he reached out and saw the mechanisms of the pulse gun as a blueprint.

The person stalked in, covered head to toe in a layer of snow and ice over a thick coat and scarf. Only a sliver of his face was visible, and his cheeks were flayed red from the wind. His green eyes glittered, and he stalked forward, undeterred when Ren's power dismantled the weapon. The weapon lay in pieces on the floor, but the man kept coming. When Ren realized he wasn't stopping, it was too late to flee, but he tried, staggering backward, tripping over the quilt Jakob left behind. His pulse raced; fear was tangible with the cold sweat at the back of his neck. Ren's feet tangled, and he fell against a chair. He let out a strangled cry as he pushed out of the man's grasp and stumbled to the staircase.

He made it up one step before the man grabbed the back of his shirt and yanked him backward. His collar dug into his throat, cutting off his air, and he slipped. Grabbing the banister, Ren held on, desperate and afraid, in his last attempt at escape.

But the intruder was stronger. He pried Ren's arms back, and then Ren was pressed hard against the wall so the back of his head knocked into it. Bruisingly tight, an arm pressed across his body. His chest heaved. He struggled weakly, gasping. The tips of his toes barely touched the wood floor. This was it! He was going to die at the hands of someone he didn't even know. He had survived capture, the citadel, mercenaries, the Phoenix Corps, only to perish in an old farmhouse, a day away from possibly finding his family.

Then he was let go. He sagged on the wall; his knees were weak.

The man pulled the scarf away from his face. His mouth was turned down in a frown; his expression was absolutely livid. He hit Ren on the back of the head.

"You idiot!" Asher said. "You left the door unlocked. Do you want to be killed? You have no idea who or what is wandering around out there. Tracking you was depressingly easy. You could have at least tried to cover your tracks."

Ren let his head thump on the wall. "Cogs, Ash! You scared the star right out of me."

"And running up the stairs? Unless you were going to jump from a window, you would have had no escape. Plus, no boots. No *trousers*. For someone who *ran away* from people who were protecting him, you have done an abysmal job of trying to keep yourself alive."

Ren slid to the floor so his bare legs stuck out. A flush worked up his neck. He was mortified to be caught half-naked, but relief won out over the humiliation.

"I could go on, but I am going to go *lock the back door*." Asher went back the way he came, passing a closet door. He grabbed the handle and wrenched it open. "Predictable hiding place, Jakob."

Ren laughed, giddy, as Jakob stepped out. Jakob shot a glare to Ren, which only made him chuckle harder as his fear morphed into lightheadedness.

The back door slammed, and Asher carried a pack into the main space. He stripped out of his own hat, scarf, gloves, and jacket. The snow clinging to Asher's boots and trousers melted into puddles as he stood near the flames.

"Where the stars do you two think you are going, anyway?"

Jakob snatched his quilt from its heap and went back to his nest on the floor next to the fire. "None of your business."

Once Ren gathered his wits, embarrassment welled through him, though Asher had seen Ren looking worse, and he quickly found his own blanket and wrapped up in it. He sat in his chair and huddled into the warmth. "Where are the others?"

"Heading toward Delphi, hopefully." Asher warmed his hands over the fire and rubbed them. His fingers were red.

"They left?"

"Rowan is justifiably furious. She says she'll meet us at Delphi and if she's not there when we get there, to wait for her."

"They let you go off alone?" Ren asked. He rested his cheek on his pulled-up knees.

"Ollie wanted to come," Asher said. He unlaced his boots and stepped out of them. His socks had a hole in the toe. "But I made him escort Rowan and Penelope back to the ship. Not that I think they couldn't take care of themselves, but because if Ollie came, then Penelope would want to come, too, and that would leave Rowan alone. She'd feel abandoned by her crew. And then I'd have to deal with that. So here I am."

"You could've announced that it was you when you came through the door. You didn't need to scare us," Jakob snapped.

A slow, cruel smile bloomed across Asher's lips. "What would have been the fun in that? Besides, you two deserved it, for sneaking off on a dumb mission for nothing."

"It's not for nothing," Ren said, quietly. "And we know where we are going."

Asher lifted an eyebrow. "You do, huh? Something you want to share?"

"Jakob found a note."

"Stars, Ren! Why don't you tell everyone? I'm sure my father wouldn't mind *since he wrote it in code.*"

Ren gestured. The blanket slipped down his shoulder. "It's Ash."

Jakob gave Asher a narrowed-eye glare. "My father left a note. We have an idea about where my family is living and we're going to check it out. You can go back to the space dock and wait for us there."

"Like hell."

"Ash," Ren said.

"No. I'm not letting you two out of my sight, even if it means staying up all night in case you get it in your heads to sneak off again."

Jakob snorted.

Ren sighed. "No need for that. You should rest. We leave at first light."

Asher studied Ren, then nodded.

Jakob grumbled as he twisted in his nest to get comfortable. Ren grasped his blanket tighter. Asher settled down, careful of the small pools from the melted snow. Ren's eyes drifted closed, and the last image he saw was the flames reflecting in Asher's gold hair.

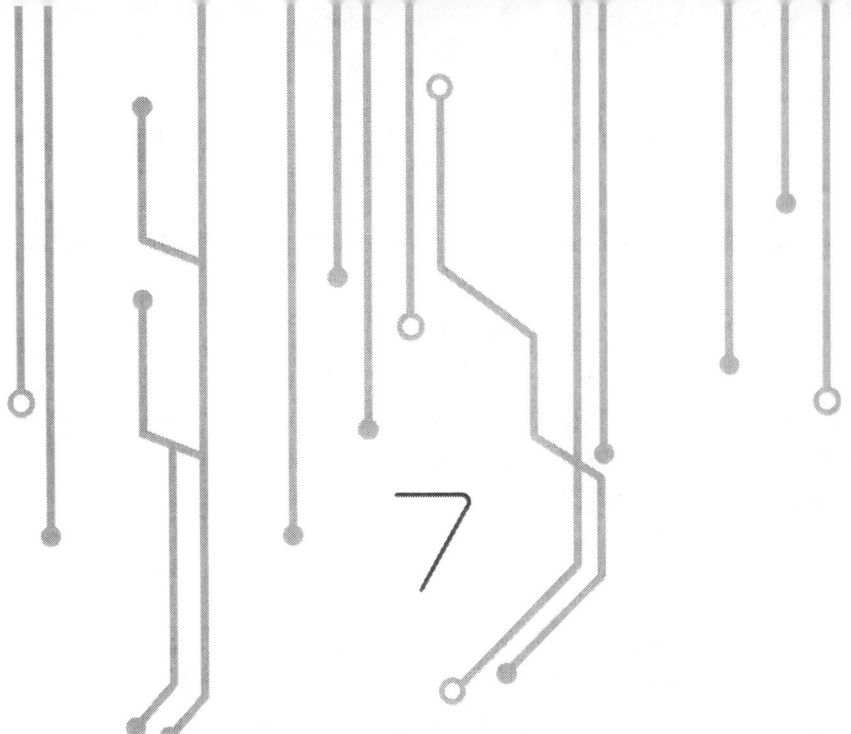

7

BUNDLED IN LAYERS AND CARRYING their packs, they left the farmhouse as the sun rose. Ren had reconstructed Asher's pulse gun, though that was more difficult than making it fall apart. It had taken a few minutes, but in the end, Ren was fairly certain it would work. Asher had it tucked near his hip, hidden beneath his bulky coat.

Ren covered up; only the barest sliver of skin was exposed to the cold and the frost. They trudged through the snow: Jakob leading, Asher a step behind, and Ren bringing up the rear. The snowstorm had died down during the night, and the sky was clear. The sun was bright and beating down on the rolling fields covered in powdery white.

Ren looked over his shoulder at the house as it diminished in the distance. He was glad to be out of there; the place had left him unsettled.

"I'm still mad at you for scaring us, by the way," Ren said, as they walked.

Asher laughed. "Well, I'm still mad at you for sneaking away from the group."

Ren hummed. "Fair, I guess. Oh, I've been meaning to ask, how did you get from the front door to the back door so fast last night?"

Asher stopped. He frowned. "I wasn't at the front door."

Ren's stomach dropped. "What?"

"I approached the house from the back when I spotted the fire through the windows. I was freezing and went for the direct route." Ren swallowed. Fear must have shown in his eyes because Asher moved close. His voice was full of concern. "Was there someone at the front door last night?"

"It must have been my imagination." The wind had been brutal. He had already been thinking of ghosts and of being watched. And only a few days ago, he'd been slowly driven insane by a spaceship.

"Are you sure?"

Ren picked up his pace and brushed past Asher. "Yeah. Let's go."

By the afternoon, Ren sweated beneath his layers from exertion and the warmth of the day. He didn't remove his scarf or coat, however, knowing that his sweat would chill and leave him colder than before.

When his stomach growled, they all stopped to eat the dried meat Penelope had packed and to drink from the canteens. The cold water chilled Ren's throat and chest, and he coughed into his fist. Before they moved on, Asher packed fresh snow into the empty canteen, then looped it over his shoulder.

The path they took wound through the countryside. They started in farm fields, but as they neared the entrance to the Laurels, they encountered a small wood. They stuck close to the edges, taking refuge under the canopy of evergreen branches. Ren didn't experience the feeling of being followed or watched again, but he occasionally prodded the area with his power to make sure. He didn't experience any feedback from tech, which put his mind somewhat at ease.

As they traveled, Ren couldn't help but remember the time he and Asher had spent days wandering the countryside on their way to a spaceport: how they had slept in a hollowed-out log, how they had bathed in a stream, how they had spent most of their days in a dazed sleepless state, how they'd kept moving out of fear and desperation. Ren had spent days watching Asher's back as he'd pushed them onward. The circumstances weren't quite the same, but the span of Asher's shoulders was no different and neither was the determined length of his strides.

Their relationship was different, though. The closeness they had found in the dungeon and in their escape had evaporated. Maybe that's all their relationship had been—born of mutual desperation. When the fighting was over, the flimsy premise had disappeared, and whatever they had been crumbled.

Ren frowned and pushed the thoughts away. It wasn't the time to dwell on the past and the things Ren couldn't change. He would always be a duster technopath, and Asher would always belong to the stars.

"We're getting close to the entrance to the Laurels," Jakob said, in the late afternoon. "We should start looking for a place to take shelter."

"I think I saw a thicket a few yards back that would be good," Ren said, pointing over his shoulder.

"We should keep going," Asher said. "And find actual shelter. I don't want to be out here in another snowstorm." Asher waited for Ren to join him. "Not that I don't think we could tough it out, but there may be better shelter ahead. I'd hate to go backward."

Ren shrugged. "Whatever you say—"

A sharp crack of a twig cut Ren off.

Asher grabbed Ren's coat and yanked him back while stepping between Ren and the place where the sound originated. A shrub rustled nearby. Footsteps approached.

Jakob joined them and crowded close. Asher had his pulse gun out of his holster. Ren reached with his star, and four pieces of tech pinged back from different directions.

"Four of them," Ren whispered. "We're surrounded."

Jakob had a knife in his hand; his gloved fingers were wrapped tight around the hilt.

"Come out," Asher called. "We know you're there."

Four figures, dressed like villagers, but wearing body armor and helmets reminiscent of the Baron's soldiers, melted out of the wood.

Three of them had prods, the fourth carried a stunner. Suddenly the thought they were being watched didn't seem so farfetched after all.

"Well, this is familiar," Jakob said, low.

The four fanned out with weapons trained on their small group.

"I can take care of this," Ren said. They had fewer weapons than the Hatfields had, and Ren's star already crackled through him, lighting up his nerves from his frozen toes to his fingers.

"No," Asher replied, voice low. "Don't reveal yourself. Not yet."

"You're trespassing," one of the group said. She stepped forward. Her red hair peeked out from beneath her helmet and trailed over her shoulders. She hefted the stunner. "Turn around and go back, and we won't hurt you."

"No weedin' way," Jakob shot back. "We're heading to the Laurels. And you're not stopping us."

"Stars," Asher said, voice low and irritated. "You want to get us captured?"

"The Laurels," the woman said. She looked them up and down, but the helmet covered her expression. "Why?"

"We're looking for someone."

Their potential captors shifted, adjusting their weapons, firmly pointing them at the group. If they weren't on edge before, they certainly were now.

"He didn't mean that in a threatening way at all," Ren said. That didn't help, especially when one of the group moved forward so his prod grazed the outer layer of Ren's coat. Ren struggled with reining in his desire to lash out, to render the weapons harmless, to protect the three of them. His eyes flashed as he blinked blue for a second. He choked back his power, packed it up, and shoved it down.

Asher looked to the sky. "Save me from idiot dusters."

"We should take them with us," one of the others said. "Let the leader handle them."

"And lead them to our camp? No. What if they are *birdmen*?"

"They don't look like birdmen."

"What the hell is a birdman?" Jakob said. He pushed his hood back and pulled the scarf from around his face. "Whatever. I don't care. I'm looking for my father and my sisters. We're not here to hurt anyone or steal anything. Okay? Just let us go."

The leader tilted her head. "You look familiar."

"Well, I am a duster from the village near the lake."

They murmured. The leader allowed the muzzle of the stunner to aim at the ground. "Surrender your weapon and come with us."

Asher resisted, standing still. He looked to Ren, read the hope apparent in Ren's expression, then spun the pulse gun in his hand and held it out to the nearest person, grip first.

The person holstered a prod and took the pulse gun, then tucked it into their belt.

"Good," the leader said with a nod. "Follow us. We'll be back to our camp before sundown."

The end of a prod pushed into Ren's back, and he lurched forward; he held his body stiff lest he sizzle with electricity. He followed the woman with the stunner into the trees. She led. Jakob and Asher and Ren walked in the middle of the cluster. The three others surrounded them and herded them.

"How long have you been tracking us?"

"A while."

"Since Roper's farm?"

The woman looked over her shoulder. "No."

Asher and Ren exchanged a glance.

There was someone else out there. Or Ren should start believing in ghosts.

An hour later, the group stopped. The wood thinned, and the evergreens and the thick bark of leafless oaks gave way to a copse of slender branched trees. Ren stepped forward and ran his hand over the smooth, white bark. The roots forked like legs and dug into the earth in a curve like the arch of a foot. The branches rose toward the sky, like arms raised in supplication to a higher being. Daphne ran, and prayed, and turned into a tree, frozen in beauty for all time.

Asher placed his own hand next to Ren's. "They're beautiful. What are they?"

"The Laurels," Ren said.

"Why are they so different from the other trees?"

The question had their captors whipping their heads around to stare at Asher. At least, that is what Ren thought they were doing. It was hard to tell through the shields of their helmets.

"There's a story," Ren said. "I'll tell you another time."

Asher realized his question had marked him as an outsider, either because he didn't know the lore or because he had limited experience with trees, which was clearly a drifter trait. Ren was afraid he'd do something rash, but instead, Asher shrank back near Ren with his shoulders hunched and his head down.

"Who did you say you were again?" the woman asked.

"We didn't," Jakob shot back.

She crossed her arms. The stunner was strapped to her back but within easy reach. The electric charge of the prods pricked the star in Ren's middle, and he sparked in response. It was only a flicker, but again, Ren blinked blue.

Asher grabbed his hand.

"I think maybe you should. Or we might decide to leave you out here to the elements."

Jakob lifted his chin. His cheeks were pink from exertion. His eyes shone a cold blue. His breath hung in clouds. "I think maybe you should fetch someone in charge if you can't decide whether to bring us to the camp or not."

Ren sighed. Asher rubbed a hand over his face. So much for keeping Jakob from being reckless.

The statement certainly struck a nerve. The leader moved forward and pushed hard on Jakob's shoulder. He took a step back to keep his balance; snow and twigs crunched under his heel.

"I *am* in charge."

"Prove it. Take us in."

She shoved a finger in his face. "You don't give me orders."

"Obviously someone does."

She bristled. "Fine, we'll go." She held up her gloved hand to silence the chatter from her men. "But if you try anything, we'll kill that one first."

She pointed to Ren.

"Fine," Jakob said.

Ren balked. "Wait, what?"

She cocked her hip, and Ren imagined her mouth in a self-satisfied smirk.

He started to protest, but was shoved in the back again, and this time Asher grabbed his arm to keep him from falling. He shot a glare to the owner of the prod before the group started moving, but received no reaction, not that he could tell. He loathed the face shields.

They continued on, following the woman along the boundary of the tree line that separated the small forest from the Laurels. The white trees on the right of their path grew thicker, until the branches intertwined, and even bare from the season, the brush was so thick it was difficult to see through. Ren didn't know how they would be able to traverse the Laurels. To complicate matters further, the snow and the white wood of the laurel trees blended, and, even squinting, Ren found it difficult to discern any passage. Other vegetation ran wild in the small spaces left—ferns and vines and briar patches. Though dormant because of the cold and the snow, they still made the area impassable. Everything was a blur of white with occasional patches of brown. If they had entered on their own, they would have been lost within minutes and would never have found their way out.

Ren's questions about the entrance were answered when they stopped in front of a thick group of trees. At their feet, almost hidden by the clinging snow, was a protection stone. Carved into the rock was the familiar lettering of the language of his ancestors. And beneath those was an X. On the note the X didn't mean to cross the Laurels. It marked the entrance.

Ren nudged Jakob and jerked his head toward the symbol.

Jakob's eyebrows shot up, and he smiled, quick and bright, then smothered it when a guard looked his way.

Their leader glanced around, and then swept back a curtain of vines to reveal a small alcove. She ushered them through, kept watch until the entire group was inside, then allowed the vines to fall back, which obscured the view and the light. Ren found himself beneath a natural arch made from two trees that had sprouted near each other and grown until their branches had become entangled. Ren couldn't tell where one tree ended and the other began.

Asher's eyes were wide, and he pushed his hood back. "This is amazing."

"Quiet, now," the woman said harshly. "Come on."

She beckoned them onward. They ducked, bodies hunched, as they walked several feet through a tunnel that was longer than Ren had thought. About the time Ren developed a crick in his neck, the tunnel opened up and revealed the head of a twisting path.

Two more guards stood waiting, weapons in their hands, helmets on. "What do you have?"

"Stragglers," she answered. "Found them wandering in the forest. They claim they're from the village by the lake."

"Really?"

One of the guards pulled off her helmet. She was impossibly young to be wielding any kind of weapon, and her wide smile when she saw Jakob made that more evident. With her wild dark hair and bright blue eyes, the resemblance was striking.

"Jakob!" she cried. She dropped her prod and her helmet in the dirty snow and leapt at her brother.

He caught her in a hug. "Ezzy!" He squeezed her tight so her feet left the ground, and they held on for a long, intense moment. When

Jakob finally set her down, he didn't let her go, but kept one arm around her shoulders.

"Ezzy, you remember Ren? Right?"

She blushed and shyly tucked a strand of hair behind her ear. "Yeah, of course. Liam's older brother."

"Is he here?" Ren asked. His pulse fluttered. Hope was present and dangerous, until she looked at the ground and shook her head.

"No, I'm sorry. But your mother and father are here."

Ren's knees went weak. His vision and hearing fuzzed out; the only sound was his heart thundering, while black dots danced across his eyes. He staggered back, dizzy, and clumsy. Asher caught him and held him up before he fell to the ground. His legs trembled and he had a stray thought about how Liam would've made fun of him for *swooning*. He chuckled and rubbed at his eyes and leaned on Asher's embrace until he regained his bearings.

"They are?" His voice was a shiver. "Where?"

"In the camp," Ezzy gestured over her shoulder. "Follow the path."

"Wait," the leader of the group that had found them said. She took off her helmet; her red hair stood on end. "How do you know these two?"

Ezzy squished into Jakob's side. "This is my older brother Jakob. Jakob, this is the leader of our guard, Beatrice."

"You're Levitt's son?"

Jakob nodded.

"Well, why in the hell didn't you say so when we met?"

"Because I didn't know who the hell you were."

"You should've said!"

"You're dressed like one of Vos's guards and you're carrying a stunner."

She made a scathing retort. They bickered, and Ren barely paid attention to the conversation. His thoughts centered on talking to his mother, on what he might say, what he might do—but his focus snapped back when he heard mention of the stronghold.

"Salvaged, from the citadel," Beatrice said, both pride and a challenge in her words.

"You go to the citadel?" Ren straightened, though he was unsteady on his feet. Asher's hand stayed on his arm.

"When we need supplies."

"So it's empty, then?"

Beatrice shrugged. "Sometimes there are birdmen hanging about, but we avoid them easily enough."

"What are birdmen? You keep mentioning them, but it's a term I'm not familiar with."

Beatrice smiled; her freckled cheeks were like apples. "It's a term we used in my village. It means the Phoenix Corps."

"There are Phoenix Corps? Here?" Asher asked.

"Unfortunately. The limited intel we gathered is that they're looking for someone or maybe a few people. We're not really sure. But they're here and they are a bunch of weeds, let me tell you."

"I need more information." Asher pointed a finger at the group.

"And who are you?" Beatrice crossed her arms and eyed Asher critically.

"He's a friend," Ren said, twining his fingers with Asher's, ignoring the way Asher startled and stared at their hands. "And we can find out more in a while, but my parents…" Ren trailed off. A lump formed in his throat. "My parents are here," he said, quiet, awed.

"Right." Asher backed down. "You should see them."

Ezzy clapped her hands and bounced on the balls of her feet. "I can take you to the camp." She looped her arm through Jakob's. "Come on. Daddy is going to fall over when he sees you."

A mixture of excitement and dread swirled in Ren's stomach as he walked down the path to the village. He was about to see his parents, about to talk to his mom. He didn't know what to say, what to reveal, if anything at all.

The path curved gently, and, when they'd stepped through another copse, the camp lay before them. The buildings were no more than shacks that looked as if they could barely bear the weight of a light snow, but there was no snow on them at all. They had been clustered in no discernible pattern. There were dozens, made from a combination of wood, metal, and blankets. Some of them shared walls the way apartments were stacked on the drifts. Which one belonged to his parents?

Cooking fires burned outside away from the wood and cloth. Tarps hung overhead in the trees as well. They reflected the smoke and the flames, and, when Ren crossed into the meadow, under the first layer of canvas, it was like walking into a wall of heat. He took off his scarf and unzipped his coat, shrugging out of the heavy fabric. Asher and Jakob did the same. At Ezzy's instruction, they dropped their winter gear into a pile, and she led them deeper into the commune.

Ren didn't know how the villagers had pulled it off, but the ground was free of frost and snow, and small gardens grew. Ren and Asher lingered. Asher bent to finger the leaves, as Ezzy and Jakob continued ahead of them.

"It's a greenhouse," Asher said. "Like on the drifts."

Ren elbowed Asher hard in the ribs and shook his head. "Keep it down. We shouldn't broadcast that you're a drifter. Keep your tags and tattoo hidden. Something's going on here."

"I noticed." He looked around, scoffing. "Birdmen? What the cogs? The Phoenix isn't just a *bird*. It's a mythological creature, and we are *soldiers*."

Ren bit back a retort. "Your ridiculous contempt for the name is noted. Now, will you *shut up*?"

Asher pouted and crossed his arms.

Sighing, Ren pushed his hair from his eyes. "I'm serious. Try to keep your drifter opinions to yourself so you don't get us thrown out of—"

"Ren?"

The voice was tentative, uncertain, but familiar. Ren snapped his head up and watched as his stepfather approached, carrying a bundle of wood. He looked the same, big and brawny. His brown hair was salted with gray, and his beard was full, as he always wore it in the winter.

"Ren, is that you?"

Ren straightened. He raised his hand in an awkward wave. "Um… hi."

The firewood tumbled to the ground, and Ren found himself caught up in a bear hug. His stepfather's arms crushed Ren to his barrel chest.

"I can't believe it."

Ren's relationship with his stepfather had been lukewarm at best, awkward and strained most of the time, and contentious every once in a while. They didn't hug. Emotion hadn't been an aspect of their association. But wrapped tight in his stepfather's arms, Ren felt tears gather because he was *safe*. For the first time in a long while, he was safe, without the throb of the star in his chest. He clutched back.

"Katherine!" he bellowed. "Kat! Come out here."

He pushed Ren to arm's length; his meaty hand curled around Ren's forearm.

"What is it, honey?" she said, a laugh on the edge of her words. Pushing back a curtain decorated with flowers, she emerged from one of the shacks nearby. "What is the fuss all about?"

She wiped her hands on her apron. Her red hair was pulled back from her face in a complicated knot, and she had streaks of gray at her temples. Her eyes were bright, but her face had aged. She looked careworn, fatigued—the price of losing her home and both of her sons.

She gasped when she saw Ren. Her hands flew to cover her open mouth. Her voice trembled. "Ren?"

"Mom."

She attacked him. It was the only way he could describe it. He wobbled backward, almost fell, but Asher supported him for a second. His palm made a reassuring pressure between Ren's shoulder blades before he stepped away.

"My boy." She cupped his face. Her hands were warm, and she kissed his forehead. "Oh, my son. How did you…? Where have you…?" She hiccupped. "I'm sorry. I can't believe it. Are you okay?"

"I'm good. I'm good." He held her hand to his face. He was good. He was bursting. All he'd wanted was to return home, and he had. He had made it. *He had made it.*

"You need a haircut. You're shaggy."

Ren laughed.

"And you need a good meal. You don't look like you've been eating."

That was true. Ren hadn't been eating on the ship. He'd been too consumed with nightmares and electricity and power. What else did she see? The circles under his eyes? Could she read the things that had happened in tense lines around his mouth or the slump of his shoulders?

"A lot has happened," he said simply.

She nodded; her smile dimmed. "It has," she confirmed. She patted his cheeks and pulled away. She wiped at her eyes, then noticed Asher for the first time. "And who is this?"

"I'm Ash," he said, holding out his hand. "I'm Ren's friend."

"We met at the citadel, when…" Ren trailed off. He didn't need to finish the sentence.

Kat pushed away Asher's arm and pulled him into a hug. Asher held his body stiff, but, after a moment, he relaxed into her embrace.

"You look like you need a good meal as well," she said, stepping back and eyeing them. "And a warm place to sleep and ward off the chill."

"That would be very nice," Asher said.

His stepfather bent to gather the wood back into his arms. "Come along, then. We'll get you both sorted."

Kat beamed. She took Ren's arm and tugged. Ren grabbed Asher's hand, and they were swept along into the camp.

⊣⊢

His parents' shack was tiny. The four of them fit, but barely, sitting on a threadbare rug on the floor. But it was cozy and warm, which was a surprise.

Ren and Asher received bowls of rich, hearty stew. The broth was fragrant, the vegetables were fresh, and the meat chunks were plentiful. Ren ate his fill, slurping from his bowl and sopping the remnants with a hunk of bread. Asher ate politely, though with zeal, and, by the end, Ren could've dozed off where he sat—warm and content and *happy* and back where he belonged, even if he wasn't so sure of that last part.

His stepfather left to tend to the fires, which was his job in the little community. When he departed after a tender pat on the head to Ren and a kiss for Ren's mother, the three of them were alone. His mother stacked the dishes, then fidgeted. She picked at a loose thread in her apron. Her fingernails were dirty. When she spoke, she didn't look at him, but stared at a spot on the packed dirt floor. "What happened, Ren? When you were taken?"

The question was tentative, as if she wasn't sure how to ask, or whether she really wanted to know.

Ren and Asher exchanged a glance, and Ren sat up straighter, keeping his legs crossed beneath him.

"You have to be more specific. So much has… it's been almost a year. It was barely spring the last time I saw you."

"The last I saw of you and Liam was when you two went to swim in the lake." Her brow furrowed, and she worried the string between her fingers. "Was Liam with you when you went to the castle?"

"No," Ren said. "I saw him in the forest. They had him, but he got away." Ren ignored the sharp glance from Asher. Asher knew the whole story, having heard it on one of the nights they'd spent locked in the dungeon. "You haven't seen him?"

"I dream about him," she said. "But no, I haven't seen him. Not since the day they took you. He must have been taken, too."

Ren pressed his lips together and took a shallow breath. "He wasn't at the citadel. Where else would he have been taken? Who other than Vos would have wanted him?"

She finally looked at him. Her eyes were green, like Liam's, but they were haunted, afraid. "There are several possibilities for people with special gifts like him. Like you."

The confession was like a stunner blast to the chest rendering him helpless. One moment, Ren's heart beat, and the next, it seized painfully. He couldn't breathe. He couldn't move. His muscles locked. He stared at her with fists clenched against his thighs, eyes burning, body rigid.

"You knew," Asher said, softly, gently accusing, but oddly compassionate, as if her knowledge was a burden.

She nodded. The gesture unlocked Ren like a key. He breathed, though it wasn't calming or even; it was ragged and distressed. Tears of anger welled in his eyes as he remembered: the confusion and the dread; the prods and the locks and the cell and the ships; the nights wondering what was happening to him and trembling with exhaustion; the panic as he slipped into the machines; being hunted across a landscape and across the cluster and not really understanding why; being overwhelmed with power and having his humanity burned out of him in waves of blue electricity; having no agency, no control; being weaponized, dehumanized, and scared, so scared; terrified he would succumb to the thrall of tech, lose his humanity, lose his mind.

Ren jumped to his feet; the action startled both his mother and Asher. He towered over her, with his shoulders hunched to keep from knocking his head on the ceiling.

"Ren?" Asher said. "Calm down."

"You didn't tell me. Why didn't you tell me?" He sparked out. His vision went blue. There was nowhere for the star to bleed to, other than Asher's pulse gun, or the tech in his shoulder. And both were too small to warrant the attention of the *rage* which throbbed through him.

His mother blinked at him. Her face was pale, and she had twin spots of red on her freckled cheeks. "It wasn't supposed to happen like this, Ren. You have to understand. There are things going on that you don't know."

"No coggin' *shit*."

"You will not take that tone with me. I am your mother, no matter what you think of me."

"What I think is that you were scared of me, like everyone else, like you *should* be, and you couldn't face that. Were you scared of Liam too? Is he like me?" Ren held out his hand. Electricity snapped and crackled down his fingers, flickering along his skin. "What didn't you tell him? *Where is he?*"

"Ren, I wasn't scared of you. I was scared *for* you."

She stood and folded her hand over Ren's, snuffing out the sparks of power. Her eyes flashed gold. Ren's star receded, tucked back into his chest, and when he squeezed his eyes shut, the blue faded. He blinked and caught the fading color in his mother's eyes.

"How did you do that?"

"There is much more going on than you understand," she repeated. "I'm sorry you had to figure it out on your own. And you must know that everything I did was to protect you and your brother." She released his hand. "Now, sit down."

Ren folded to the floor, partly in shock, partly from compulsion. Ren had always attributed his power to his nonexistent father. It hadn't crossed his mind that his mother would be the one. He should've known.

Asher patted his arm, a gesture that didn't go unnoticed by his mother. "Do you want me to step outside?" he asked.

"No. You should hear this too," Ren said. He lifted his chin and waited for his mother to argue, but she did not.

"I'm not powerful," she said. "And I can only comfort and calm. When you were small, you toddled to one of your toys, touched it, and your eyes went blue. When that happened, I had your stepfather throw out all of the limited tech we had. And we kept it that way."

"I figured it out in Vos's dungeon. Why we didn't have tech. Why you wouldn't let me go to the space docks." His throat went tight. He had guessed about his mother's knowledge all those months ago, but to hear it confirmed was entirely different. "Why didn't you tell me? Why did you hide it?"

"I was hoping you would never be forced to know. I was hoping that it would pass you by, and you would never know the star that pulsed within you."

Asher raised an eyebrow. "Your plan was that you hoped he wouldn't need to use it? Wouldn't be captured? Even though you knew there was a chance? That is the worst plan. That's not even a plan. And what if he wanted to leave?"

She stared at Asher with a flat expression.

Ren turned his head away, against the realization that all his aspirations, all his hopes of leaving Erden would have never manifested if he hadn't been taken by the soldiers. Liam had been right: His dreams were dust.

"I was never going to leave here," he said softly. "You condemned me to a life on this weedin' planet, in this stupid village, because you were afraid."

"This is a wonderful life, Ren. This isn't anything to be ashamed of, even if drifters deem it backward or spacers don't understand."

Ren didn't respond. He couldn't. He didn't know what to say. He bowed his head and stared at the dirt floor.

"You couldn't have left, Ren. You needed to stay here and remain hidden. There are things you don't know. Things about us, about star hosts, and what we had to do to survive."

"I can't listen to any more." Ren stood. "I'm going for a walk."

"I think I'll join you," Asher said, also standing.

His mother got to her feet, and the three of them huddled in the shack. The air was too close; the secrets were too thick.

"You have to listen to me, Ren. You need the whole story."

Ren shook his head. "I've been figuring it out on my own. I can figure out the rest, too." He brushed past Asher, pushed the blanket curtain aside, and left the shack. He heaved a breath of the crisp, unfiltered air.

"Your son is wonderful and amazing and brave. He's incredibly brave. I wish you could've seen that while he was here and trusted him enough to tell him what he needed to know. He's survived, but not without cost, and that could have been prevented."

"That's easy for you to say, as someone not burdened with the gift of the stars."

"No, it's easy for me to say as someone who cares for him."

Ren sucked in a breath.

Asher left the shack with a determined stride and stopped short. "I thought you would've walked a little farther away." His cheeks bloomed with a pink flush.

Ren licked his lips; his pulse beat hard beneath his skin. "You care for me?"

"Of course, you know that."

Ren did. Away from the ship, away from tech, this fact was a solid, irrefutable presence in his middle, separate from the star. It had its own space, its own force, and Ren could've cried from the warmth. He lifted his hand, curled it around the nape of Asher's neck, and drew him close. The kiss was soft, not filled with the desperation of their other kisses, but significant all the same. It took a moment for Asher to respond, and, when he did, he sank into it, relaxed the tense line of his shoulders, and pulled Ren closer with an arm around his waist.

They kissed in front of the home where Ren's parents lived, in the middle of a community of which Ren never really was a member. They kissed and didn't care who saw, and while they did, while Ren's lips molded to Asher's mouth, he was at peace. The turmoil which constantly threatened to break him into pieces was soothed, and the universe shrank to Asher's hand combing through his hair, and the movement of Asher's mouth on his, and the beat of Asher's pulse beneath Ren's fingertips.

It was Asher who broke away, too soon, and Ren wasn't prepared to relinquish the quiet thrum of intimacy, of affection.

"Does this mean I'm forgiven for being an arrogant drifter *birdman*?" Asher's words vibrated against Ren's mouth; his breath ghosted over Ren's cheek.

Ren huffed a laugh. "We'll work on it." He pressed a quick kiss to Asher's cheek. "What about me? Does this mean I'm forgiven for being an unpredictable, sometimes homicidal, star host?"

"We'll work on it."

Ren smiled, and it wasn't brittle. He didn't feel as if he'd break.

"I haven't seen you smile in so long," Asher whispered; he touched the corner of Ren's mouth with his fingertips. "I had forgotten what it looked like."

Ren clutched Asher tighter, prepared to continue working on forgiveness, but a hurried crunch of footsteps and a loud voice stopped him.

"Oh, thank the stars!" Jakob yelled. "I need to talk to both of you, right now."

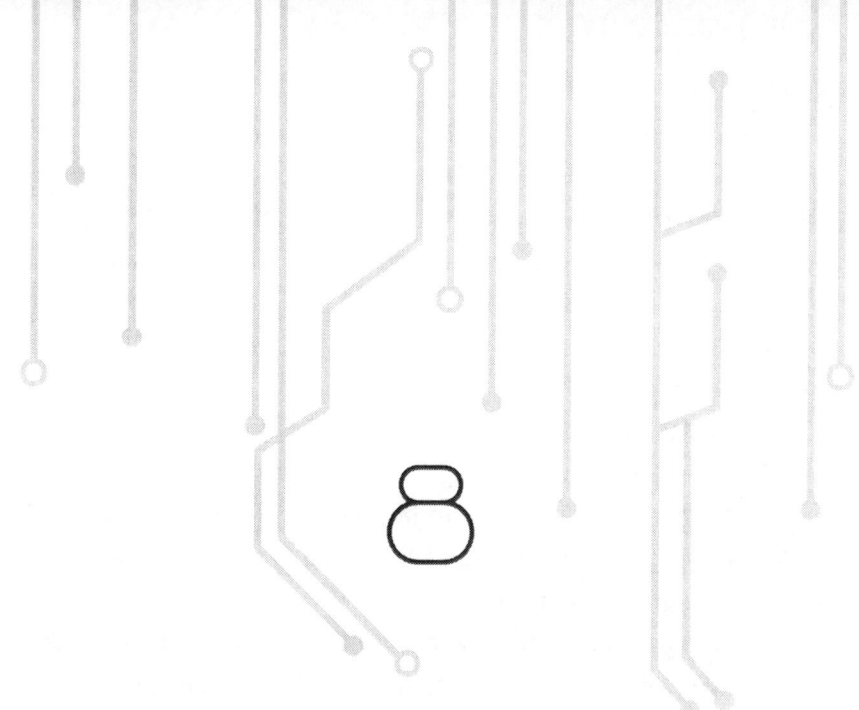

8

THEY FOUND A FIRE AND a ring of rocks. No one was nearby, which was a blessing, and the fire was large enough that it created a comfortable circumference of heat. They sat down, and Jakob kicked a bundle of firewood.

"I've been here less than a day and I already want to get the hell out of here."

"Me, too," Ren said quietly. He rubbed his hands together, then splayed his fingers toward the fire.

"My father wanted to know why I didn't come back sooner. He said I had shirked my duties here and said I was a coward for staying away so long." Jakob crossed his arms and frowned. "It's not like I almost *died* or anything."

Jakob's admission was a surprise. To Ren, Jakob had led a charmed life of privilege, the only son of the head of the village council, the wealthiest man in the village. But there was more to the story, and, seeing Jakob hunched over his knees, Ren empathized.

"We could leave," Ren said softly.

Asher snapped his gaze to him. "I thought you would want to stay. Coming home was what you wanted from the beginning."

Ren furrowed his brow. "I have wanted to come home. I've wanted to find Liam. But this isn't my home. My home doesn't exist anymore."

"No, it doesn't," Jakob said.

Asher looked at them. "If you don't want to be here, we don't have to stay. We could head back to the port and find transport."

Jakob shifted. He stared at the fire. "I don't know."

Asher gazed at Ren, searching.

Ren shrugged. "I don't want to be stuck here. And if I stay, I will be. And I… I don't want to lose you. And the family I've built."

"Are you sure?" Asher asked.

"No. I'm not." Ren took a breath. "I'm not well on the ship. I'm a liability, a prisoner to the Corps there. But I don't belong here either." He swallowed. "I've outgrown it here. And Liam is still out there. But I…." Ren trailed off.

"Face it, Ren. We don't belong here. I don't want to leave my sisters, but they are safe. And I have other things to look for."

Ren nodded. "Yeah. Yeah." He scrubbed a hand over his eyes. "I wish I had a place where I belonged."

Asher touched the back of Ren's hand. "We'll leave and if we don't find a place, we'll make one."

"But what about…" Ren trailed off. He hadn't heard anyone mention Sorcha's name.

Jakob kicked the firewood again. "She's not here, Ren. No one has seen her. I asked about her family and… well… apparently there is a gravesite at the village."

"I know."

Jakob pressed his lips together. "You didn't tell me."

"Because I didn't want to take away your hope."

Jakob nodded. He tossed a twig into the flames. "I am going to keep looking for her. I'm not going to give up." He sighed. "So what happened with you? I saw you two had made up."

"We're working on it," Asher said.

"My mother and I had an argument," Ren said. He tilted his head and looked at the canvas above him. It blocked the stars. A spot in Ren's chest ached because he couldn't trace the familiar patterns. "About what I am."

"She knew, huh?"

"Yeah."

"Sucks."

"Understatement."

They sat in silence, the only sound the crackling of the fire, and the distant hum of the encampment. Asher held out his arm, and Ren squirmed to his side, enjoying the closeness while lost in his thoughts. He laid his head on Asher's shoulder and watched the flickering flames. His eyes became heavy-lidded. Emotional and physical exhaustion caught up with him. He slipped into a doze, curled into Asher's body.

Ren dreamed. He couldn't make out the setting. The area was dark save for a small light. But he wasn't afraid. The dark wasn't ominous, but merely there, a void. He squinted into the distance, and a blob of color appeared, but it had no shape, and the longer Ren stared, the harder it was to discern anything about the figure. However, he would swear he heard Liam's voice. "This is much harder when you're not connected to your own power."

"Liam?"

Before he could receive a response, Ren was shaken awake, and he snapped to the present.

"Ren?"

"I'm awake," he grumbled.

"Sure you are," the voice was not Asher's or Jakob's.

Ren craned his neck to see Beatrice, her hands on her hips, her red hair spilling over her shoulders and sticking up in places to create a halo in the firelight.

"I hear you weeds want to get out of here."

"Where did you hear that?" Ren asked. He sat up, pulled from Asher's embrace, self-conscious under her knowing stare.

"A little bird told me. Sound travels in the hot box. Might want to keep your voices down next time."

"What's it to you?" Jakob said.

Beatrice arched an eyebrow. "We're going on a supply run to the castle in the morning. If you haven't noticed, we could do with comms and alarm systems, maybe even force-field tech for the entrance. You weeds want to come?"

Jakob and Ren exchanged a look. It would give them a purpose, at least for a while, and delay them having to make a decision to leave Erden altogether. They could help the encampment while using the time to think about their own destinies.

"You could look for clues," Ren said. "Maybe find a trail from where Sorcha escaped."

Ren knew any trail would be long gone, trampled over, broken up by weather and the change of the seasons, but Ren couldn't take away Jakob's hope, not when Ren clung to his own.

"And you could have breathing space," Jakob replied.

Ren gathered his legs beneath him and stood. He was slightly taller than Beatrice, and she crossed her arms.

"We'll go."

"Good. We'll leave first thing in the morning."

"Do you have a place where we can sleep?"

She raised her eyebrows, but didn't question that they would not sleep with their families.

"We have a communal area with free beds. You can doze there."

They followed Beatrice into the heart of the camp. Asher placed a hand on Ren's shoulder, and Ren was bolstered by the touch.

Ren settled down at Asher's side in the communal tent. Though he was exhausted, Ren couldn't sleep, but Asher's soft snores were a calming rhythm in his ear. His mind flitted from thought to thought, flinched from his mother's duplicity, and wondered what his brother could do, whether he knew his power, and where he might possibly be. He thought about going back to the citadel, and asked himself if that was a wise choice. Maybe they should go to the spaceport instead and leave, leave this place where Ren didn't fit, where Ren would remain for his lifetime, if his family had their choice.

That was what stung the most. He had talked nonstop about leaving, about working on the drifts, about honing a skill that would be marketable, that would earn him passage. His parents had heard every word, often at the dinner table after a long day of shearing or planting or harvesting. What had they thought when he babbled about the contrails he had seen that day? Why had they remained silent? Had they cared? Ren gave up trying to sleep. He slid off the cot and the blanket and stood.

Asher stirred immediately. His eyes blinked open in the low light of the banked fires. "Ren?" He smacked his lips. "You okay?"

"Fine. Stretching. Go back to sleep."

Asher huffed. "You sure?"

"Yeah."

Asher rolled over, pulled the thin blanket up to his ears, and dropped into sleep on the next snore.

Ren left the communal area, which was just a large tent in the middle of the camp with several beds. Beatrice explained it was a good place for guards on duty to sleep between shifts and a transitional place for new refugees before their own accommodations could be arranged. They'd had a steady stream of new people for a while, from different villages, but the numbers had decreased once winter struck. Ren understood why. He wouldn't have wanted to search for a hidden encampment in the middle of winter either, unless he absolutely had to.

Ren wandered a few feet from the tent and stretched his arms over his head. His shirt rode up; goosebumps bloomed over the skin of his stomach in the cooler air away from the fires. He yawned and sighed and looked up at the canvas. He frowned. As silly as it seemed, he did miss the view of the stars. He sighed and imagined the twinkle of the constellations against the blue-black sky.

A twig snapped to Ren's left, and he turned quickly, peering into the darkness. "Is someone there?" he whispered. He took a few steps toward the sound. His bare feet were noiseless on the packed dirt and moss. "Hello—"

A hand clamped over his mouth, cutting off his speech and his air, and a strong arm wrapped around his middle, pinning his arms to his sides. He yelled against the gloved palm, twisted and turned in the iron grip, but his captor lifted Ren off the ground. He fought, kicked his legs, and threw his head back only to find a hard shoulder, but the arms held him, crushing Ren to a strong chest. Fingers dug into his jaw, and it hurt.

Ren lashed out with his power, but found no tech, nowhere for his star to go. He could only thrash and make noise as he was dragged to the outskirts of the camp, out of sight of the communal tent, away from the banked fires.

"Quit struggling." The voice was frustrated and fierce, loud in the shell of Ren's ear, but hushed.

Ren froze. His stepfather's large hands clutched him, and they were not gentle, but Ren didn't think he would hurt him. He held himself stiff and tense, waiting. His stepfather dragged him to the very edge of the encampment, where the trees began to grow thick and the canvas drooped. A line of snow marked the end of the hot box, and Ren shivered as they crossed it. They came to a small break in the branches, and his stepfather stopped.

"Set him down."

Ren's bare feet sank into the snow. The cold stung his skin, and when he was finally let go, he wrapped his arms around his body. His breath came in fraught, cloudy puffs.

"Mom?"

She held a candle but it barely illuminated the space. The darkness was dense under the twined branches of the Laurels. Ren glanced up and spied the broken moon.

"Yes. I needed to talk to you."

Ren's mouth dropped open, and he settled his incredulous gaze on the cloaked figure of his mother. "Are you *serious*? You had to kidnap me? What the *weedin'* hell?"

"I had to get you away from that birdman you are traveling with. I couldn't talk to you in front of him."

Ren narrowed his eyes, but didn't confirm Asher's identity. Beatrice had warned them sound traveled in the hot box, and it seemed his mother had heard Asher refer to himself as Phoenix Corps. Ren looked at his stepfather, who stood nearby, arms crossed, watching intently, and his expression was confirmation.

"And the best way to do that was to make me think I was being captured again?"

"We don't have time for you to be difficult."

Irritation flared, but Ren didn't speak. He clenched his jaw and gestured for her to continue.

"You cannot trust the Phoenix Corps." She stepped forward and grasped Ren's wrist. "I know you want to, but you cannot trust him."

"Why?"

"Because he does not have your best interests at heart."

Ren pulled his hand away. "And you do? I'm supposed to believe you?"

"You don't know everything that has happened."

"Then tell me," Ren shot back. "Stop being cryptic and stop thinking I'm too young or I can't handle it, because I can. I've been kidnapped, tortured, threatened, and I've been possessed by a ship which has slowly driven me insane. I think I deserve a reason."

"You do. I'm sorry for everything that has happened. It wasn't my intention for you to ever have to be involved with all of this." She cast a glance around them. "When the technopaths were destroyed after they rose against the drifters, the other star hosts fled to the planets. Our ancestors dispersed, hid themselves, and destroyed any record of their existence. They disappeared among the dusters and passed down their history and knowledge through stories."

"They became myths like the ones you used to tell me and Liam."

She nodded. "Yes. It was their way of hiding while The Phoenix Corps hunted them."

Ren furrowed his brow. "The Phoenix Corps hates coming planetside. They don't want to meddle in our affairs. That's how Vos managed to get away with what he was doing for so long."

His mother shook her head. "Vos knew the truth to the legends. He knew that there were star hosts on this planet and on others. He knew that they would be the key to his plans. But with his rash actions, and, I wager, due to your own experiences with the Corps, the birdmen are back and searching."

Ren swallowed. "Vos's soldiers told Jakob they destroyed the village looking for me. Is that true?" Ren asked, voice low. "Who killed Sorcha's family?"

"Do you really want to know?"

"Yes."

Ren steeled himself for the answer he already knew. Vos had lied before; it wouldn't have been out of character for him to lie again to ensure allegiance, to crush the recruits' hopes.

"Vos's soldiers did come back looking for more recruits. But that was normal. They came, took what they wanted, and left."

"The Corps came later." Ren's voice was thick; he choked on the words.

"A few months after Vos retreated. They had already destroyed some of the other villages in the fiefs, so we were prepared. The Laurels was already set as one of the encampments."

Ren's knees went weak. He grasped one of the trees, felt the bark smooth beneath his palm, and fell heavily against it. The cold was forgotten.

"They cannot be trusted, Ren. They are here to find others like you, like us, and destroy us before we can destroy them."

Ren rubbed a hand over his chest. "But the scrap of cloth you keep, the insignia. My father."

"That is how I know you cannot trust your friend. I loved your father. I trusted him. But he was Corps and here for a reason. When he tried to betray me, your stepfather intervened."

Ren shifted. His feet burned from the cold. His arms were numb. His thoughts were in turmoil. He looked at his stepfather. "Did you kill him?" His throat worked, and he glared, looking for anything in his expression that might tell him the truth. "*Did you kill him*?" Ren said again, voice hard, incensed.

"Ren! Ren! Where are you?"

Worried and sharp, Asher's voice pierced through the trees.

"What other encampments? There are others? Where?"

His stepfather spoke. "I'll not allow you to lead him to the others. It's bad enough he knows of us."

"Are you going to kill him, too?" Ren snapped.

His stepfather bristled, but Ren ignored him. He turned back to his mother. "I'm leaving in the morning. I won't ever be back. I'm going to find Liam. I'm going to find a place to belong."

"You can stay with us, love. You can always stay."

"No."

Jakob's voice joined Asher's, calling out for Ren.

"When I was in that cell and scared and wondering what was going on with me, I wished, I wished so much that I could be home, that I could see you again, that you could at least know what happened to me. Even though I never fit in here, even though I dreamed of leaving, I thought if I could get home, everything would be okay. But this whole time, all you've done is lie to me and manipulate me. You're just like Vos. You're just like the Corps."

"We're nothing like them. We love you and we only have your best interests at heart. We want you to be safe."

Ren laughed, the sound hollow. "That's what I thought I wanted, too. But being safe here is just another prison. I'd rather take my chances out there. At least I'll be free."

"You can be free here." Her voice took on a pleading edge.

"No. I can't. I've done so much, seen so much, met so many people who do care for me. I can't imagine staying here."

Tears spilled down his mother's cheeks, and she didn't wipe them away. They glistened in the candlelight. When she reached for him, he didn't move, didn't flinch. He allowed the hug, allowed her to clutch her hands in the back of his shirt and rest her forehead on his shoulder. He allowed it, but he didn't hug her back. He stood unmoving as stone and waited for her to say goodbye. When she let go, Ren gave her a nod. He left the small clearing, passed his stepfather without saying a word, and stepped back into the hot box.

Asher's voice echoed in the enclosed area. Chest tight, body taut, Ren was a powder keg, but he clamped down on the emotions threatening to overwhelm him. He bit his lip and followed Asher's frenzied voice. He was unable to call back lest the sobs building in his throat let loose.

"There you are!" Asher said, striding toward him, wrapping him in an embrace. "Stars, you're freezing." Asher rubbed Ren's arms; his palms swept over the chilled skin. "Where have you been? You left and never came back. Jakob and I have been looking all over for you."

Ren pitched forward, planted his face in Asher's chest, and shook. The terror at being taken again mixed with the crushing truths from his parents overwhelmed him.

"Hey, hey, you're okay." Asher pulled Ren close. "What happened? Was it a dream? Sleepwalking?"

Ren stilled. Pressed close to Asher's body, it would be easy to give into the urge to tell him everything, to spill the truth about what his parents had said about the Corps and the star hosts, and the history his life was mired in. But his mother's words lingered in the back of his mind, and Ren remembered how Asher had sided with VanMeerten so many times since the debacle on the drift. Asher was Phoenix Corps, through and through. His allegiance was split, torn between Ren and his duty as a soldier. And how much did he know? Was Asher aware that the first mission of the Corps was to hunt down the scattered remnants of the star hosts? Or did he only know what he had been told, like the rest of them?

Ren heaved a breath, pulled himself together, and stepped away. He wiped at his eyes.

"I had another talk with my mother," he said.

Asher raised an eyebrow. "Oh?"

"Yeah. It didn't go well."

"What did she say?"

"Goodbye."

Asher's expression shifted from disdainful caution to sympathy, and the corners of his mouth turned down. "I'm sorry."

Ren waved him off. "It's fine."

"It's really not."

Ren scrubbed at his face. He yawned and his jaw cracked. "I should try to get some sleep. It's still early."

"Good idea. I'll let Jakob know you're okay."

"Thanks."

Ren shuffled away, but Asher's voice stopped him. "And Ren? It'll be okay. We'll help your village, and then we'll go back to the ship. We'll figure it out."

Ren's stomach roiled: back to the ship, back to being a different kind of prisoner. "Okay."

Asher smiled.

Ren forced a grin, and went to his cot.

He tossed and turned until the sky lightened with the dawn.

"We're going in that?" Jakob pointed to a beat-up floater half-hidden under a pile of leaves and bracken. The hover transport was rusted in some places and dented in others, and the vehicle's cab sported cracked glass. "We'll die."

Wrapped in his winter clothes, Ren peeked over his collar and eyed the run-down equipment with trepidation. He didn't think they would die, but they definitely would make a lot of noise. It could garner unwanted attention. They would probably go faster walking.

Beatrice crossed her arms over her own overstuffed coat. Her wild red hair was captured in a braid. "We've used it before, and it worked fine. Or would you rather walk?"

"Walk. I would really rather walk," Jakob said.

"Fine, then. You can walk. And Ezzy and I will take the floater."

Asher's breath was a gust of hot air on Ren's neck. "Can you fix it?"

Ren was exhausted. His head was fuzzy, but, as ever, the star burned inside him and easily flooded to his fingertips. He didn't need to pull off his glove, but he did anyway. The chill in the air nipped at his exposed fingers when he held them out and closed his eyes.

The floater was junk, battered and old. However, Beatrice was correct. It did run.

"What's he doing?" she asked. "Is he addled?"

Ren cracked open an eye and frowned. He stalked forward, brushing past the group, and slapped his palm onto the cold metal of the transport. He let go and poured his power into the circuits and mechanisms. He could fix it. As he raced along the broken wires and repaired them, and as he rerouted power around components that were too damaged to save, Ren was free from mortal concerns. He was happy, unburdened from impending decisions and from his loss, and content to stay there. His star hummed throughout his body and throughout the floater. Once he was finished, he flicked on the power source.

The floater lifted under his hand and the thrusters engaged, propelling the hunk of metal a few feet off the ground. He reveled in the whir of engines and the thrum of power in his veins. Satisfied, he eased off the power, allowed the floater to settle to the ground, and pulled out of the circuits.

Beatrice stared at him with wide eyes and an open mouth. Ezzy grinned, her face lit up.

"What are you?" Beatrice asked.

"I'm a technopath."

"A star host," she said, awed. "An actual star host."

Jakob laughed. He walked past Beatrice with a smug look. "Did you hear that engine purr?"

She snapped her mouth shut and glared.

They all squeezed onto the front bench seat. It was a tight fit, but Ezzy was small and half sat on Jakob's lap. After an argument over who would drive, Beatrice started the floater, and they eased out of its hiding spot in a copse outside the dense crush of the Laurels.

"Ren fixed it," Jakob said, leaning over and jostling the rest of them. "You can go faster."

Beatrice scowled, but she picked up speed, and soon the floater hurtled over the landscape. Scenery passed in a blur of snow and sky.

"We'll have to ditch the floater before we get too close to the walls," Beatrice said, her voice carrying in the wind. "In case there are birdmen around. Our patrols didn't report seeing any in the woods last night, but we can't be too careful."

"What would happen if they saw us?" Jakob asked.

She kept her gaze on the sprawl of the land in front of them, but she lifted her eyebrow.

"They'll kill us," she said.

Ezzy nodded. Her gloved hands were wrapped tight around the nearby handles. "Or they'll take us and ask us questions and then kill us."

"Surely that's a rumor," Asher said. "The Corps has no interest in dusters. They're probably here looking for Vos."

"Vos is gone," Beatrice replied. "He cleared out with his troops and never returned. Everyone knows that. And the leaders of our village told them so, but that didn't stop them from burning it to the ground."

Ren winced.

"It was the Corps that destroyed your village?" Asher asked, tone brittle.

"Yeah, and all the villages around it." She stared at Ren. "Including yours."

"They wouldn't do that," Asher said. He turned to Ren. "They wouldn't do that," he repeated, though his voice was softer. "Would they?"

Ren shrugged. "I'm sorry, Asher. But it looks like they did."

"What is your problem?" Beatrice asked, staring at Asher. "Are you some kind of birdman sympathizer? Or are you one of those, 'they are only following orders' people?" She kept one hand on the steering stick and placed the other on her throat. She fluttered her eyelashes. "They're good people, honestly." She talked softly with a strange accent. "It's not their fault. They have to do what they are told."

Ezzy snickered.

Asher paled. "Stop. Just stop."

Beatrice batted her eyelashes again, then dropped her hand and sneered. "What the stars is your problem?"

"Drop it, Bea," Jakob said. "You can understand it's a touchy subject. And we're all on edge. The three of us were actually held in the citadel, you know. I almost died there. This isn't a fun jaunt across the countryside for us, whatever it might be for you."

Beatrice huffed and rolled her eyes. "Fine. Whatever."

Asher looked stricken, with eyebrows drawn together, mouth in a tense line, and eyes shadowed. Ren interlaced their fingers. He gave a comforting squeeze, but Asher didn't respond. His gaze was far away, unfocused, as the terrain passed beneath them.

The next few hours were spent in awkward silence as Beatrice drove on, except for Ezzy, who updated Jakob on all the gossip of the encampment, leading Ren to believe Ezzy was the "little bird" who'd spilled their desire to leave. Eventually, Beatrice changed course.

Ren roused from half-sleep and squinted. The sun shone high above them in the middle of the day and illuminated the snow-laden fields. The citadel rose above them, dark against the gray sky. The stone castle loomed over the landscape. The sheer outer wall was formidable and familiar. Turrets pierced the clouds, and from their tops the Baron's standards flapped in the wind. Ren shivered, remembering the first time he had seen them almost a year ago.

Beatrice guided the floater parallel to the front of the castle and to a small gathering of trees. Ren recognized the woods he'd seen Sorcha run for, and he tried not to think about what might have happened to her. Jakob may have hope that he would see her again, but Ren wasn't so sure.

Beatrice settled the floater on the tree line. The transport was too big to fit between the bushes and trees. The group climbed out and Ren stretched his arms, glad to walk after the ride. The floater stood out against the snow and the barren trees.

"We're just going to leave it?" Jakob asked.

"Yes."

"So someone can come along and steal it?"

Beatrice ignored the question, grabbed her bag, and slung it over her shoulder. Ezzy did the same. They each took a weapon—Ezzy a prod and Beatrice the stunner—but they left the body armor and helmets behind.

"No armor?" Ren asked.

Beatrice's gaze flicked to Ren. "We don't need it."

"Are you sure?"

"Yeah, I'm sure."

"I think, maybe, it would be a good idea—"

"You know, Ezzy and I have been doing this for months," Beatrice snapped. "We haven't been killed, yet. I think we know what we're doing."

Jakob didn't look pleased. "It's a wonder how you haven't been. We're not only advertising that someone with a floater is *here,* but we're leaving it unlocked. And you're not even worried!"

"I don't think I like your tone, Jakob."

"Yeah, I don't think I like that you've been endangering my little sister."

"I've been protecting your sister because you weren't here to do it."

Jakob turned a dangerous shade of red; his muscles tensed. Asher grabbed his arm to keep him from advancing.

"Can Ren do something to it?" Ezzy asked. "To keep it from starting in case someone comes along?"

"Yeah. Yeah, I can." Ren reached for his power and blocked the path from the power source to the ignition. It only took a few seconds, and then Ren retreated. He took a moment to take stock, to indulge in his ritual of counting his heartbeats. His consciousness settled back into his body. "It's done."

"Your eyes glow blue," Ezzy breathed. "They're beautiful." Her cheeks reddened, and her eyes went wide. "Not that they aren't always beautiful. I mean, I've never seen someone do that."

Jakob pulled his own pack and weapon from the back, then wrapped his arm around Ezzy's shoulders. "Get used to it. He does it a lot."

"Let's get going," Beatrice grumbled. She broke off from the group and trudged through the snow.

Asher followed her, uncharacteristically silent.

"How are we going in?" Ren asked.

"The front door, of course."

"Do you think that's safe?"

Beatrice threw up her hands. "Your little group really is a bunch of weeds. Can you just let me lead and stop questioning everything? Like I said, Ezzy and I have done this before. We'll be fine."

Ren sighed. There was another way in, the siege door that Asher and he had escaped through, but even if Ren could lower the force field, they didn't have a key for the iron doors. And if they couldn't get through, trying would waste more time. He nodded, acquiescing to Beatrice's experience.

"Good. Now follow me. Keep your eyes open and your mouths shut. Ezzy, take the rear and make sure your weed of a brother stays out of trouble."

Jakob glared, but kept his lips pressed together so hard they turned white.

They crept across the open countryside that surrounded the towering walls of the citadel. The stone was stark against the wispy snow clouds and the occasional sliver of blue in the sky. It didn't seem safe. Ren swore he was being watched, and his skin prickled with the sensation.

He reached out, searching for weapons or energy signals, but his power balked. His senses fuzzed out as his star twisted and writhed, tangling up. His head buzzed, and his vision went blue. Static overwhelmed him and tingled through his body down to his toes. He tasted electricity and colors and smelled sound, and the citadel vibrated in his bones. He clapped his gloved hands over his ears and hunched forward, gritting his teeth—none of which quelled the all-consuming whine of white noise invading his head.

Ren let out a whimper. Despite being invaded, he felt hands on his shoulders, someone pulling him up, then fabric against his cheeks.

He didn't realize he had clenched his eyes shut until a voice asked him to open them. He did, and Asher's face took shape: a blurry impression amid the blurred lines of blue and black and white.

"What's going on?" Asher said.

Ren furrowed his brow, not able to speak as his power went haywire. Ren flinched, but the action made everything worse, and he realized fighting or hiding wasn't going to work. Instead of withdrawing from the signal, he opened to it. He engaged with it. His star was a throbbing pressure in his chest. His body shivered and shook, his muscles tensed, his joints locked. But despite the assault on his senses, the more Ren succumbed to it, the clearer it became.

Vos's voice. Repeating a warning in Ren's head.

Asher shook him, and Ren's teeth clacked. "Ren? What is going on? Are you okay?"

"Do you hear it?" he asked, his voice far away, blunted, barely a sound in the noise.

"No. No, we don't hear anything. What do you hear?"

Stay away. Stay away. Not safe. Report to other base. Leave.

"A warning," he managed to grit out. "From Vos. A signal."

"This is why we need comms," Beatrice said. "I bet we would pick it up on those."

Asher ignored her. "Can you block it out?" His touch was gentle on Ren's face. "Ren?"

Ren scrunched his eyes shut, but the message was insidious. It overran his mind and echoed through his thoughts.

Stay away. Stay away. Not safe. Report to other base. Leave.

Except you.

Ren shivered. The last words were softer, an intimate whisper in the shell of Ren's ear, an invitation. Abiathar's voice was a caress; his power of suggestion was present within the sound, and Ren was certain those words would not be picked up on any comm system. Fear crept down his spine as the phrase appeared again in the static.

Except you. Come in.

No. No!

Ren wrenched from Asher's grip and broke away from the group. He ran, kicking up snow behind him, and sprinted across the wide-open area toward the stone.

He had to shut it off.

He had to shut it off.

He had to—

Come in.

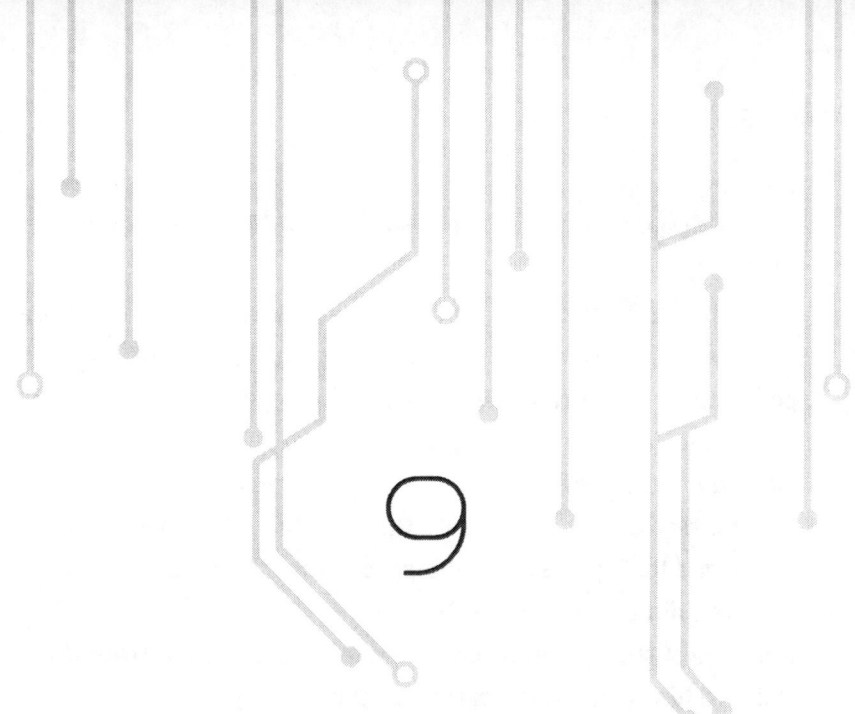

9

Ren had no idea what he was doing, but he knew he had to push Vos and Abiathar out of his head. He got to the shadows cast by the towers and blindly felt along the stone edges. Not finding what he needed, he pulled off his gloves, ignored the shouts of the others behind him, and ran farther, trailing his hand along the citadel's wall. The stone was cold and it scratched his palm, but he had to find it, had to find the source. He had to shut it off.

Come in. Come in.

"No!"

Ren stumbled to the castle gate. The portcullis was propped open and the heavy doors swung wide on broken hinges. The force field wasn't active but the system was enough.

Ren slammed his power into it and raced through the wires and the circuits, up into the stone, through the courtyard, into the keep. He climbed and climbed, hopping from system to system, until he found the communications. Set in the highest tower, the beacon blared, alerting stragglers of Vos's empire to their orders. It must've run for months, since Vos had left and Abiathar, his lead general, took the army to the drifts.

With a surge, Ren cut it off. He silenced the bleating repetition of words.

One second, the static consumed him, and in the next, it was gone. Ren was flesh and bone, weary, breathing hard from running. He sagged against the wall and slid down. Sitting in the snow, knees bent, he waited for the others to catch up.

He had outrun them all, and the group approached, weapons out and at the ready. Ren didn't miss the fact that while Asher, Jakob, and Ezzy had their pulse guns and prods pointed outward, Beatrice's stunner was aimed squarely at Ren.

Ren's chest stung from the cold, and his hands bled from a few scratches. He warily eyed Beatrice as they approached. Though he could disable the weapon with a blink, she didn't know that, and he didn't know if he could stop her if she chose to pull the trigger with no warning.

The massive wooden door that Ren had walked through almost a year ago banged against the stone wall in a gust of the bitter wind. It sounded suspiciously like *come in*, but Ren shook his head, clearing away the clutter of words.

"What the stars was that?" Beatrice barked. "Are you trying to get us killed? If there were any birdmen around they would've picked you off for sure. Are you addled?"

Ren pushed his hair from his eyes.

"Your eyes are blue."

"My eyes are brown."

"She means you're glowing, Ren," Jakob said.

"Oh. I'm detangling." Ren's consciousness was stretched from the entrance to the tower, and he slowly contracted, pulled himself out of the remnants of the castle systems.

Ezzy's eyes were bright, and her mouth was slightly open. "What did you do?"

"I turned off the signal," Ren said. "I had to. It was… too much."

"Are you okay?" Asher knelt, placed his hand on Ren's shoulder, and squeezed.

"Yeah, I'm all right." Ren tugged and he slotted back into his physical self. He took stock, counted his pulse, and wiggled his fingers.

Come in.

"For good measure, can you ask me an impossible question?"

Asher narrowed his eyes. "What happens when an unstoppable force meets an immovable object?"

The question chimed sharply in Ren's mind. "Paradox."

"Good."

Beatrice heaved a sigh. "Well, any cover we had was blown as soon as you took off running. We might as well go in."

"Any cover we had was gone the minute we stepped out of the floater," Asher said. He stood and slid his pulse gun back into his holster. "If anyone wanted us dead, we would be. But that doesn't mean we should throw caution into an air recycler."

Beatrice raised an eyebrow. "Wind."

"What?"

"Throw caution to the wind. Why would you throw caution into an air recycler?"

"I… what?"

"Weeds, you're a drifter, aren't you?" She pointed her finger at Asher's chest. "That's why you have such a problem with the truth about the Corps. You're spoiled drifter trash."

His jaw clenching, Asher visibly restrained himself from commenting. Ren rested a hand on his arm before rolling his eyes and sharing a commiserating look with Jakob. Ren stood, and Jakob shouldered between Asher and Beatrice.

"Can we finish what we came here to do? I don't know about you, but I don't want to have to spend the night here. Let's go." Jakob brushed through the center of the group, breaking the tension.

"I'm leading," Beatrice said. "And you three better start paying attention or you're going to end up dust."

They inched toward the opening to the courtyard. They stepped around the heavy wooden doors, and then ducked under the portcullis, which was pried open so its slats rested on a tower of pilfered stone. Beatrice led, checking around corners, with her weapon out and ready. Asher moved in tandem with her, inspecting corners and passageways. Beatrice remained stone-faced, but after putting together that Asher was a drifter, and the way he moved and handled his pulse gun, it was only a matter of moments before she figured out he was Phoenix Corps.

But Ren had bigger things to worry about for the moment.

Come in.

Past the threshold, the entryway split. The left led to the keep. The right took them to the courtyard.

Beatrice eyed him. "We've already picked the courtyard clean, and so has everyone else. We need to go into the keep."

"We can get into the keep from the courtyard and then into the barracks. Jakob knows the way. So does Ren."

She huffed. "Fine."

The group moved to the right, quietly, on edge.

The courtyard was eerily silent. The sun was high; the walls cast shadows. The raised platform stood in the middle, looming over the closed-in area. Ren swallowed the lump in his throat, and Jakob crowded close to Ren's side as he stared at the wooden structure.

"I died there."

Ren cautiously touched Jakob's shoulder, remembering when the soldiers had tortured Jakob in front of him for attempting escape, how Jakob's cries had echoed through the courtyard, how his body had hung so limply. "Don't look at it."

"Hard not to."

"I know."

Ren looked at the corner where he'd spent his days. The bench was there. The buckets of broken tech were turned over and rooted through. He hefted the container onto the wooden board that used to be his desk.

"That stuff is junk," Ezzy said, coming to stand at his elbow. She had her prod leaning on one shoulder.

Ren shifted the broken pieces and in the bottom he found a comm. It was indeed broken, but, with a flash of his star, he fixed it. He handed it to Ezzy. The small green light around the rim indicated it was on and working.

"Whoa," she said. "You fixed it."

"Yeah. It's working now. We only need to find a few more and tune the frequencies."

"You're amazing," she said, cheeks red.

Ren laughed. "Not really."

"Yes, you are. I noticed, even when we lived in the village, before everything." She cleared her throat. "I used to watch you work. I could see the fields from my window and the livery."

Ren's eyebrows shot up. He ran a hand through his hair and laughed.

"Aren't you… uh… young to… uh…" Ren cast a helpless look around the courtyard, but the others were busy. Beatrice stood watch, while Asher and Jakob looked for tech in any of the mess left behind. "Notice people?"

"I'm thirteen," she said.

"Oh. We should find more tech." Ren walked away to join Asher. His limbs moved awkwardly, and he felt heat in his cheeks.

Asher handed Ren another comm. "Found it in the dirt. Can you fix it?"

Ren nodded. Distracted though he was, it flared to life in his palm, and a voice came across loud and clear.

"Fox, you see anything? Over."

"Saw a group go in through the front. Not birds. Didn't see if they went to the stone or the dirt. Be careful. Over."

"Okay. Might be friendlies. We'll be careful. Over."

"Comm if you need me. I'll be watching. Over."

"In the tunnel, heading in. Radio silence for now. Out."

Ren and Asher exchanged a glance. "Someone's coming!" Asher said, harshly. "Come on. Under the arch."

Beatrice, Ezzy, and Jakob ran to the shelter and crowded in. It was the arch Ren had walked through every morning and night of his captivity and it only offered minimal shelter. They could hide, but only if the group didn't walk directly in front of them. Pressed against the stone, in the shadows, Ren held the comm in his fist, while Asher peeked out. The sun lit a slant across Asher's features. The tension in the small corridor was thick as the group held its collective breath.

"What's happening?" Ezzy whispered.

Jakob shushed her, and she made a face and opened her mouth to retort, but Asher waved her quiet.

"Weapons ready," the female voice from the comm said. "Fox saw a group. Not birds, but we're not taking any chances."

Jakob went still, then he pushed away from the wall where he had been squished between Ezzy and Beatrice.

"I know that voice." Jakob stepped toward the opening.

"Jakob, no," Asher said. He reached out to grab Jakob's sleeve, but Jakob was too quick. He pulled his arm away and ran into the sunlight.

Ren watched as Jakob put his hands up, and he felt the weapons charge, heard the loud hum of the energy, and smelled the slight ozone tinge of the air. Ren gathered his power and waited, body coiled as a spring, ready if he needed to defend Jakob.

"Wait," the voice said. There was a charged moment, and then a timid, "Jakob?"

"Sorcha," he said.

Sorcha!

Ren's body unlocked, and he vaulted from the wall and into the sunlight. He skidded to a stop next to Jakob.

The sunlight blinded him for a brief terrifying second, but then he found himself staring at a ragtag group of dusters with Sorcha at the lead. Her white-blonde hair was cut short; her blue eyes were large in her round face. She had her head tilted and her weapon pointed to the ground, but the group behind her had their stunners trained on the pair of them.

Ren ignored the cursing coming from the tunnel and grinned at her. He belatedly raised his hands in surrender, and that had Sorcha's lips twitching into an amused smile.

"Ren," she greeted.

"Sorcha."

"Is it really you two?" she asked. She took a step forward, her boots crunching in the snow.

Jakob trembled. "Is it really you?" His voice shook, and Sorcha's expression softened. "I've been looking for you," he continued. "We came back for you. I came back for you."

Sorcha dropped her stunner. It fell to the snow, and she gave up any pretense of caution. She threw her arms around Jakob's neck, and he grabbed her, threaded his gloved hands through her short hair, and held on.

"I thought you were dead," she said, words thick and muffled by Jakob's coat.

"I thought *you* were dead," he replied in kind.

"We went to the village," Ren said. "We saw and we didn't know if…"

She lifted her head from Jakob's shoulder, and met Ren's gaze. She held out an arm. Ren leaned into it and she embraced both of them, then clung to them.

"I've missed you. I've missed you both so much."

Ren closed his eyes and sighed, happy to be with his friends, the two people who had started the journey with him. They were together, though in the place they didn't want to ever see again.

Sorcha pulled away. "Where's Asher?"

There was an annoyed sigh, and a shuffle of footsteps.

"Right here."

Sorcha beamed at him. "You've taken care of him. Good job."

"It's been difficult," Asher said. "I'm glad to see you," he added sincerely.

Sorcha laughed. "I'm glad to see you too, Ash."

Their reunion was cut short when someone behind them cleared their throat. "Sorcha?"

"Oh." She turned around and addressed the group of five behind her. "They're friendlies. No worries here."

They relaxed and holstered their weapons. "So what are we doing?"

"We're going to scavenge like we came to do. But we might be staying the night. What do you say to that?" She looked to Jakob.

"Yeah. We are too."

"Since when?" Beatrice asked, stepping out of the alcove.

"Since now."

Jakob glared at her, daring her to protest, but she didn't. Her gaze dropped to Jakob's fingers laced with Sorcha's, and she acquiesced with an annoyed grunt.

"Fine."

⊣⊢

Beatrice and Ezzy disappeared into the keep with Matt, one of Sorcha's men who knew the way. He was another teenager who had escaped with Ren and Asher the last time they had been at the castle. Asher, Jakob, and Sorcha ventured into the barracks and tunnels that led to the kitchens and dungeons.

Ren set up his old workstation and inspected tech the others brought. He fixed what he could and junked what he couldn't.

Between the two groups, Ren fixed several comms, which allowed everyone to be in touch. He helped Asher and Jakob pry the force-field tech out of the stone at the siege tunnel. With three points of contact, Ren was certain someone mechanically inclined could set it up at the entrance of the encampment. Not him, though. He wasn't going back to the Laurels, to his family. He was certain of that now.

Ren worked, and the others worked, and soon they had a pile of tech that would be of good use. They also had clothes, rugs, and pots and pans. There were some dried stores in sacks. There was a single prod, which Ren managed to get to spark.

As night began to fall, so did the temperature, and the groups agreed to take respite from the cold inside the keep. They hauled their bounty inside and assembled in a large room with a fireplace. A rug that was too big to move lay on a stack of rushes. The doors were intact and they closed. Sturdy chairs were dragged in front of them to provide protection, however inadequate.

Ren wasn't worried. He had Asher, Jakob, Beatrice, Sorcha, all equipped with weapons, and all hardened by their experiences.

They started a fire and gathered around it. Jakob stayed close to Sorcha's side. They shared provisions from their packs and from the stores they had found in the kitchens. As in the farmhouse, Ren was surrounded by stories and ghosts, the echoes of the people who had been here before him. He could feel them in the electricity in the air, in the systems in the walls, in the lights which glowed, and in the reflections in the glass of the high windows.

Come find me.

"So you found Ren on a drift?"

Jakob nodded and drank from a bottle of wine he had found in the stores. "Yeah. He and Asher were mounting this rescue that had ridiculously bad odds."

"Shut up, Jakob," Ren said, though he smiled. "We won, didn't we?"

"Barely."

"What happened to you, Sorcha? Where did you go?"

She took the bottle from Jakob and had a long pull. She wiped her mouth with the back of her sleeve. "I never made it back home. I'm sorry," she said to Ren. "I never found your parents or your brother, but I made it to another village, and they took me and a bunch of the others in. They hid us when the soldiers came. And after Vos left and the birds came…" She trailed off. "We're in a safe place now, but for a while it was almost as bad as when we were here."

"And Sorcha became our drift-kickin' leader," a voice chimed out. "Took charge, and even the council listened to her!"

The group cheered and laughed, and Sorcha ducked her head. "I did what I needed to do to protect my new family, so be quiet, you weeds."

Jakob took her hand. "We're glad you didn't make it home. We're happy you're safe. I'm happy I found you."

She blushed; the pink in her cheeks was evident in the firelight. "I'm glad of that, too."

Beatrice made a noise, stood, and left the group. Ezzy shot Ren a look that he couldn't decipher, and Ren scooted closer to Asher's side. Asher raised an eyebrow, and offered Ren the bottle Sorcha had passed. Ren shook his head. Asher took a swig, coughed, and then handed it off to another person whose name Ren didn't know.

"Are you okay?"

"Yeah," Ren said. He was—in both his power and in his decisions. "I'm happy they found each other."

Ren looked back to where Jakob and Sorcha sat and startled when he saw them kissing. Jakob's hand cupped Sorcha's cheek, and she gripped Jakob's jacket; her fingers twisted in his collar. They kissed as if they were dying for it, and Ren flushed and looked away.

"Oh," Asher said. "We should give them some privacy. Probably?"

"Yeah." Ren nodded. "I need air anyway."

Ren stumbled to his feet. The main entrance to the room was blocked, but next to the fireplace he found an ornate wooden double-leaf door with decorative iron scrolls and swirling images carved into the wood. He pulled on the knocker, and the right side opened with a creak. The lights embedded in the stone lit as Ren entered and wandered past them, giving the space an eerie glow. Ren trailed his fingers along the wall and followed the path. He heard Asher behind him, but Ren kept going, pushed forward by an inkling, an urge.

Come find me.

"I'm coming," Ren said softly.

The voice insisted, and Ren followed, and the passageway guided him to another open area. The lights were on there, too. The room was circular, with a desk, tapestries, and another door, which led farther into the castle. There were chairs along the walls, but the desk, heavy and lavish, had a screen embedded in the top. It glowed, and Ren approached it warily.

It wasn't Abiathar's room, which Ren remembered, with the tapestry that depicted sword and sorcery and with the lavish trappings.

No, this room was plainer, not as decadent—a room of a tactician, of a planner, of a leader. This was the room of Vos, a man with a mission, who wanted little distraction as he calculated his odds, his losses, his moves.

Ren sat in the uncomfortable chair behind the desk and stared down at the screen. It beckoned him.

You found me.

Ren touched the tech, and it hummed to life under his palm. His star engaged in his chest and Ren found himself standing in a room, a virtual area, with a green grid under his feet and walls of electric blue all around him.

In front of him stood a young man. Abiathar's voice may have compelled him here, but that wasn't who stood in front of him now. He wore simple clothes, like a duster: trousers and a homespun shirt overlaid with a black vest. His face was narrow, and his body was tall and thin. His chin was pointed, and he wore a mustache and a patch of a beard beneath his lower lip. His hair was long, brushing his shoulders, and black, and it curled at the ends.

"Who are you?" Ren's voice echoed, bounced around like static. The sound sizzled.

The man smiled. He waved a hand, and the light from the grid reflected from a large ring, a signet ring, black and red, like the standards that flapped on top of the towers.

"You know who I am." His voice rang out, deep and resonate, a vibration in the virtual space.

"Vos?"

"Baron Vos. To you, though, I'm a program. An illusion. Nothing for you to fear." He walked around the space and approached Ren.

Ren blinked and took a step back. "You're young."

"Not as young as you."

"That's not saying much."

Vos smiled.

"What is this?" Ren asked, looking around. "Why did you want me here?"

"You're thinking, why the program? Why am I here waiting in this castle? This was not made specifically for anyone, though there are a few of you that I wager will come back here to find answers. That's why I left the message, why I had Abiathar record a few words to call to you. As you know, he can only compel fellow hosts."

Ren pushed his hair from his eyes. This message wasn't only for him. It was for anyone with power, any star host. And Vos mentioned others, more who might have been here, who looked for answers. Who else had seen this?

The virtual Vos stalked around the room, and Ren spun to follow it, to keep his eyes on the figure.

"Some of you have always known the legends that surround your kind. Others have had their origin, their legends, hidden. I'm here to educate you, to give more information for you to join our cause of your own free will. By this time, I've either taken over the first few drifts, or I was defeated for a time and have gone to regroup at my base on Crei."

Ren snapped to attention. Millicent's home world! He was there. He was there, and maybe Liam was there as well. If he had another base, another army, and Liam had been captured…

"You have been made to hide all your lives because of the Phoenix Corps. They've hunted you, destroyed your homes. Even now, as I am certain that some of you have revealed yourselves to them and you're being pursued or captured. You contain the power of the stars, and they are afraid of you. They want to wipe you out, make sure no one else can threaten them with your fantastic abilities.

"You must make a choice. Stand with me, and, together, we can make sure you will never have to hide again. You will never need to restrain yourself. You can give in to your power, become what you were made to be."

Ren swallowed.

Vos stepped close to him. The figure almost touched Ren's body, and his presence crackled through Ren and pierced almost as fiercely as his words. It brushed through Ren's hand, and Ren's skin tingled.

"You could rule," Vos said, black eyes boring into Ren's. "You could make them cower. You could live a quiet life wherever you wanted. You could touch the stars. You could be safe. You could do *anything*." He took a breath. "You could be free."

Ren shuddered. He could be free. He could join Vos at Crei and be *free*. He could find Liam and run away, the two of them, away from Erden, their parents, away from the *Star Stream*, away from the Corps. The only thing Ren ever wanted was to be free, to make his own choices. This could be that choice.

The program smiled, knowing, but genuine. The image flickered, and Ren blinked. Vos wavered, became a blur, then focused again.

"You have a choice, star host. Make the right one."

Then Ren was back in the chair, staring down at the console, and Asher stood next to him with his hand on Ren's arm.

"Ren?"

Ren looked up into Asher's concerned gaze. "Yes?"

"You okay?"

"I'm fine."

"What did you find in the system?"

Ren focused on Asher's touch, clammy and warm, on the back of his hand. He focused on the cold air. There was no heat in this part of the citadel, and he had goosebumps on his arms.

"Nothing really." He didn't stumble over the lie. "I looked at that beacon again. We could send someone up to the tower to retrieve it. It'd be a way for the encampments to communicate with each other."

Asher eyed him. "That's a good idea." He nodded at the console. "Anything about Vos's plans in there?"

"Nothing but what that message said. To report somewhere else."

"Huh. That's unfortunate."

"Yeah."

Ren stood. His middle fluttered at the pointed look in Asher's eyes.

"You know," Asher said, pulling Ren close. "It would be a shame to waste this secluded room in an abandoned citadel where we used to be prisoners."

Ren laughed, his lie momentarily forgotten. "Was that a horrible pickup line?"

"Did it work?"

"Yeah, it did."

Asher pulled Ren away from the console, then backed him up against the wall, caging him in. He splayed his fingers over Ren's jaw and tilted it up. "You're cold."

"Are you going to warm me up?"

"Now that was a bad line."

Ren laughed breathlessly. "Well, you know what they say about—"

Asher sealed his mouth over Ren's, cutting him off, kissing him softly, thoroughly.

After a few long moments, Asher broke away. His eyes were bright in the artificial glow of the lights, and his expression was not one that Ren wanted to see after kissing.

"What's wrong?"

Asher met Ren's gaze, unflinching. "I just… don't know what I would do if I lost you."

The statement was so earnest that Ren's heart stuttered with affection and then sank. His and Asher's relationship was never going to be easy, not like Sorcha's and Jakob's. It would always be in question, especially while Asher remained in the Corps and Ren was a star host. That much had been proven to Ren months ago on Mykonos and confirmed along the way—aboard the *Star Stream*, by VanMeerten, by his parents' confession, by the message from Vos. There would always be doubt, suspicion, distrust, and Ren couldn't promise Asher anything. He couldn't promise that he wouldn't burn up from the inside or that he wouldn't detach completely, so his humanity would be lost, and everything that made Ren himself would be gone in a spark and a bang.

"You haven't lost me yet," Ren said. "Despite my best efforts."

Asher kissed him again, surged forward, and captured Ren's lips with renewed desperation. Whatever this was, whatever feelings were warring within Asher, be it hope because of Jakob's and Sorcha's reunion, or despair at the revelation of the Corps' actions, or even simple nostalgia at revisiting the site where they first met, Ren didn't know. And he didn't need to know.

He sank into the kiss, wrapped his arms around Asher's shoulders, and hung on.

It was nice to be a teenager, to forget all that awaited them outside the door, and to give in to being alone, in the dark, with someone he was attracted to, held affection for, and wanted to be with. Any ties to the program, the beacon, the citadel, fell away, and all Ren could feel was the pass of Asher's lips over his own, the heat of Asher's body so close, and the ache in his chest that this may be taken away from him, too.

They kissed until they heard footsteps in the hallway and hushed voices and saw the approaching glow of a light.

Ezzy appeared in Vos's office, holding a torch above her head. Beatrice was a step behind.

"There you are," Beatrice said, hands on her hips. "Just as I thought."

Asher stepped away, straightened his clothes and cleared his throat. Ren smoothed his hair, but he couldn't hide his kiss-swollen mouth or the pink of his cheeks.

Ezzy's gaze flickered between them and she frowned, confused at first, then embarrassed when she realized what she had walked in on, and then heart-broken. She bit her lip and blinked rapidly. Her hand shook as it held the torch. Ren's shoulders slumped, and he looked away; he couldn't watch the tearful expression on Ezzy's features. He awkwardly shuffled farther from Asher and rubbed the back of his hand over his tingling mouth.

"We're setting up a watch rotation. Do you want first or last?" Beatrice didn't notice Ezzy's demeanor, and Ren didn't want to draw attention to it.

"I'll take first," Asher said. "Ren needs to sleep, since he didn't last night."

"Okay. I'll take last. Jakob can have the middle. I'm sure he and his girlfriend will be awake anyway."

"What about me?" Ezzy piped up, brandishing the torch while flames dripped onto the stone floor. "I want to take watch."

Beatrice smirked and messed up Ezzy's hair. "Believe me, it's better to sleep, kid."

Ezzy flushed, indignant.

"I'm not a *kid*. I can do the job. I don't need protecting."

"Fine, whatever, let's go back to the main hall." Beatrice turned away from Ezzy and rolled her eyes at Asher and Ren.

Asher ignored the gesture. "We need to discuss getting that beacon down from the tower tomorrow. Ren says it would be a good way to connect the two different encampments and maybe find others."

Nodding sharply, Beatrice walked down the hall, and they followed with Ezzy trailing behind.

Once back in the main room, they gathered around the fire and talked about the day ahead. Ren nodded off several times before Asher suggested he go to bed. Ren didn't argue. He didn't have the energy.

Suddenly exhausted from the day, he found a blanket and an empty spot on the rug next to the fire and fell into sleep. The chatter of the others was his lullaby.

⊣⊢

Ren woke from a dream suddenly, disoriented. He blinked his eyes in the low light; the only glow came from the embers of the fire and the low-slung pink of dawn through the large window. His thoughts were in a fog. What had pulled him out of sleep? The rest of the group was still and quiet; no one stirred. Ren was curled in a ball next to the fireplace under his blanket with his pack for a pillow. He lifted his head and found Asher at his back and Jakob spooned around Sorcha nearby, but all asleep. Ren was drifting back to sleep when he heard it.

"Ren." The voice was muffled from static.

Ren sat up slightly and found a comm next to his pack. He hadn't put it there the night before, but he recognized it as one he and Ezzy had found together.

Ezzy. "Ren, please. Please wake up. Please."

Ren grabbed it. "Ezzy?" His voice was rough from sleep and loud in the quiet. Asher stirred beside him.

"Oh, thank the stars." She sounded strange, as if she were scared of getting in trouble,

"Where are you?"

"In the tower, getting the beacon."

Ren rubbed the sleep from his eyes. "Why are you in the tower? We decided Jakob and Asher would bring it down. And why are you whispering?"

"Because they're here. Ren, they're everywhere."

"Who?"

"The birdmen."

Ren snapped to full wakefulness. He pushed off the blanket and scrambled from the makeshift bed. He accidentally kicked Asher, who grunted and opened his eyes, scowling.

"Okay, first thing, are you safe?"

"I think so."

"Okay, second, are we safe?"

She didn't answer for a long moment. "No."

Asher jumped to his feet. He woke Jakob first, then Sorcha, and in moments they were all mobilized, quietly but quickly packing and preparing.

Jakob hung over Ren's shoulder.

"What do you see, Ezzy?"

Her harsh stuttering breath came over the comm. "I see them all around the castle and in the courtyard. And some of them went into the keep and..." She started to cry, and Jakob snatched the comm.

Ren handed over comforting duties to someone better equipped and turned to the others. "What do we do?"

"I can't raise Fox," Sorcha said, her own comm in her hand. "He's not answering."

"Which means what?" Asher asked.

Sorcha's mouth turned down. "They've got him."

"Where's Beatrice? I thought she was on watch."

"How did Ezzy get out if the door was shut and barricaded?"

"We are coming to get you," Jakob said, over the din of their questions. "Don't worry. Stay put. Shut yourself in or whatever you have to do. But I am going to come get you, okay?"

"Okay."

"You're in the highest tower, right?"

"Yes."

"There is a good chance they won't come up there. So you'll be fine. You'll be fine."

Jakob's tone didn't waver or tremble, but his hand clenched the comm tight, and his jaw clenched with worry.

Sorcha strode toward the main door, where the barricade of chairs and tables was in place. "We've got to figure out where they are and get everyone out of here." She grabbed a stunner and hefted it. "We have weapons but I'd rather—"

She was cut off by a loud knocking on the door.

Everyone froze as if they were playing some child's game. They waited.

There were voices and footsteps and the scuffle of people—and a long pause. Ren held his breath. Asher squeezed Ren's hand. The noise on the other side of the barrier ceased. Ren tensed, his muscles taut, his heart pounding so loud he could feel the pulse in his ears. Then he heard the high whine of weapons charging swiftly followed by a bang.

The door heaved inward; the wood cracked and splintered under the assault, and the group leapt into action. They picked up bags and weapons and ran from the entrance to gather behind Ren, Asher and Sorcha.

"Well," she said wryly, "we're not going out that way."

The door bulged against another loud push and clatter. Ren heard the charge of weapons and smelled the burning wood.

Asher pulled his pulse gun.

Ren reached for his power and let it warm him from his core to his toes and fingertips. He succumbed to it; his vision washed blue.

"As much as I want to play 'last stand' with you all right now, I think it might be better if we run," Jakob said, prod in one hand, comm in the other.

The door splintered, and there were shouts from the other side from several voices.

Ren swallowed and poked with his star, and the ping back from the weapons almost overwhelmed him. "There's too many. We won't stand a chance in this open area."

"Into the passageway," Asher commanded. "Go. Now. Run!"

The door fell in.

They ran. Ren shoved the younger kids in first, through the partial doorway, and then he ducked in, clambering through the small space. As they moved, Ren smacked into Beatrice returning from down the corridor. He skidded and almost lost his balance before righting his body. Asher was the last in, ducking behind a piece of the door. He held onto the iron ring of the knocker and pulled it shut as a stunner blast rocketed into the wood. Splinters rained on the floor.

"What is going on?" she shouted.

"Where have you been?" Ren grabbed her and turned her around, pushing her away from the half-open door and out of the line of fire toward the wall. "I thought you were on watch."

"I was, but then I saw Ezzy was gone and went to look for her."

"She's in the high tower," Jakob said.

"What the hell is she doing up there?"

"Trying to prove herself."

There was another blast, this time closer.

Ren readied to send a burst of power, his fingers outstretched, but Asher grabbed his hand and shook his head.

"Not yet. We may be able to talk our way out of this, and we don't want to give you away if we don't have to."

"Talk our way out of this? They're shooting at us, Ash. In case you didn't notice." Jakob clenched the comm in his hand. "And my sister is out there."

"All the more reason for me to try and talk."

"Asher will stall," Sorcha said, tucking a wayward strand of her short hair behind her ear, then hefting her weapon. "Jakob and I will find Ezzy's route and lead the others out of the citadel. Bea, you stay here and be Ash's back up in case this strategy doesn't work."

"I don't take orders from—" Another blast into the wood cut her off and everyone ducked away.

"I'm staying with Ash," Ren said. He took the comm Sorcha slapped into his hand.

"That was never a question. We'll keep in touch."

They didn't have time for a touching goodbye. Jakob's punch to his arm and Sorcha's quick kiss to his cheek would have to do. And then they were gone, disappearing down the corridor, leading the rest of Sorcha's small group to find Ezzy and escape.

Beatrice pulled her weapon from the holster on her back. "Okay, what's your plan?"

Asher pulled out the shiny metal tags he always wore. He slipped the chain over his head, and, with a quick breath, he kissed the twin pendants. He stood from a crouch from behind the half-closed door and tossed the tags into the main room.

"Wish me luck," he said.

"No! Ash! What? What are you doing?" Ren whispered harshly, but Asher had already stepped into the line of fire, hands raised.

"Don't shoot. I am Corporal Asher Morgan with the Phoenix Corps, stationed on Mykonos Drift, under the command of General VanMeerten."

Ren scooted closer to the door and closer to Asher. He couldn't see into the room. He didn't know what weapons were leveled at Asher. He didn't know how many of the Corps had entered and were facing Asher down. All he could see was the profile of Asher's face, and it wasn't enough to gauge what was happening. His military mask had fallen into place.

Beatrice huddled next to Ren.

"Be ready," Ren said, voice low.

"To run?"

"To save him."

"You didn't tell me he's Corps."

"Shut up."

Asher took a step forward. There was no verbal response, but Ren heard the scrape of boots on stone, and then the jangle of medal.

"You are far away from home, Corporal Morgan."

"I'm on a special assignment. These people are under my protection."

"Scan these," the voice said.

Ren swallowed, throat tight. He hated not being able to see the soldiers, hated relying only on what he could hear and the nuances of Asher's flat expression. He was difficult to read, and Ren didn't want to miss a tell or hesitate a second too long and have Asher injured.

"I'd like to know whom I am talking to," Asher said.

The leader scoffed. "I'm Corporal Chase Zag."

"How did you know we were here?"

"My scouts have been tracking a small group of potential revolutionaries for days. We lost them for a day or so, but thank you for turning off the beacon. That was a sure sign they'd made their way into the citadel."

"They are not revolutionaries. They are citizens of this planet."

"Anyone caught scavenging tech is considered dangerous. Not that I have to explain anything to you, Asher Morgan, since I'll be taking you into custody now."

"Into custody? On what charge?"

"A quick scan of your identifications shows you've gone AWOL."

"That's a mistake," Asher protested. His brow furrowed, and he changed the grip on his pulse gun slightly. "I'm on a special assignment ordered by General VanMeerten."

"Huh. I guess it's pretty funny that her signature is on this order of capture."

"It's an error."

"Then you can take it up with her. Now, the question is, are you going to come quietly, or is this going to get messy?"

Ren coiled his legs beneath him and called his power to his fingertips. He closed his eyes and sent out a wave to pinpoint the weapons. Five. Only five. Where had the others gone? He looked up at Asher and saw the slight shift in his posture.

"I don't want to cause any trouble," Asher said evenly.

"Shame," the voice said, closer than before. "I like it when they fight."

Asher slid his foot slowly back. "I have no intention of fighting."

Corporal Zag made a disappointed noise.

"But you'll be happy to know," Asher continued, inching gradually backward, his body clearing the plane of the door. "I do plan to run."

Ren sprang. He jumped in front of Asher and pushed a blast of power outward, disabling the weapons in the immediate area. He grabbed the other leaf of the double door and slammed it shut. Beatrice jammed her weapon into the brackets on the back, effectively locking the door from the inside.

A loud thud echoed as a body hit the door, and the wood rattled in the frame.

"That's not going to hold them long."

"No. Let's go."

They ran to Vos's office and through the exit at the back of the rounded room, firmly shutting the door behind them.

They were in another passageway, this one long and arched, with doors down either side.

"Oh, cogs," Asher breathed. "How do we get out of here?"

"Ezzy found a way; so can we."

Ren lifted the comm to his mouth. "Sorcha? Report. Um… over."

"We're outside," she said, tone hushed. "Safe for the moment. Hidden. But they're everywhere. Ren, we need help, your help, or we're not getting out of here. Over."

Ren shuddered. "Okay. Tell us how to get to you and we'll be there in a flash. Over."

"Fourth door on the right."

They didn't hesitate.

With Sorcha giving them directions, they found their way through the labyrinth of the keep. Ren kept his hand on the comm, leading Beatrice, with Asher bringing up the rear. After one final turn, Ren stopped and recognized the corridor.

"You should be close," Sorcha said. "Over."

"Yeah, I recognize this place. I know the way from here. Over." Ren had spent most of his captivity memorizing the way from the dungeon to the courtyard, and now it was coming to good use.

"Good, because..." She trailed off, and there was the sound of a scuffle before the transmission cut off.

Asher crowded next to Ren's shoulder, staring into Ren's palm where the device glowed. Ren willed Sorcha to speak, to come back, and when she did, her voice was hushed.

"Hurry. We're about to be—" She stopped, breathless, and then yelled. "Jakob! No!"

Ren didn't wait to hear any more. He ran.

Beatrice and Asher yelled after him, but he didn't stop, skidding along the stone of the floor. He took a sharp turn and spied the arch that led to the courtyard. It glowed with sunlight, and Ren didn't slow down, though a Corps soldier stood in silhouette in front of him.

Ren lowered his shoulder, fully prepared to barrel into him and take him down as he had with the troops who'd wanted to take his brother. A shot from behind him rendered his foolhardy idea moot, and the Corps member crumpled forward with a smoking hole in the back of his shoulder from a pulse gun.

Asher.

Ren rushed past the body, which was knocked out, not dead, not dead, not dead, because Ren couldn't think about the consequences of that. He was too busy. His body worked, heart pounding, blood pumping, adrenaline rushing, joints and muscles and tendons stretching and contracting. His mind ran through scenarios, bleak and terrifying, and his star swelled, infusing him wholly. When he broke into the blindingly bright courtyard, he shouldn't have been able to see, but his vision was blue, and his eyes blazed. As frightening as was the ring of Corps troops surrounding his friends, *he* was more so.

Every piece of tech in the courtyard sang to him—the weapons, the comms, the wires in the stone, the pirated pieces in their packs—everything was a part of him. The power tangled within him, and he pushed out. The feedback loops flowed through his body, then outward, and back. He was a nexus of blue threads, of star, of machine, of electricity.

The Corps had his friends. Ezzy, Jakob, Sorcha, and the rest of the group. Ezzy sat in the snow and clutched the beacon; her arms were wrapped around it, and its base sat between her knees. A trickle of red dripped from the corner of her mouth and splattered on her chin, and Ren's gaze zeroed in on the line of blood, on the offense.

He *burned*.

"Let them go." His voice reverberated through the comms and boomed from the beacon, and the captives clapped their hands over their ears. The Corpsmen visibly flinched, and Ren smiled, a grim manic pull of his mouth.

"Or what?" Corporal Zag stepped forward, unafraid, his pulse gun trained on Sorcha. Then he moved it to Jakob, then Ezzy. "Think you can stop a shot, star host? Are you willing to risk it? What about her?" He lifted it to point over Ren's shoulder, where Beatrice stood behind him. "Or him?" He swung his arm, pointing the weapon at Asher.

As the Corporal taunted, Ren slowly tilted his head. With tactical clarity, he assessed and catalogued. Scattered along the ground were the remains of the tech from the packs the soldiers had upended, and lined in a haphazard row were the force-field points he and Jakob had removed from the stone. Each of the corpsmen held a weapon or had a comm on their uniform. His group of friends huddled together, and Jakob eyed Ren knowingly. Ren smirked. Jakob smiled in return.

Zag changed tactics and leveled his weapon at Ren. "Or maybe I'll kill you. I might even get a medal for it." He narrowed his eyes. "All I would need is one shot to wipe that smile off your face."

Plan firmly in place, Ren gritted his teeth. "You'll regret threatening my friends."

Zag chuckled, his gun arm steady. "I don't think so." His finger twitched on the trigger.

Ren blinked.

Several things happened at once. The force fields engaged. All the weapons shorted. The comms blasted static. Zag shot. And the group of captives scattered.

Chaos reigned.

Ren poured his power outward. The force field created a partial wall between the captives and the Corps. The comms shrieked. The pulse guns spat electricity, came alive in the hands of those who wielded them, and sparked and sputtered, shocking the Corpsmen with forks and tangles of electricity. They fell, writhing on the ground, even Zag. Ren vibrated with their screams, tasted the burn of skin and hair, but it wasn't enough.

They had destroyed his home. They had made it so Ren could never return to what he was before. They had scared Ezzy, who was only a girl with a crush, who wanted to prove herself capable in a war zone when she should've been learning at school, playing in the woods, swimming in the lake, or blushing around boys. They had threatened them, frightened them, and they would *burn*, as Ren did, blaze in misery and despair, and thrash in pain until their veins blackened and peeled like wires, until their bones glowed like circuits.

The power flowed from him in a torrent, and he pushed it, and pushed it. He ensured those responsible were filled until they burst, until their souls were scorched out of them, until their humanity had crumbled to dust as his had.

"Ren!"

"Don't touch him, Sorcha!"

"But he's—"

"Ash, what do we do?"

"I can't touch him. My shoulder—"

Ren heard a desperate sob. It broke into his concentration, traveled through the din of the static and the crackle of the air. He turned a bit, and it came again, harder, sharper.

Ezzy. She cried, and Ren pulled back. Why was she crying? He had saved her. He had saved the group. She didn't need to be afraid.

He lowered his arms from out in front of him; his joints ached. He turned fully and took in the scene through clouded eyes, and the tendrils of power receded, fled back into his chest. Ren blinked, and the haze retreated.

Around him the soldiers lay in heaps—not dead, not dead, not dead—their weapons smoked, bodies twitched. The force field hummed, but the comms were silent. The air smelled like ozone and smoke.

And Ezzy cried.

Zag's shot, the one meant for Ren, had gone wide. Beatrice lay in the snow, eyes open and unseeing, and Ezzy clutched at her coat with hands twisted in the fabric and sobbed.

"Ren?" Sorcha asked softly.

"We need to leave," he croaked. "We need to run."

"No!" Ezzy yelled. "We're not leaving her. We're not leaving her."

A soldier stirred.

"Jakob," Ren said.

Jakob nodded, his face pale, his mouth flattened in a grim line. He hauled Ezzy to her feet and pulled her away from Beatrice's body. She fought him, but not hard; her sharp cries gave way to low, shuddering sobs. She covered her face with her hands and allowed Jakob to guide her away.

Someone groaned. Another soldier rolled to his back.

"Run," Asher said, grabbing a shocked Sorcha by her shoulders. "Through the siege tunnel. Go!"

She moved, slowly at first, with her eyes wide and locked on Ren, but after another shove from Asher, she shook her head. The key to the heavy lock already in her hand, she beckoned her group, and they sprinted across the courtyard.

Ren followed on unsteady legs. His chest heaved. His hands shook. Asher covered them with his weapon out. It was an unnecessary precaution. With the entire regiment on the ground, their weapons sizzling and smoke curling in the crisp winter air, they were not a threat. Yet.

Ren had guaranteed that.

"But what about the stuff? The whole reason we came?" Matt asked. He stuck close to Sorcha's side and stared at Ren in awe, and fear, and admiration.

Sorcha pushed him into the siege tunnel. "Don't worry about it."

Ren licked his lips. "It's garbage anyway. I destroyed it all."

He waited for Beatrice's groan, her snappy comeback, her cutting remark, her fire. There was only silence, a void where her voice should've been. Ren looked back and saw her body in the snow; her red hair was stark against the white. For a second, he agreed with Ezzy. They couldn't leave her. They shouldn't leave her. Why were they leaving her?

"Ren," Asher said, his hand gentle on Ren's shoulder. "We need to go."

Ren nodded.

The sound of the metal grate closing behind them echoed in the small stone space, the same tunnel that he had escaped through forever ago. But this time, as he fled with Asher and Sorcha, he couldn't pinpoint exactly whom he ran from, or whom he needed to run to.

If this was a fairytale, or a nightmare, or one of the old myths his mother used to tell him, he didn't know who the villain was. But it wasn't a story, it was his life. And replaying the last several minutes in his head like a vid, he couldn't help but think, perhaps, the villain was him.

10

When the group reached the floater, they piled in, and it took a moment for Ren to realize that Beatrice had driven them there and they would need a new driver.

Sorcha took over. Ezzy continued sobbing. When Sorcha tried to power the engine, it did nothing, and Ren realized he'd have to fix the block he'd put on it. The thought of using his star made him sick. He pressed his lips together and accessed his power, tasting bile in his throat as he did. The engine roared to life.

Sorcha took a breath. "Where are we going? Where am I taking you?"

"I'm not going anywhere without you," Jakob said. He had his arm around Ezzy, and he held his sister close to his side. "I've found you and I'm not letting you go." He dropped a kiss to Ezzy's hair. "Either of you."

Sorcha gave him a soft, fond smile. Ren crossed his arms, clutched at his body, and hoped to hold himself together.

"Ren and I need a spaceport. We have to leave. There's no question now," Asher said.

"Why? Why can't Ren stay with us?" Jakob demanded. "He belongs on Erden. We'll protect him."

Ren shuddered. "Because they won't stop looking if they think I'm here," Ren said, softly. "They'll burn all of Erden to the ground searching. You'll all be at risk."

"Let them try. We'll fight. We'll keep you safe."

"No, no, please. I can't… I don't want to be responsible for anyone else's death." Ren blinked; the image of Beatrice lifeless in the snow flashed in front of him.

Jakob's gaze flickered between Ren and Asher. Ren saw sorrow, fear, and protest in the angry twist of his mouth and the glitter of his blue eyes.

But Sorcha nodded. "I can get you close to a port." She paused. "Ren?"

"Yeah," he said, nodding. "Yeah, that's good. I'm good. I'm sorry. I'm sorry that I couldn't do the things everyone needed me to do."

"It's okay," she squeezed his hand. "We've survived without you and we will continue to survive. You've brought Jakob back to me. You've given us a chance to unite the encampments, if not the tech. And we have a floater. That's more than what we had."

Ren nodded. The platitudes was an insufficient balm for the turmoil that swirled within him, but at least it soothed him for a moment.

Sorcha eased the floater out of the small hiding place on the edge of the woods. With part of the group piled in the front cab and the rest in the flat bed, Sorcha piloted slowly, carefully. She was unused to the controls, but grew more confident.

Ren lost track of time. It was an instant and an eternity when Sorcha eased the floater to a stop.

"We risk too much going farther," she said. "The port is over the hill and down."

"We know," Asher said. He disembarked, stepping over Jakob and Ezzy and jumping down to the ground. Ren followed.

Jakob untangled from Ezzy's grip and stepped out of the cab, hopping down into the leaves. "Ren," he said. He toed the ground, leaving scuffs in the snow and dirt. "Thank you for helping me, for being my friend."

Ren swallowed around a tight throat. "You, too."

Jakob chuckled. "Who'd have thought I'd be best friends with the weird kid?"

Ren shrugged. "Who'd have thought I'd be best friends with the rich kid with the big mouth?" he said, mustering a smile.

Jakob laughed outright. "Come here, you weed." He pulled Ren into a tight hug. Ren returned it heartily, holding on a fraction longer than necessary. Shared grief and a tinge of desperation were in the clutch of their arms.

"You be careful," Jakob said, low. "And if things don't work out with Asher, you can marry Ezzy and be my brother."

"I don't need to marry Ezzy to be your brother."

"You're absolutely right." Jakob squeezed hard and then let go and stepped away.

Ren nodded toward the floater. "Take care of them."

"I think Sorcha has that covered, but I'll try not to hinder her too much." Jakob climbed back into the floater and settled in the seat. He gave Asher a nod, then winked at Ren, gracing him with a final smirk.

Ren's heart squeezed. They were the last remnants of his home, and he didn't know if he'd see them again. He took a stuttered breath. "Goodbye, Jakob."

"None of that. I'll see you later, Ren. I will."

Ren forced a smile. "Okay. Later. Until then."

Jakob grinned. He patted the side of the floater, and Sorcha pulled away. Ren watched them leave, streaking across the landscape, until they were a speck on the horizon.

Ren turned to see Asher disappearing into a nearby bunch of trees. Ren followed; standing in the middle of the road wasn't such a great idea, especially now.

Asher stopped in a small space between the trees and let out a loud sigh. He kicked a pile of snow and dead leaves. His anger finally spilling out. He rubbed a hand over his eyes. "I'm listed as coggin' AWOL. AWOL, Ren."

Ren leaned on a tree. He was exhausted; the last hours were catching up to him as his adrenaline rush receded like the tide.

"I don't know what that means, Ash."

"Absent without leave! It means I've abandoned my post, my duty. I'm a *deserter*."

Ren's shoulders sagged. He rolled his head back against the bark. He was cold, and his breath hung in clouds. They should've stayed with Sorcha and Jakob, at least for the night; the sun now edged toward the horizon.

"Is that such a bad thing?" Ren's head was fuzzy, and tiredness made his tongue loose.

The question went over as well as a lead balloon.

Asher moved quickly, suddenly looming in front of him. "What the stars does that mean? Of course it's bad."

"Are you sure? Or have you forgotten the part where the Corps left you on a planet by yourself *for a year*. Not to mention the fact that it's obviously not the white tower of moral right you think it is."

"You don't get it. The Corps was everything I had. It was my family and my home. And now, I'm cast out, a fugitive. I can be arrested, captured, taken prisoner."

Emboldened by his fatigue, Ren pushed off from the tree and stepped into Asher's space. "Wow, I wonder how that feels?"

"It's not the same thing, Ren. I'm not—"

"What? A star host? A *threat?*"

Asher clenched his jaw. His face flushed. His fingers curled into fists at his side.

Ren circled him, taunting, devastated yet unafraid. "You're not *dangerous*, like me?"

"Fine," Asher faced him. He jabbed his finger in Ren's chest. "You want to go there? You want to have that argument right now?"

"Sure," Ren shot back. He knocked Asher's hand away. His body shook with spent adrenaline, exhaustion, and grief. "Right now. Let's talk about how the organization that you hold the most allegiance to is here and *killing* people. They killed Beatrice, and they would have killed you today, if given the chance."

"Okay, then let's talk about why they are here. They're here because you stupid dusters can't govern your own damn planet and spawned a lunatic like Vos. The drifts were attacked, and they have every right to make sure that doesn't happen again."

"Really? That's why you think they're here? Because of Vos?"

"Why the stars else? It's not like anyone wants to come to this backwater dirt sphere."

Ren laughed. "Wow. And I thought I was kept in the dark. You couldn't be more wrong."

Asher crossed his arms. "So you know information I don't? I thought we were done keeping secrets."

Ren scoffed. "As if you're not keeping secrets from me."

"If I am, it's for your own good."

"You're an ass. You're an arrogant drifter jerk, and sometimes there are moments when you fool me, and I think: No, he's not so bad. But then you say crap like that."

"Oh, come off it, Ren. If you know something, say it, or keep your mouth shut."

Ren shook, and not from the cold. "They're here to hunt star hosts. Happy now? They're here to find people like me and wipe us out because that has been their purpose from day one, and because I *saved a drift*. They are terrified there are more like me out there, that there are more like me here, in hiding."

Asher rolled his eyes. "Whoever told you that was lying. Stars, you're gullible."

"My parents are liars now?"

"Yes. Or did they not lie to you for most of your life already?"

"They did. So what? The Phoenix Corps killed Beatrice in front of us. They chased us and they tried to kill a young girl because she had tech they wanted. You can't deny that."

"You're right, I can't." Asher said. He turned away. "But you can't deny that Millicent killed people, too, or that you were ready to kill when the star possessed you, that you may have killed at the citadel just now."

Ren seethed. No, he couldn't deny it, and the knowledge threatened to sink him. *He* was the reason the Corps was on Erden, no one else. He thought about the dream he'd had, about being pulled under the lake, about being held down, about thrashing uselessly, unable to change anything. That was what guilt felt like—like drowning. He bit back a yell of utter frustration. He shoved his hands into his pockets and gnawed his lip, trying not to erupt with anger.

Asher paced nearby, ignoring Ren, muttering to himself. Ren was glad of it. Maybe they would calm down and begin to think logically again and find a way back to the drifts.

"How are we going to get on a ship? How are we going to get to Delphi?" Asher looked up and pinned Ren with an irritated glare. "We're literally right back where we started when we escaped the first time."

"Fate's a cog," Ren said, his voice a knife's edge.

"This is your fault, you know."

Ren sighed. They weren't finished then. "My fault? How is this my fault?"

"If you and Jakob hadn't decided to go off on your own, I'd be back on the ship and able to report. I wouldn't be AWOL. But no, you two had to trudge off into a snowstorm."

"You didn't have to follow. I didn't ask you to follow."

"You knew I would."

"Yes, because you can't let a prisoner out of your sight. Couldn't let me get away, or you'd be in trouble with your frightening boss."

Asher blew a breath out through his nose. He looked like a bull. "No, because I care for you and I didn't want you to die. But sure, blame it on that. Blame it on VanMeerten and on me. That's what you're good at."

"What the cogs does that mean?"

Asher didn't answer, just pressed his lips together. He put his hands on his hips and stared off into the distance.

But Ren wasn't going to be ignored. He approached on wobbly legs and pushed his finger into Asher's chest. "Hey, I'm talking to you. What does that mean? Huh?"

"Leave it, Ren."

He should've. He really should've, but he was *boiling*. His fury was hot as the sun. He pushed Asher's shoulder again, harder. "You started this fight. So finish it. What does that mean? Come on, Ash. Don't spare my feelings. Out with it. Tell me. I want you to—"

"You didn't see yourself! Okay?" Asher exploded, knocking Ren's hand away. "It means that you didn't see what I did, what the others did. It means that you haven't seen anything clearly since we left Mykonos. You're erratic and—" Asher fought for the words. "And *paranoid*. You're a ghost. You don't sleep. You don't eat. On the ship, you barely talked. You walked around at all hours with your eyes constantly blazing blue."

"My eyes are brown."

"They were blue," Asher said his voice dropping so low Ren strained to hear. "More often than not. And when they were, you just," he shrugged, helpless, subdued. "You weren't there."

Ren's heart pounded. His throat went dry. A shiver sliced down his body and wracked his frame. The lost time, the lack of sleep, the intimacy with the ship all pointed to Asher telling the truth. "That's not…" He swallowed. "That's not… You didn't tell me."

"I tried, but you… you interpreted concern as… something else. And I didn't do a good job of showing it either. I was afraid."

Ren's knees went weak, and he stumbled, sinking to the ground. He sat in the snow and let the cold leech into the fabric of his trousers, into his skin. The feeling steadied him, reminded him that he existed in his body. "Of me?"

"Sometimes," Asher said. He crouched. "But mainly I was afraid we were losing you." Ducking his head, he met Ren's gaze head on; his expression was haunted. "I was losing you."

Suddenly exhausted, Ren dropped his head into his hands. "I'm sorry." The words came out muffled by his palms. "I never wanted any of this."

Ren heard the crunch of snow and the thud of Asher sitting next to him. His leg bumped into Ren's, and the body heat was welcome in the cold.

"I can't imagine the power you have inside of you. I can't imagine what it must be like. And I have done my best to try and help, and I know it hasn't always been what you think is right."

Ren raised his head. "This," he said, gesturing between the two of them, "has been harder than I thought it would be."

Asher looked away. "Yeah." He cleared his throat. "We can't stay here. We need to get going and meet Rowan. She'll want to know everything."

Ren stood and reached out. Asher took his hand, and Ren hauled him to his feet. He didn't let go of Asher's hand. They didn't speak. Silence pervaded the woods; all sound was dampened by the drifts of snow.

Ren lifted the side of his mouth and managed a laugh. "As you pointed out, we've done this before."

Asher's lips twitched into a small smile. "We have," he said.

"We can do it again."

"We can."

Ren nodded. He dropped Asher's hand and shoved his own hands into his pockets. "Okay, then. Let's find a ship."

Asher's grin turned wry. "Let's try not to find one with a crew who will try to ransom you."

Ren brushed the snow from the back of his trousers and sighed. "That's an excellent plan."

⏻

The journey from Erden wasn't nearly as stressful as the last time. They entered the spaceport and kept their heads down. Ren didn't spark. Asher didn't run into any Phoenix Corps members. They found a ship headed to Delphi and booked passage without a problem. Asher's active credit chip surely helped.

They boarded and shared a room. Ren was silent. Asher brooded.

Asher resisted sending a message to Rowan, scared that the Corps would be looking for them and monitoring transmissions to and from the *Star Stream*.

Ren didn't care. He slept in the bed. Asher slept on the floor. They ate with the crew, but there was no fear of discovery of Ren's powers. He kept everything bound tight, and when he did merge, he did so discreetly, and only to see if there were warrants for them. There weren't, meaning the Corps wanted to keep Asher's AWOL status a secret except in the organization.

Ren had been worried about being on a ship again, but he didn't find it difficult, which was strange. He wasn't tempted as he had been on the *Star Stream*. This ship didn't live and breathe, didn't flood Ren's veins, didn't call to him when he slept. That didn't stop Asher from staying awake at night to ensure Ren didn't accidentally cause an emergency, but when Ren slept, he didn't dream. He slept hard, and deep, and woke up rested.

Asher's words rang in Ren's head, so he made sure to eat. He talked. It was inane chatter, but Asher barely listened, anyway.

Ren tried not to think about Beatrice in the snow.

He missed Jakob, his brusque attitude and his unwavering friendship, with a fierceness that surprised him. He hoped Ezzy was okay. He knew Sorcha would take care of them all. He didn't think about his parents.

Now, Ren's gaze turned from Erden and into space, toward finding his brother. He might be on Crei. He might be anywhere, if Asher's ideas about a larger conspiracy against the drifts were true. Ren didn't offer his opinion. Asher wouldn't appreciate it, especially since Ren could no longer tell who was in the right. Vos and his parents had planted the seed that the Corps was corrupt, and Zag's attack on them at the citadel only made that seed grow.

But Ren couldn't support Vos, either. He had taken Ren from his home and had forced Ren to expose his existence to the drifts, and, because of him, Ren couldn't live a normal life, no matter how much he wanted to.

However, Ren's objective had remained steadfast since the beginning—protect his brother. And he would. He had to. If he could find him.

They docked at Delphi. Ren and Asher disembarked without incident, though Asher radiated anxiety. He kept his head down and shoulders up, hunched in a worn jacket that had seen better days.

The drift was as Ren remembered, not remarkably different from the other drifts he had visited: a little smaller than Mykonos, but as vibrant and loud, spinning slowly in the middle of the dark of space. It bustled with activity. People from all over brushed past Ren, knocking shoulders with him.

Asher left Ren standing in an alcove near benches and plants framing a large viewing window. The sky slid past him; stars twinkled from far away. Ships eased into docks and blasted off, leaving trails of particles behind them. Checking the drift's time, Ren found it was the middle of their day, though it seemed to him it should be the middle of the night. He stifled a yawn, covering his mouth with the back of his hand. He could use a nap, and food—he was tired of rations and stale bread.

The first time he had been on Delphi, Asher had snuck him off the ship and taken him to a buffet. At the memory, Ren perked up.

Asher approached, mouth pulled into a frown. "The ship isn't here," he said. "Info says they should be back in two days. I sent Rowan a vague message." Asher looked over his shoulder and ducked his head when a few Corpsmen sauntered past. "We need to find a place to lie low."

Ren nodded. Hands in the pockets of his trousers and long-sleeved shirt pulled down over his wrists, he looked every inch a duster. Asher didn't look much better. They stuck out, even among some of the more outrageous of the drifters.

"I want to see Nadie."

Asher lifted an eyebrow. He grabbed Ren's shirt and pulled him close. "Are you serious?" he said, voice low and harsh. "Are you addled?"

"You don't have to come with me, but I want to see her. She could have information for me. She could know something I don't."

"What is this about, Ren? What do you have in your head?"

"Can you trust me?"

Asher sighed. He put his hands on his hips and studied Ren. His gaze pierced Ren to his core, then swept up and down his frame, finally studied the color of his eyes. They were the familiar brown. Ren was sure. He didn't feel as though his hold had slipped or that he was sparking anywhere. Yes, the drift buzzed around him, spoke to him on levels that Asher couldn't hear, but so did the people, the low hum of movement, the burst of voices, the rustle of fabric.

"What could she know that we don't?"

"The future."

Asher rolled his eyes. "Really?"

Ren's lips almost brushed Asher's jaw. "I control technology. You've met a man who can influence others with his voice. And for some reason, you still can't believe that she can see glimpses of the future."

"Is there a question in there?"

Ren stepped out of the alcove, knocking into Asher's shoulder. "I'm going."

"I'm not stopping you."

"Good." Ren looked down the outer curve of the drift floor and took a step. He stopped, looked to the inner spoke, and then back to the other side. He huffed, annoyed. "I don't know where her office is."

Asher smiled, smug and irritating. "It's three floors down."

Ren grumbled under his breath and marched to the nearest lift. During the ride down, Ren turned off the cameras with a tendril of his power, in case anyone was looking.

When they arrived where Nadie's office used to be, all they found was a cracked window and a torn sign. Ren peered through the frosted glass and could see nothing of the eccentric room that had greeted them last time. He tried the knob and found it locked, but at a push the door fell away from the frame on broken hinges.

The mess that greeted them reminded Ren of his childhood home—broken objects, scattered papers covered in scrawled predictions, items tossed everywhere. Her business, her home, her *life* had been destroyed. Ren froze; fear shivered down his spine, but he had to know. Maybe she'd escaped, too. Maybe she had been warned. Maybe there was a coded message here, too. Anything. There had to be *something*.

Brow furrowed, Ren stepped in, but Asher's hand on his forearm stopped him. "Don't," he said, voice low, full of warning.

"Why?"

"We're being watched."

Asher kept his chin tucked down, but jerked his head toward the middle of the drift floor. Sure enough, two *birdmen* watched with interest. Their hands were near their weapons; their body armor was snug around their torsos. The symbol of their institution blazed stark red on their shoulders—the phoenix with wings outspread, talons hooked, rising from flames.

The image of Beatrice's red hair spread out against the snow flashed in Ren's mind, and he shook with anger. He clenched his hands, and bit his lip, and fought against the swell of power that rose in him.

"Ren," Asher whispered fiercely. "Stop whatever you're doing."

Ren blinked, turned away, and covered his face with his hands. "We should walk away."

"Good idea."

Asher jerked on Ren's arm, pulled him away from the broken entrance of Nadie's office, and led him parallel to the wall, back to the lifts.

They went a few steps, then passed a dark alcove, and a hand shot out, gripping Ren's shirt. Elegant fingers with long fingernails and adorned with jewelry tugged Ren out of Asher's grasp and then let go. Twin red orbs stared out from the darkness, and Ren remembered how Nadie's eyes glowed red when she used her power, as his glowed blue.

"Nadie?" he asked. He moved into the alcove with Asher a hot presence at his back. "Is that you?"

"Why are you here?" Her voice was deep and resonant, as if several people spoke at once, echoing in the small space.

"I wanted to see you."

"Do not seek him out. Do not find him."

Ren moved closer. In the sparse light, he saw that the elegant, ageless lady he had met before was gone. Instead, a haggard woman with glowing eyes and tangled hair stood in front of him. Her dress was tattered, though colorful, and she walked with halting steps; her bare feet slid backward along the deck plate as she drew them farther into the alcove.

Asher stiffened behind Ren, but Ren followed her.

"Why not?"

She didn't answer; her gaze shifted to Asher. "You have left the flames," she said.

"Yeah. Not quite by choice."

"You will watch him cross. In your arms. After you cross him. He will leave, but don't let go. Don't let go. To the ship."

"What do you mean? Who will leave? Ren?"

She shook her head and the long tresses of her black hair swung at her hips. She rolled her neck and moaned, then moved her lips soundlessly. She pushed the heels of her hands into her eyes, and then laughed as she swayed. Then abruptly, she stopped. She dropped her hands and raised her head. Her eyes were dark. Nadie blinked, looked around the alcove, and scanned the area.

She leveled her gaze at Asher. "You again. If you're here to arrest me, I'm not going without a fight, Phoenix."

Asher raised his hands. "I'm not here for you."

"Then why are you here?" She jerked her chin toward the main floor. "Are they still out there?"

"Yes," Asher said.

She stiffened. "They've been there for days, since they destroyed my office, my life."

Ren stepped closer. "What happened to you, Nadie?"

She cut her gaze to Ren. Her eyes flickered, shifting from red to black, before blazing.

"I saw them. I saw them. I saw them. I saw them." She laughed again, wildly, terrifying. "They have come for me. I hid in the shadows, waiting for you. You have come."

Ren stiffened. "Why did you wait for me?"

She stood motionless for a long moment, and then lunged. Ren scrambled backward, but hit Asher's chest. She grabbed him, nails digging into his skin, and she smiled, a crooked, broken expression that made Ren shudder in her grip.

"Do not seek him out. Do not let her guide you. Find the star when it happens. Find it and be safe. Be safe. Be safe. Be safe."

She released him and went back to mumbling incoherently. She drew her nails up her arm and down again, leaving scratches. "I had a life," she said softly. "I had a life. I wanted a life."

Ren's heart sank. "Cassandra," he whispered.

She snapped to attention and stared at him with eyes like dying embers that slowly turned to ash. She lifted a trembling finger to her pale mouth, and took a breath. "You need to leave, young star. You're putting us both in danger."

"Come with us," Ren said. "We can help you. We can hide you."

Her lips pulled into a smirk. "I don't need your help. My alter ego may be dramatic but I am prepared. I have a plan. You must go. Remember whatever I told you. I am rarely wrong."

"No," Ren said. He shook off the hand that Asher placed on his shoulder. "No, I'm not leaving you. We can help each other."

She narrowed her eyes. "Save me from idiots," she said softly. "I am not afraid. I am not helpless."

"No, but—"

Then she screamed and her eyes glowed red.

Ren flinched backward, bumping into Asher's chest. His eardrums rattled as she screamed and screamed. Her voice pierced Ren's core and vibrated there, as if he were made of glass she could shatter. He and Asher scrambled from the alcove and bolted to the side as the members of the Phoenix Corps swarmed toward them.

Asher pulled Ren close, and they left the scene.

Nadie continued to scream, high-pitched, hysterical, *insane*.

Ren peeked over his shoulder and watched as the Corpsmen pulled her from the alcove. She shrieked and clawed and cried. Her eyes were red as fire and her body writhed as she saw a future no one else could. Ren hid his face as they marched her away, dragged her when she wouldn't walk, took her away from her home to only she knew where. She had seen her own future, and now it enveloped her, overwhelmed her, and she succumbed to it. But as she had in the alcove, she stopped and suddenly broke their hold. She cackled as she raced away with her long black hair a streak behind her.

With the Corpsmen focused elsewhere, Ren slammed a hand on the wall, released his power and plunged the drift into darkness for the count of two breaths. Then he brought the lights back up, silencing the panicked cries of the populace.

Nadie was gone.

Asher grabbed Ren by the shoulders and pushed him into the crowd. They blended in and disappeared, and only when they were certain no birdmen were watching, they slowed.

"Ash," Ren said. "She hid and waited for us. They drove her from her business, her home, and she waited for us. To warn us."

"I wish you would stop believing everything you hear," Asher said. He pulled Ren farther down the outside curve of the drift and then to a lift. He shoved Ren inside. Asher leveled a glare at the lone occupant, who scurried out. Asher slammed his hand on the close-door button. "Turn it off."

Ren nodded, cutting the video feeds. They rode in silence; the lift took them up and up and up to the higher levels of the drift.

"She said—"

"I don't care." Asher cut Ren off. "What the hell were you thinking?"

"I had to help her."

"No, you didn't."

"She was right before."

"Well, she wasn't glowing and *crazy* last time, was she? Did you not see her, Ren? She had clearly lost whatever tenuous connection she had to humanity. She was star."

"That doesn't mean she wasn't accurate. If anything, it meant she was more so."

"Who knew what she saw? That could've been minutes into the future, or hours, or *decades*."

"So you admit that she was seeing the future?"

Asher set his jaw. He watched the numbers tick by.

"You… you didn't like seeing her like that, did you? It reminded you of me."

Tapping his foot, Asher breathed heavily through his nose. "Yes," he finally said, clipped, strained.

"She was driven to that. The Corps had obviously been watching her, and they drove her into hiding, which makes what she said even more important. She waited for us, Ash. She was compelled to tell us those things."

"She made no sense. It was a jumbled mess. What does watch you cross mean? Huh? After I cross you? It was nonsense."

"It wasn't nonsense."

Asher spun on his heel. He crowded close, pushed Ren to the wall of the lift with his body. Ren was suddenly overcome by the heat of him, the smell of his skin, the warmth of his breath puffing against Ren's neck.

"What do you want me to say? That I'll betray you? That you'll betray me while you're in my arms? Do you want that future?"

Ren shivered. "No, No."

"Then don't."

"Don't what?"

"Don't believe her. Don't make it a self-fulfilling prophecy." He swallowed. "Don't keep secrets."

Ren met Asher's gaze; Nadie's words rang in his ears. Asher will cross him—betray him—to the Phoenix Corps, to get his rank back, his family back. Asher had already shown more allegiance to the organization that had taken him in as a teenager than to anyone else. And Ren was… Ren was a stupid duster who had been nothing but trouble—a star host, a being who skirted humanity, a person whom people feared. "I'm not keeping any," Ren lied, voice even.

Asher dropped his head and sighed. He nodded and pushed away as the lift dinged and slowed to a stop. "Okay," he said. He rolled his shoulder and stepped out into the bustling corridor. "Okay," he repeated.

Hollowed out and rattled, with Nadie's glowing eyes vivid in his mind's eye, Ren followed.

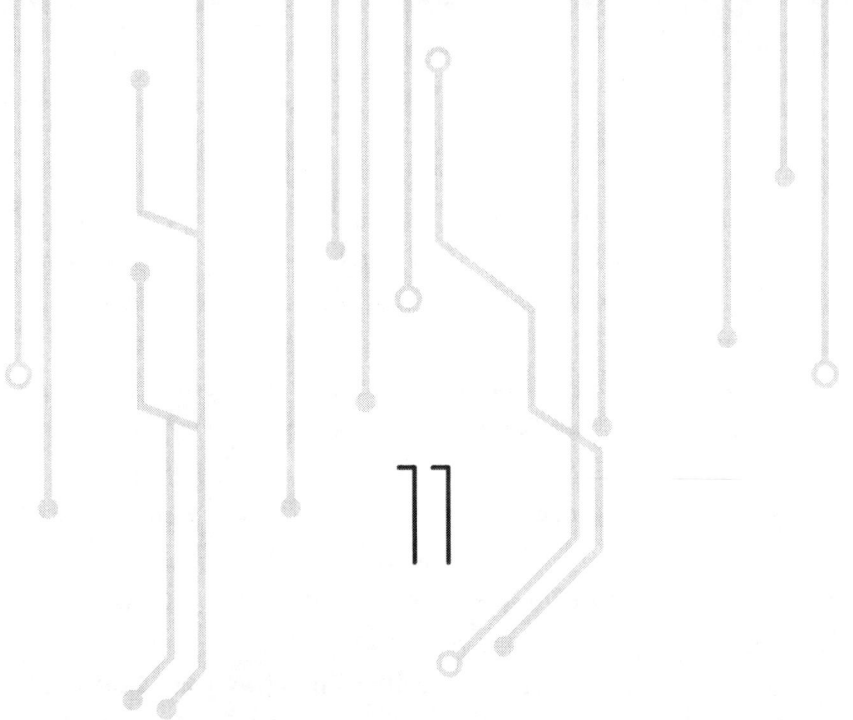

11

"That's for running off!" Rowan said.

A slap to the back of the head wasn't quite what Ren was expecting when he saw Rowan again, but he couldn't complain. Well, he could, but it wouldn't be a good course of action. Instead, he silently rubbed the sore spot and stared at the floor, trying to convey a mixture of guilt and apology. He didn't pull it off, if Ollie's snort was anything to go by.

She smacked Ren again, and he ducked out of her reach. Then she did same to Asher, two quick taps to the side of his head.

"Hey!" he yelled. He pushed her shoulder. "What did I do?"

"That's for making me worry." Rowan put her hands on her hips. "Honestly, I don't know what to do with the three of you."

"How about not hit us?" Asher said, rubbing the spot above his ear. "We've had a difficult week, thanks."

Ren bit his lip. Difficult was an understatement. He and Asher had hidden for two days while Rowan made her way back to Delphi. Staying below the radar was tougher than they'd first thought. Nadie had been able to hide as long as she did because she could see the future. But Asher was an AWOL Phoenix Corps soldier and somewhat of a celebrity, as the son of a high-ranking official. Ren didn't stand out, but the Corps under VanMeerten knew every angle of his face, and though Ren could monitor vid feeds and comm systems, he wasn't clairvoyant.

Two days of using fake names, a credit chip, and the little charm they had, got them rooms in two different hotels. They'd changed after the first night, just in case. They didn't leave their room unless it was necessary, and thus spent two long, tense twenty-four-hour drift cycles sleeping and staring at each other. It was maddening, especially since Ren held a secret, and Asher was determined to pretend he wasn't aware of it.

Also, Ren couldn't shake Nadie's visions. They pierced him; the truth of her words sank into his bones and made him wary and afraid.

"What were you *thinking*?" Rowan asked, moving back into Ren's personal space. She gripped him by the collar of his jacket and shook him like a naughty puppy. "You could've gotten yourself killed. You could've gotten Asher killed. And where is Jakob? I need to yell at him, too." She whirled around, finger pointed, looking behind the pair of them. When she found nothing, she froze, and her eyes went wide. "Where is he? Is he okay?"

"He stayed behind," Ren said. "We found Sorcha, a friend of ours, and his sisters. He couldn't leave them again."

Rowan nodded, then tugged on her golden braid. Her relief that Jakob was alive was evident. "I'm glad for him. He'll be missed. He was good crew. But I'm happy he found what he was looking for."

"Yeah," Ren said, throat tight.

"And you? Did you find…?"

"Not here," Asher said, breaking his silence. He gestured at the open ramp, at the life and energy of the drift within arm's reach, as well as vid feeds and comms.

"Fine. Come on in. Though if you weren't family and you couldn't turn my own ship against me with a thought, I'd draw this out a little more. I'm still angry at both of you. Keep that in mind."

"Your stubbornness has been noted and will be filed in the proper receptacle," Asher said.

Rowan made a rude gesture. Asher smiled smugly. Siblings.

Ren's stomach ached.

Rowan led them into the cargo bay, and Ollie shut the doors behind them. The yellow light from above cast them in a warm glow, though it didn't do much to illuminate the rest of the area. After the kinetic atmosphere of the drift, the dim surroundings and the silence of the closed cargo bay were a reprieve. Ren breathed slowly. Being back on the *Star Stream* gave him a sense of peace he hadn't felt recently. It was more home than anywhere else now, and Ren was happy to be back, happy to be in a place where he knew every wire, every conduit. It was familiar and comforting, and Ren cloaked himself in it, wrapped it around him like a blanket, and indulged in the systems that welcomed him.

"Ren?" Rowan hedged, touching his sleeve. "You okay?"

Ren sucked in air. "I'm fine. Why?"

Rowan stared at him, brow furrowed. Ollie towered next to her with arms crossed over his chest and muscles bulging beneath his brown skin. He also seemed concerned. "I've asked you the same question three times, and you haven't answered. You stared off into space and glowed."

"Oh," Ren said. He shook his head and cleared his mind of the ever-present crackle of the comm system and the glitch in the starboard thruster. "What?"

"I said, did you find what you were looking for? I hope your insubordination had a payoff."

"I found my parents."

"Oh, that's… good? You don't sound like it was good."

"It wasn't really."

Rowan raised an eyebrow. "I'm missing something."

"You're missing several things," Asher said. He crossed his arms. "To make a long story short, the Phoenix Corps believes I've abandoned my post and that I've gone AWOL. They are all over Erden looking for Vos and now us. And Ren is keeping information from me."

Ren glared. "Your short stories suck. First, the Phoenix Corps is all over Erden looking for star hosts and killing residents because they believe that there are more people like me hiding in the population. Second, we went to see Nadie."

Rowan's eyebrows shot up. "The seer?"

"Yes, and she warned me that Asher is going to cross me and that I'm going to cross him. So I'm sorry if I don't feel like sharing all the information I have right now."

Rowan looked at them, mouth pulled in a frown. "Seriously? You're back to fighting? I'd hoped time alone together would have led to making up."

"That's not your business."

"It *is* my business when you two act like children and keep making me intervene. Also, when your relationship with a powerful being threatens my actual money-making business, then it is my business."

"Can we stop saying business?"

"I swear to the stars you two will be the end of me. One of you start making sense. *Now.*"

"The Phoenix Corps is evil," Ren said. He stared at the deck plate. "They killed a friend of mine. They're looking for a way to rid the cluster of people like me. And they're doing it by killing innocents."

"Says your parents. Who *lied* to you your whole life," Asher said, sharply.

"Says my parents and *Vos.*"

Asher dropped his arms. Ollie's mouth fell open. Rowan's eyebrows shot up.

"When the hell did you talk to Vos?" Asher demanded. He crowded into Ren's space. His expression was flat. "Is that why you needed the beacon? To contact him? Is that why Beatrice died?"

Ren lashed out, shoving Asher away from him. Asher took a step back, and Ren followed, pushing again, with his palms flat on Asher's shoulder. He shoved and shoved and *shoved*.

"Ren!"

Ollie grabbed him and pinned his arms down at his sides. Ren twisted in Ollie's grip. His star throbbed in anger; his vision washed blue.

"How *dare* you?" Ren spat. "How dare you say her name when it was your beloved Corps that killed her. They killed her. Not Vos. Not me."

"If you hadn't turned off that stupid message, they wouldn't have known we were there."

"Don't take your utter denial about your place in all of this out on me."

"My place? What? Do you think I'm like Zag? That I went to planets and murdered people?"

"You were a Phoenix Corps soldier. How do I know what you did while under orders?"

"Do you of all people want to talk about murderers? That's slippery ground for your kind."

"That's enough!" Rowan barked. Her hand splayed across Asher's chest, keeping him in place. She looked at them with lips thinned and eyes narrowed. "Ren, stand down. Asher, go to your quarters."

"What?" Asher's jaw clenched. His cheeks reddened. "Why? Are you siding with him?"

"Are you questioning an order from your captain? Because let me remind you how utterly pissed I am at you and how I can have Ollie throw you back out onto that drift into the waiting arms of the Corps."

Asher's gaze flickered to Ollie. Ren couldn't see Ollie's expression, but Asher paled. Still shaking with anger, and with one last glare in Ren's direction, Asher stalked off into the belly of the ship. His stomps echoed, and Rowan sighed. She rubbed her temple.

"Little brothers."

Ren blinked. The phrase wiped away his anger and reminded him of his purpose. He sagged in Ollie's arms and scrubbed a hand over his eyes. "I'm sorry."

Rowan waved off the apology. "Just tell me the facts, and we won't have a problem."

Ren nodded, and after a quick walk to the common area and after sinking into the lumpy couch cushions with a cup of tea, he did. He told Rowan and Ollie everything. He talked about Beatrice and the program of Vos and the possible outpost on Crei. He talked about the ghosts in the farmhouse which could've been birdmen—Rowan snorted at the nickname—and the blaring message at the castle. He told them about Sorcha and Jakob and Ezzy and about Zag and the shot meant for him.

When he finished his tea, Ollie handed him a trinket from the broke-box. Ren spun the old tool in his hands and fiddled with it as he continued, fixing it with barely a thought as the words poured from him.

He talked about failure and fear and seeing Nadie driven mad and how Asher had told him he hadn't been much different.

He talked about Liam.

He talked about his parents, about their beliefs, their warnings, about how Asher had reprimanded his mother. He talked about the story of his kind, of the star hosts, how they'd been driven to the planets to hide. And then he stopped, throat parched, with the words drying up in his mouth.

Rowan crossed from the table and sat beside Ren on the couch. She rested her hand over his; her palm was cool and comforting on his knuckles.

"I'm sorry, Ren." She closed her eyes, took a breath, and her hand closed over his a little tighter. "One of the hardest lessons I learned when I was younger was that sometimes the people you want to believe in and look up to aren't who you think they are. Sometimes the people you love aren't good people. And it's awful. It's hard to reconcile the image you had with the things you know. But hard as that is, the good news is that you don't have to follow in their footsteps."

"And you get to make your own family," Ollie added. "And those kinds of family, the ones you choose, are the best kinds." Ollie took the now-fixed tool from Ren's fingers and slipped another item from the box into his free hand.

Ren swallowed. He turned his hand over and gripped Rowan's. "Thank you."

She smiled. "I would say it's no problem, but you've been a cog in the system since you stepped on board. And I'm still angry with you, but you do have a place here, if you want it."

"I want to find my brother."

"I know. And you really think he's on Crei? With Vos?"

Ren shrugged. "I'm not sure, but I think Vos might know where he is. If he doesn't, we might be able to find a clue."

"I'll have to think about it, Ren. I can't endanger the crew. Again. And I have to think about Asher, too. He's my brother and he's considered AWOL. We may be able to get that reversed, but I don't know what it will cost him."

Ren looked away. "I know."

"I don't think you do. Look, stars know he can be a jerk, and arrogant, and a standoffish cog. But when he ran away from our mom at sixteen and joined the Phoenix Corps, they took him in. They became his family of choice. And he needed that. So if what you say is true, about what they've been secretly doing for years, and with him witnessing the events with Zag, he has things to work through. You may have found out that your parents weren't shining examples of humanity, but Asher also found out that the organization he holds allegiance to is shady and corrupt. And you know he has to be replaying all the missions he's been on, questioning if he's contributed to the destruction of your kind."

That was true. Asher was probably in his room, head in his hands, eyes scrunched shut, agonizing over every detail.

"Yeah."

"I'm going to go talk to him. Hang out here with Ollie and—" she picked up a broken spanner— "fix things. Honestly, I don't understand boys at all." She stood and dropped the tool onto the couch. She straightened her shirt, tugged it down, and smoothed out the nonexistent wrinkles.

Ren mustered a smile. "It seems I don't get them either."

Rowan laughed. "Idiot. Don't worry. It will all work out. You're both under stress, and I know from experience that stress makes the pair of you stupid."

Ren didn't argue, but history had proven otherwise. They worked well under duress. They clicked when things around them fell apart. It was all the other times when they couldn't get along. Ren rubbed the end of his sleeve over his face. He didn't know how they could go from kissing in the midst of a life-or-death crisis to being safe on the ship and at each other's throats.

Rowan left, and Ollie moved from his position on the arm of the couch to the cushion next to Ren.

"So you want to go to Crei?"

Ren nodded. He handed Ollie the repaired spanner and accepted the next broken item. He was thankful for Ollie's strong and steady presence. It calmed him, and the mindless work kept his star occupied while he tried to think.

"Yeah."

"Are you sure? What if you find something you don't want to? Like with your parents."

Ren shrugged. "I want to find Liam."

Ollie nodded. He handed Ren a part from an air recycler. "I understand. If Pen were missing, I wouldn't stop looking, either."

"I don't know how I'll get there if Rowan decides she won't risk it."

"Rowan has two weaknesses," Ollie said, rooting through the broken box. "Asher being one."

"And the other?"

Ollie smiled. "Credits."

"Well, I can't pay her."

"You let me handle it."

Ren looked up from his hands and met Ollie's gaze. "You'll help me?"

Ollie knocked shoulders with Ren, and Ren fell sideways onto the cushions. Ollie laughed, then shrugged.

"You're family."

"You barely know me."

"I know you. I know you want to do the right thing and you want to protect the people closest to you, even if that means giving yourself up. And I know if Asher decides to expend energy and emotion on you, then you must be someone worthy of it."

Ren blushed and ducked his head. "Even if that emotion is anger?"

"Anger isn't the opposite of love. Indifference is. He wouldn't be upset if he didn't care for you."

Ren didn't quite buy into Ollie's logic, but he appreciated the sentiment, and he was buoyed by the fact that Ollie wanted to help him. He'd have to repay Ollie's kindness, if he ever could. He sat up from his sprawl.

"How do you know?"

"Because I'm old and wise."

Ren scoffed. "You're not old."

"I'm old enough to have a younger sister who is married and to have experienced lots of things, some even weirder than you. So trust me, okay?"

"I do," Ren said.

"Good." Ollie looked into the box. "I'll go add this to your pile of sellable junk. And I'll restock the box up here for you."

Ollie stood. He ruffled Ren's hair, grinning down on Ren as an older brother would.

"Don't worry, Ren. I'm sure we'll get everything sorted."

"Thanks, Ollie."

Ollie waved him off and lifted the box. He left the common area, and Ren leaned back on the couch.

Lighter now that he had revealed everything to Rowan, Ren tipped his head back to stare at the ceiling. Sharing his burdens had eased the tightness in his chest and the tense line of his shoulders. However, he couldn't shake Nadie's prophecy. Somehow, Asher and Ren would cross each other, and Ren didn't want to believe it would be intentional, but Rowan confirmed his fears. Asher had lost his chosen family, his purpose. That would be difficult to get over, even if the Corps proved to be as sinister as Ren believed.

Ren's quarters were as he had left them. The blanket was halfway off his bed, trailing on the floor. A pile of clothes in a corner needed to be washed. His sparse belongings were on the shelf, and his pillow was a misshapen lump on the bunk.

He reached into his jacket and pulled out the crumpled picture he'd found in his family home. Amazed it had lasted through the time on the planet, Ren smoothed it out on the top of his dresser. The cheap comic book Ren had taken from the remnants of Liam's room hadn't fared well. The pages were bent and the ink had bled, but he set it next to the picture.

Ren toed off his boots and jumped on the bed, shoved his face into the pillow, and inhaled its familiar scent. It wasn't until he was wrapped in the blanket and staring up at the picture Jakob had drawn that he realized how much he had missed his bed.

He missed Jakob, too. The sharp pang of loss made him gasp as he thought of his friend, but at least Jakob was with Sorcha and Ezzy. The three of them would be okay as long as they looked after each other. He clung to that hope.

Ren was half-asleep when his door opened. He sat up, startled, as Millicent walked into the room. Her long hair hung in limp strands to the small of her back. Her feet were bare as she picked her way into the room, toes sliding along the floor, always connected to the ship. Her eyes were large and faintly glowing, and she stared at Ren.

"A knock would have been polite," Ren said.

She tilted her head, watching him. Her lips were pale and chapped, and Ren watched her with narrowed eyes. He gripped his pillow with fingers curled tight in the fabric.

"Millicent?"

"The ship missed you," she said.

"I missed the ship."

She swayed where she stood; the hem of her dark dress brushed her ankles. "You were disconnected. I couldn't find you in the wires, but you've returned. Do you feel it? How the systems longed for you?"

Ren pressed one hand to the hull. "When I came back on board."

She took a step closer to him and then another. She pressed her face to Ren's neck and inhaled.

Ren tensed and sat still as stone, unsure how to respond. He was used to her being odd, but this was… this was above her usual level of weirdness.

"Millie?"

"You smell like dust. Like planet."

Ren scooted back, uncomfortable, and she followed, her knees making indents on the mattress. "I showered on the drift," he said.

"You don't belong with the dust. You belong among the stars. In the ship. In the wires. Free in the circuits." She hovered over him, straddling his legs, her hands on his chest.

"Um… this is weird and inappropriate."

"There you are!" Penelope's voice was loud, and Ren sagged in relief. "Pen!"

She entered the room, and Lucas popped his head around the door frame. His red hair stuck up everywhere; his complexion was even paler than usual. Ren had never been more relieved to see the goggles on Lucas's head and Penelope's unimpressed expression.

Penelope gently took Millicent by the bicep and pulled her off. "Now, now, Millicent. That's not polite."

Ren mouthed a thank you to Penelope as she guided Millicent away.

"Are you okay, Ren?" Lucas asked.

He cleared his throat. "Yeah," he said, his voice coming out far higher than he would've liked. "What's going on?"

"She's been a little out of sorts since you left," Penelope said, smiling tightly. "It's been a challenge."

"Yeah. Thanks for leaving me with her for those first few days," Lucas said, also wearing a forced smile. "It was a laugh a minute."

Penelope shot him a harsh look with her dark eyes narrowed. "Are you going to bring it up constantly? Because we've apologized. Several times."

"And you'll continue to apologize, because it was quite a traumatic experience." Lucas kept his frozen smile, but twin spots of red appeared on his cheeks.

Ren didn't want to know.

Millicent blinked for the first time since she had entered Ren's room. She looked around. "How did I get in here?"

Penelope's expression softened. "Oh, dear."

Millicent's gaze found Ren and she smiled the little half-smile she usually wore. "You're back."

"Yeah."

"Welcome home." Her smile became sharper and knowing, and a chill worked down Ren's spine.

"Ren must be tired. Let's leave him be until dinner." Penelope tugged on Millicent and pushed her out of the room. Penelope shared a wide-eyed, exasperated look with Ren before stepping from the room.

"Glad you're back, Ren," Lucas said, waving.

"Thanks. Me, too."

Ren stood and crossed the room and closed the door behind the trio. He engaged the lock, though it wouldn't stop Millicent if she wanted to come in again.

What had happened while he was gone? What had pushed Millicent to be stranger than ever?

He flopped onto his bed and stared up at the picture. Ren closed his eyes and relaxed into the bunk. There were so many things to figure out—Liam and Crei and Vos and Millicent. *Asher*. Ren didn't have the energy, and let his mind and power drift until he fell asleep.

⊣⊢

"Weeds, you are a hard person to get in touch with. It's easier when you're connected to your own power."

The area was low-lit, and Ren squinted. The floors were metal as were the walls. The only light came from tech in the ceiling. Ren could see a shadow in front of him and walls to the sides, and when he looked behind him, he found another wall. He couldn't discern a door.

"Where am I?"

"I don't know."

"Liam?" Ren stepped forward. The light overhead followed him; the darkness receded as he walked, as if fleeing from his footsteps.

A few more paces, and Liam appeared in front of him. He was fair-skinned and freckled; his red hair was slicked back as though he'd been swimming in the lake.

"Hey," Liam said, a smile breaking over his face. "You look awful. Seriously. When was the last time you ate anything? Or had a haircut?"

"You look the same."

"Well, I'm a projection. I'm letting you see what I want you to."

"Are you saying you're not well?"

"I honestly don't know."

Ren crossed the space between them. He brushed his fingers over Liam's hand, and he felt solid, corporeal. This wasn't a program like Vos, and Ren looked around and reached out with his star to find the trick. But there was nothing. No tech. Even the light in the room didn't respond to him.

"Is this real?"

"It's a dream."

"You're in my dream?"

Liam smiled. "Yeah. It's kind of my thing."

Ren's eyes widened. "It's your power. Your star. You can enter dreams?"

Hands in his pockets, Liam shrugged. "I'm still figuring it all out."

Ren laughed. "Me, too."

"Yeah, I've heard a little about a powerful star host who saved a drift. It figures; you finally leave home, and the first thing you do is save people. Good job there, bro."

"You heard about that?"

"Oh, yeah," Liam said smiling. "You were all the talk."

Ren laughed, giddy, relieved. "All this time I've been searching for you, and you've been coming to me in my dreams. Why couldn't I figure it out?"

"You're an idiot, that's why."

Ren laughed again. He marveled. Their environment was a mixture of real and unreal. The metal of the floor was cool on his bare feet, but the light and the shadows moved oddly. He breathed, but couldn't smell anything.

Giving into impulse, Ren closed the gap between him and Liam and grabbed Liam in a tight hug. Liam gasped and laughed and returned the embrace. He was real. He was *real*. After a long moment, they disengaged.

Ren wiped at his eyes. "Where are you?"

At the question, Liam dropped his gaze and scuffed his shoe on the floor. "I don't know."

"But you knew you weren't at the lake? On Erden?"

"Yeah, I knew I wasn't there. I'm not home. But the people who took me have given me no indication where I am."

Anger swelled in Ren. "Took you?"

"You didn't think I ran away from Erden on my own, did you? I'm not you. I didn't want to leave, but I didn't hide well enough apparently."

Ren bristled and reached for his star. He found nothing, no conduit for his power. He was useless. He deflated, shoulders drooping. "Are you okay? Have they made you do anything?"

Liam's face went red. "Weeds, Ren. You weren't ever this protective at home."

"I didn't have to be. Now, answer the question."

"It's okay. I have a room, a bed, and I get three meals a day. But I can't leave. I've gone into people's dreams and gathered information from their subconscious. It's not been all that bad. I mean, it's not what I would've chosen to do, but you know, in the grand scheme." Liam shrugged again.

"Do you want to leave?"

"Yes." The sound was an urgent gasp. "Yes. I want to go home."

Ren didn't tell Liam about how home wasn't there any longer, or about their parents, or their village. It wasn't the time.

"Can they hear this? Can they see me?"

"They monitor me, so probably."

Ren looked around the room and focused on the light. Even though it didn't respond as real tech would, that didn't mean he couldn't posture. He allowed his star to flood him and let his eyes glow blue. His power burned and pulsed in him. He clenched his hands and imagined the tendrils of electricity dripping from him, down his limbs, lighting up his bones.

"I'm coming for my brother," he said. "Understand? I'm coming, and you will not be able to stop me. I will destroy anyone who stands in my way."

"Weeds, Ren. Dramatic much?"

Ren turned back to Liam, and Liam took a step back, his face paling even further.

"I'm going to find you and free you."

Liam swallowed; his throat bobbed. "I think they are counting on that."

"Good. I want the challenge."

Liam nodded and wiped at his eyes. "Okay. Okay. I look forward to leaving. Stars, when did you get so scary? The only fight you were ever in was when Zeke pelted us with snowballs, and even then we ran away."

Ren pulled back. He packed away the power and blinked. "That better?"

"Yes." Liam's voice shook. "Stars, Ren."

Ren patted Liam's shoulder. "They can't stop me."

"I should go. I need to go before the other one shows up."

"Huh? Other?"

The light overhead flickered, and Liam started to fade. "I'll see you around, big brother. Don't do anything too stupid."

"Liam? Wait! Can you come back?

Liam waved and said something, but he faded too quickly for Ren to hear.

⼀⊩

Ren woke up with the sheets tangled around his legs and sweat slicking his hairline, but there were no alarms. Nothing blared. No one pounded at his door. He wasn't trying to kill the crew. That was a bonus.

He pushed up to sitting and checked ship's time. He had napped for a few hours, though his interaction with Liam had been only a few minutes long, and he hadn't missed dinner. He had seen Liam. Liam was alive. Liam could contact him. Liam was okay, if imprisoned. And Ren was going to find him and save him. They would be family again. Ren was even more determined to get to Crei.

His stomach growled. Ren sniffed his shirt. He didn't smell like dirt, but he had time for a quick shower anyway—probably for the best.

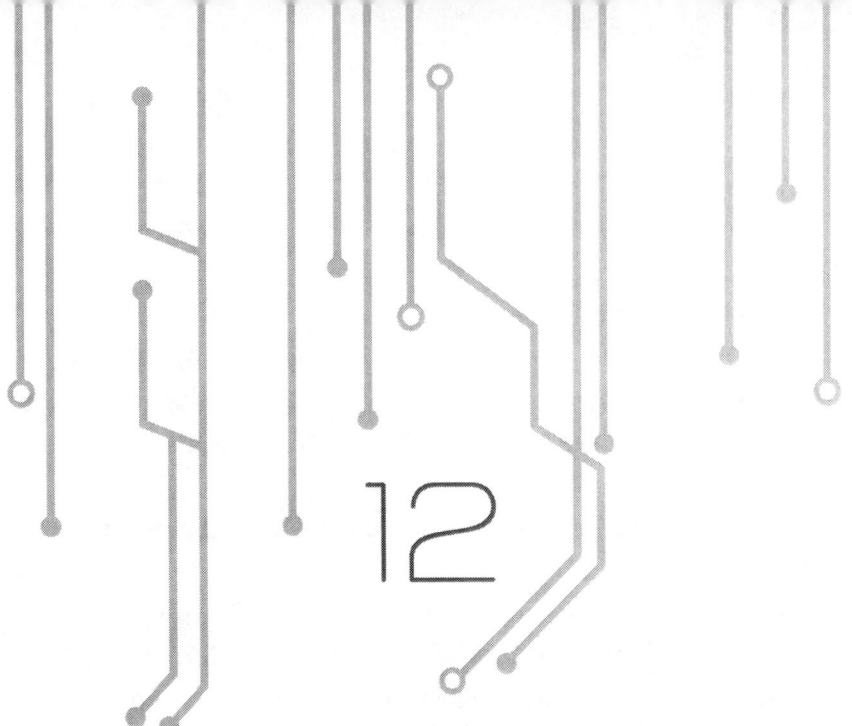

12

"I got us work," Ollie said, shoveling food into his mouth. He addressed the group around a bite of casserole.

"That's great!" Lucas said, full of false cheer. He nodded to Penelope; his goggles slipped a little to the side. "I love work."

Rowan raised an eyebrow, but said nothing. The group had gathered around the scarred table in the mismatched chairs. Millicent ate from the pink chipped plate that everyone else avoided, except she didn't really eat, but stared at her mass of noodles and sauce. She delicately picked up her bread and took a small bite.

Asher sat at his usual place with his shoulders hunched up around his ears and his elbows on the table. He didn't wear his uniform, and the stretched collar of his shirt slipped down to reveal a peek at the color of his ruined tattoo. Ren gulped at the sliver of skin, scar, and ink. He grabbed his drink and guzzled it, looking away. Water ran down his chin, and when he set the cup down and wiped his mouth with his sleeve, everyone stared.

"What?"

"Anyway," Rowan said, setting down her fork. She tented her fingers. "What is this work and where is it taking us?"

"Cargo run. Taking tech to Crei."

Ren snapped his head up. Millicent's head swiveled, and she stared at Ollie with her wide, unnatural eyes faintly glowing. Asher stiffened and lifted his head slowly, and Ren felt his hot gaze on the side of his face before Asher ducked back down. He idly moved the crust of his bread in a puddle of sauce.

"Do you think that is wise?" Asher said, his voice clipped. "I hear there might be political unrest there."

Rowan dabbed her mouth with her napkin, her lips were pressed into a thin line, as her face slowly turned red. She flicked her braid over her shoulder. Her expression was difficult to read, but from the way Ollie watched her, Ren guessed that Ollie hadn't alerted Rowan to his plan. But she wasn't going to say that, not in front of the rest of the crew. Not in front of Asher.

She ignored Asher's question. "What's the take?"

Ollie held up the credit chip in his fingers. "Half paid for already. We get the rest when we get there. I already have the coordinates."

Rowan's eyebrows twitched. "Well then, since we've already been paid."

"I don't want to go," Millicent said. "I left there."

Asher stood; his chair scraped across the floor. He dropped his napkin and left the room without a word.

"Well," Lucas said, "it seems we have dissension."

"I'm the captain. I'll say what jobs we take and where we go." Rowan's words were in response to Lucas, but they were for everyone.

Ollie had overstepped on Ren's behalf, and Ren wouldn't ever be able to repay him.

"No argument here, Captain," Lucas said, holding up his hands. "I think it's a great idea. Another planet. Wow! Who would have thought? More green things."

"You're overselling it, honey," Penelope said quietly. "But yes, great. Work is good. Credits are good."

Rowan's eyes narrowed.

"I don't want to go," Millicent said again.

Penelope patted her hand. "It'll be all right. We'll all be there. Even Ren. Right?"

"Oh, yes, sure. Yes." He sounded awkward to his own ears. "I'm along for the ride."

Millicent set her napkin on the table. "I'm finished. Thank you." She stood and lightly stepped into the corridor.

Once her footsteps retreated, Lucas sighed. "She has gotten so much weirder. Ever since we landed at Erden."

"She needs a break from the ship," Ren said. "I've been thinking about it. When I disconnected and was planetside, I could think clearer. The same may work for her. If we can get her on Crei, she may be able to… reset."

"Is that what you did?" Penelope asked. "I mean, you seem more… yourself."

Ren flexed his hands, feeling the smooth wood of the table beneath his fingertips. He focused on his lungs expanding and contracting, the hum of the air recyclers, the scrape of Ollie's fork on his plate, and the scent of the garlic in the bread. And in the far off recesses of his mind existed the pulse of the electricity, the whir of systems, the living mechanisms of the ship.

"I am myself," Ren said. "I was always myself, just a little off balance."

"Okay," Penelope said, always tactful. "And you think having Millicent go planetside will help her balance?"

"It couldn't hurt," Lucas muttered. Penelope elbowed him in the side. "What? Oh come on! You all left me with her, and she went a little loopy. It was strange, and I am not equipped to deal with weird girls. I'm the pilot. I'm awkward. I wear *goggles*. I even tried the paradoxes, and they didn't work."

Ollie snorted. "You? Awkward? Never would have guessed."

"Oh, shut up. Your sister married me."

"That's enough," Rowan said. Her tone was sharp, but her smile belied any real annoyance. "Honestly. Children. All of you."

"So we're really going? To Crei?"

"Yes." Rowan folded her hands in front of her, back straight. "We're going. But we have a slight problem."

"Another one? More problems than a star host who is acting strangely? And another one who is wanted by the Phoenix Corps?"

"I'm wanted?"

Lucas leveled Ren with a disbelieving look. "Um... yeah. You could say that."

"That's the problem," Rowan said. "We have on board two star hosts and an AWOL Corpsman. The Corps hasn't bothered them or us since we've docked, but I doubt they'll let us *leave*."

"Why haven't they approached us? What are they playing at?" Lucas asked.

Rowan shook her head. "They're waiting us out. They're waiting for us to crack under the pressure and make a move."

"And going to Crei is our move," Ollie said, confident.

Rowan sighed. "We're going to have to talk with VanMeerten."

"No." Ren's protest was immediate and raw. He couldn't. He wouldn't. No. "*Beatrice.*"

"I know, Ren. I know, but they're not going to let us gallivant off to another planet. Not after last time. We'll have to negotiate."

"Then leave me out of it."

"Okay," Rowan said with a sympathetic look. "Okay. I'll do my best."

Lucas leaned over to Penelope. "Who is Beatrice?"

Penelope shrugged.

Ren couldn't take it. Sorrow and guilt rose in his gullet and overwhelmed him; he pushed his plate away. He stood, and as Asher and Millicent had before him, he walked out.

A few hours later, there was a knock on his door. Ren sighed. He pulled out of the *Star Stream's* systems, where he'd been fine-tuning them since he had been gone for a while and wanted them in perfect shape for the trip to Crei, and settled into his body.

It wasn't Millicent, because the person knocked.

"Come in," Ren said, disengaging the lock from his bunk.

Rowan walked in. She stopped at the threshold, hovering in the doorway. She wrinkled her nose at the state of the room, and Ren flushed.

"Yes?" he croaked.

"We're leaving for Crei as soon as Lucas puts in the coordinates."

Ren frowned. "The Corps is letting us leave?"

"Yes," she said.

"What did you do?"

"I didn't do anything."

Ren's throat went tight. "Asher."

"Yes."

Ren imagined scenarios where Asher was imprisoned or disciplined. Bread and water and stew flashed in his mind's eye, and he ached thinking of Asher in a cell again.

"How?"

"You'll have to ask him, but he's not in the best mood. I'd wait until later. It's a bit of a trip. You'll have time."

"He's on the ship?"

"Yes." Rowan's green eyes flashed. "I hope you find what you're looking for there."

Rowan had two weaknesses—money and Asher. And Ren stared right at a crack in her brash and confident demeanor due to the latter.

"He didn't need to. I could've… I could've given myself up. I could've disabled the drift and the dock and anyone else for us to leave. I could've done something. He didn't need to."

"He did," she said simply.

Ren swallowed. "Okay."

"If anything happens to him because of this, because of you, I want you gone. Understand? I want you and Millicent out of my sight. I've done everything I can for you. I've risked this crew and my ship. I won't risk Asher. Not again. I allowed it before because he cares for you, but since he's met you, he hasn't made the greatest choices. And I won't allow him to die for you or for anyone."

Ren's heart stuttered. His stomach knotted. Obviously Rowan didn't adhere to Ollie's sense of chosen family as staunchly as he did.

"Okay," he said again.

"Good. I'm sorry."

"I know." He licked his dry lips. "Thank you. For everything."

Her expression softened. "I care for you too, Ren. But you have to know that this life isn't easy, and I have a responsibility to Pen and Lucas and Ollie."

"I admire you."

"Don't." She crossed her arms. "I'm not worthy of a pedestal. Don't put me on one."

Ren didn't agree, but he wasn't going to argue. "I'll make sure the ship is ready for us to depart."

"Okay."

She looked at Ren's ceiling and saw the picture taped there and the stick figure with a yellow braid and a pulse gun strapped to its side. "I miss that cog," she said softly, smiling, eyes shining. "He would've made an excellent drifter, if he could've shaken the dust off."

She talked as if Jakob had died, and, in a way, he had. Rowan would never see him again. There would be no reason for their paths to cross.

"He might still."

She didn't respond, merely nodded, before turning on her heel and leaving Ren's room. She shut the door behind her, and Ren engaged the lock again.

Flopping back to the mattress, Ren tossed his arm over his eyes and fled into the ship. At least there, things made sense, were in a predictable order, worked in a way Ren understood.

He couldn't say the same for humanity.

⏻

The route to Crei was long and uneventful. Lucas piloted. Penelope prepared. Ollie engaged Ren in a few social activities, and they worked together on the box of broken tech. It occupied Ren, and he enjoyed the comforting presence and silence around Ollie.

Ren avoided Millicent. Her behavior unnerved him. He hoped going planetside would wrest control of her body away from her star, and she would be more human. Her eyes constantly glowed now, faintly, and she moved around the ship like a ghost. Ren didn't know what Rowan said to her, but she didn't protest their destination again. Ren silently feared she would take action against the ship and kept a vigilant watch on the systems, but he detected nothing.

Ren shuddered to think that a few weeks ago, he was in a similar state. He was more grounded now. He tried to keep his excursions into the ship minimal, only going in when he needed to fix a component or needed a break from thinking too much.

Asher and he didn't talk. They passed by each other in the hallways, and the one time Ren attempted to speak to him, Asher shook his head.

"Ash, please."

"*I can't.*"

"Why? I'm sorry, okay? For what I said. For what I've done. For everything. Please."

"Ren, I can't. Don't."

And then he walked away, in strides on the verge of a full-out run, before disappearing around a corner.

Ren didn't try again.

⏻

The landing on Crei went as well as could be expected. Lucas did what he could, but the atmosphere and the pull of the gravity made the ship shudder and shake. The vid screen clouded with fog, which worried Ren. But Lucas was an expert, and he relied on the instruments and his skill to pilot them to the station. Ren gritted his teeth and did what he could with his power to aid the descent.

They docked at the station, a tower which rose from the landscape, stark against the orange sky. The slip was an open platform buttressed by huge metal girders, with a shed-like roof to protect them from the elements. Unlike the drifts and the port on Erden, it wasn't enclosed.

Lucas slid expertly into the tiny spot between another merchant-class ship and a smaller planet-bound transport. The group waited in the cargo bay for pressurization, and, once they had the signal, Ollie opened the bay doors.

He covered his mouth, and coughed, pinching his nose as he stepped out. They followed. Ren took a breath and immediately regretted it. He gagged and choked and slapped both hands over his mouth and nose. "What the stars?" Ren coughed around the words.

Penelope used the collar of her shirt to cover her face. "It's like when Lucas eats onions."

"Oh, my stars, I'm going to die. I'm getting back on the ship." Lucas pulled his goggles down over his nose. "Or I'm going to throw up."

Rowan shot him a clearly annoyed look, but waved him back. Penelope went with him, not waiting for permission, and, once they disappeared into the ship, the doors to the *Star Stream* closed tight. Ren's chest pricked when the on-board air recyclers kicked on high.

Millicent stepped daintily along the platform and walked across to the center tower. She hit the button for the lift and waited; she tapped her foot, and the hem of her dress caught on the laces of her boots. "Home," she said simply.

Crei was not green, as Ren learned. Crei was covered in metal, concrete, and factories that spit smoke in the air. Black tendrils curled through the atmosphere and blotted out the orange and pink sky. The world smelled like ash, and the air tasted like metal; the bite of it was sharp on Ren's tongue.

Ren followed on Millicent's heels, as did the others, and slipped through the doors of the lift. The lift sat in a cylinder in the middle of the landing tower. It descended quickly, and Ren grabbed onto the wall and pushed his star into the mechanisms to slow it down.

Millicent shot him a look, but with half of their group turning green from the smell, a quick drop would probably end in vomit. The lift went down and down and down, and with the descent the temperature dropped.

Ren had learned his lesson on Erden and wore a thick jacket, but he tugged it closed and fastened it as they continued.

"Are we underground?" Rowan shivered.

Millicent didn't answer.

Asher absently rubbed his shoulder. "I read that most of the populace lives in underground tunnels due to the pollution. Most of Crei's surface is uninhabitable."

The corner of Ollie's mouth lifted. "You read?"

Asher crossed his arms. "You're lucky I do."

The lift reached the end of its run, and Ren detangled from the system. When the door opened, there was a crowd waiting. Ren squeezed past bodies to get out of the lift before it went up again. Ollie grabbed his arm and pulled, and Ren popped out before the doors closed.

"What the weeds?"

Millicent rolled her head. "Personal space is not a concept here." She shuddered and craned her neck to look toward the ceiling.

She was right. Now Ren understood why she had volunteered for Vos's vision, at least on one level. Hands roamed over Ren's body, elbows jutted into his sides, shoulders brushed his chest and arms. He shrank into himself and pushed the more aggressive hands off, pressing close to Ollie's side. Ollie's size and the look on his face kept the people back, but even with the occasional force of a shove they couldn't go far.

Crei's underground was packed to the walls with people. Where there wasn't a person, there was a transport, or a vendor stall, or a pillar which shot up from the concrete ground to support the roof. Parts of the tunnel were concrete slab, others were metal, and a few walls were natural carved rock. There was no view of the sky, and if there had been a viewing portal, Ren wouldn't have been able to see the stars through the ever-present haze.

"Watch for pickpockets," Rowan said, smacking the hands of a man away from her pulse gun. "And creeps."

"Is there anywhere to get personal space?"

Millicent cocked her head, her eyes narrowed. "Space is expensive."

"I don't care," Rowan said. "I need to find our contact and I can't do it without getting my bearings."

Millicent nodded. "Follow me." A creature fluent in the living pulse of the underground society, she moved through the crowd. Her movements were a dance, and, try as he might, Ren couldn't copy it; he bumped into almost every person he passed. Ollie, a familiar presence within the heaving mass, walked at his back. Once, they were jostled apart, and Asher snapped his hand out and grabbed Ren's wrist to pull him back to the group. They didn't make eye contact, and as soon as Ren was back with the others Asher dropped his hand as if burned.

It took an eternity to walk a few yards to where Millicent stopped in front of a chained-off entrance. Ren heard the hum of a light source inside and stepped closer to look around the frame. He touched the chain, and it blared an alarm and flashed a red warning light.

Ren jumped back, startled.

Rowan raised an eyebrow. "What do we do?"

"Slide your credit chip." Millicent pointed to a reader near the end of the chain.

Rowan rooted down into her trouser pocket and yanked out a chip. She held it in front of the reader. It scanned, and then the chain dropped to the ground. Millicent skittered across and the rest of them followed. A second later, the barrier yanked back up.

"I don't like this place," Ollie said.

"I don't think anyone does." Asher said, arms crossed. "What do we do now? How are we going to find anyone in this mass of people?"

"Well, we've bought space. Let's go talk it out."

They shuffled into the building and found a large lounge with sofas and chairs. Radiation lamps in the ceiling provided artificial sunlight. Ren basked in the warmth and stretched out his arms in the empty air. In the entire space, there were only two others, and one of them obviously worked there—he carried a tray of drinks.

They found a couch and a couple of chairs and sat.

"Don't get too comfortable," Rowan muttered. "I'm certain I'm being charged by the minute."

"We should go back to the ship," Asher said. "We're not going to find anything down here and we're wasting money."

"We're not backing out of the deal we made, despotic governments or not. These are the coordinates we were given, so our contact is here somewhere."

Ollie stretched back onto the plush cushions and straightened his legs. "It's pretty coggin' genius if you think about it."

"Think about what?" Asher asked.

"Vos. Coming here."

Asher sighed and leaned forward. "No, I think it's coggin' stupid. There's no room for a base or an army or a training ground in these tunnels. There's no tactical advantage here."

Ollie shook his head. "You have a populace full of people who probably want to escape this polluted, cramped planet and would be willing to sign up for any insane cause to do so," he said, nodding at Millicent. She merely blinked. "You have tunnels and a mass of humanity to hide in. And didn't you say the populace lives mostly underground? That leaves an entire deserted surface for a training ground and a base of operation."

"He's on the surface," Rowan said. "Cogs. He's on the surface. Coming down here was a bad idea."

"No," Ren said, leaning on his bent knees. "This is perfect. On Erden, there was a message emanating from a beacon, and I found it without even trying. If Millicent could show us a place to go up, and I could have a comm of some sort, I could find him."

Rowan looked doubtful. "This isn't a small planet, Ren. Do you think you could really scan the surface and locate him? It's like finding a speck among asteroids."

"I transported a ship across a cluster. I can disable weapons with a glance and turn them against their owners with a thought. I can find a signal."

"And what are you going to do when you find it?" Asher asked. He pierced Ren with a hard gaze. "Arrest him? Talk to him? *Join* him?"

Ren narrowed his eyes. "He might have information about my brother."

"And if he doesn't?"

"I will walk away."

"Are you sure?" Asher said, tone dark. "You believe Nadie's words. She said not to seek him out, if you remember. She said not to follow—" he stopped and cut his gaze to Millicent.

"The past is fixed, but I can influence the future."

Asher rolled his eyes. "You're naïve."

"And you're a jerk."

"Stop it. Both of you." Rowan's gaze bored into Ren's. He stared back, unflinching; their conversation about Asher echoed between them. "Ollie and I will find the merchant for the tech. You, Asher, and Millicent will find a way to track the signal. Nothing more. Understood? I don't want you going off on your own without Ollie and me."

Ren wanted to protest. The words were on the tip of his tongue, but Ollie slapped his shoulder. "Trust us. We've got your back."

Ren swallowed. "Okay."

"Meet us at the dock for dinner. Ship's time." She pointed a finger at Asher, then at Ren. "Keep each other safe. Don't eat or drink anything you're unsure of. Don't get involved with anything other than what you're here to do, and, for the love of the stars, don't do anything stupid."

Asher frowned, but nodded.

Rowan and Ollie left together. Rowan sauntered out, straightening her clothes and checking her weapon before leaving the building and going beyond the chain. Ollie was right behind her, and he tossed a wave and a grin over his shoulder before disappearing.

Ren sat stiff in his chair. The awkward silence was stifling, and he would've preferred the cacophony beyond the rope. Asher continued to frown. Millicent sat blankly.

"So," Ren started.

Millicent abruptly stood. "I know a place."

She tiptoed her way to the door and Ren scrambled to follow with Asher next to him. They bumped shoulders. Asher glared. Ren's heart sank. Rowan's fierce words rang in Ren's ears.

This was going to be impossible.

Millicent led them to a row of turnstiles. She flitted to one, trailed her fingers along the mechanism, and made it turn. Ren followed, using a tendril of power to allow him to pass. He did the same for Asher, and then the three of them were on a platform with a transport in front of them.

"This way," Millicent said.

The doors opened. A stream of people piled out of the train, and Millicent squirmed between them, hopping on. Ren and Asher made it through as the doors slid closed; the back of Ren's jacket caught between them. He tugged it free, bumped into several people, and stammered apologies as he made his way to Millicent.

"Where are we going?" Ren asked, grabbing for the pole next to him as the transport lurched forward.

Millicent half-smiled. "To the end of the line."

"And how long will that take?" Asher shuffled closer to Ren as a few people moved to empty seats. Ren did his best not to lean into him.

"A while."

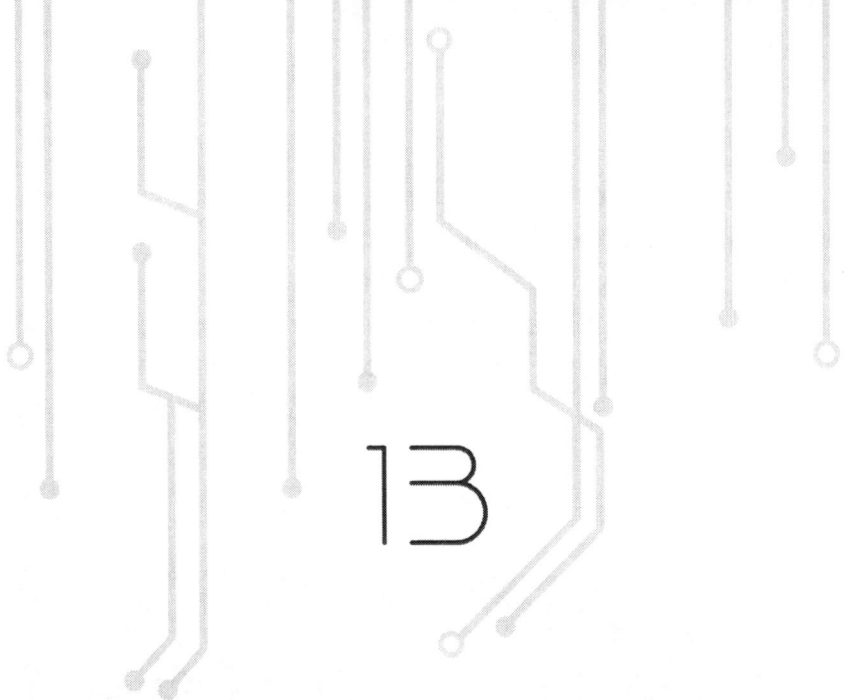

13

By the time the transport pulled to a screeching stop hours later, Ren, Millicent, and Asher were the only ones left in the car save for an individual stretched along the back wall asleep. Millicent stepped to the door and waited for it to open. A comm crackled to life, and the conductor's voice filled the metal tube, issuing a warning.

"This is the end of the line. Proceed at your own risk. These tunnels are exposed to the atmosphere. This transport will now return to base."

The doors slid jerkily open. They stepped out. The station was dark, but not abandoned. A few people milled around the space. A few boarded the train, and others wandered, talking to people, dragging boxes and sacks of items. They wore goggles and fabric tied tightly around their noses and mouths. They had hats or head coverings, and their clothes covered them from neck to toes, even their hands.

"Scavengers from the surface," Millicent whispered.

"Should we be dressed like that?" Ren asked.

"We'll be fine," she said, leading them across the station and into another tunnel.

Ren exchanged a glance with Asher. Asher shrugged and brushed past him, following Millicent farther into the dark.

Ren sighed. They were definitely not making it back to the *Star Stream* in time for dinner. Rowan would be furious.

They walked for several meters and the air became thicker, heavier. Ren squinted and saw spots of natural light beaming in through cracks in the ceiling. Pulling up the collar of his shirt, Ren placed it over his mouth and nose as they ventured deeper. The smell gradually became oppressive, as it had been on the landing pad, and Asher's face grew more pinched the farther they went..

Ren settled into his power, allowed it to flood through him, and probed the surrounding area, looking for whatever Millicent was leading them to. It didn't take him long to figure it out.

"I feel it," he said. He walked faster, jogged ahead of Millicent and Asher.

He sensed it. Pulsing with power and electricity, the blueprint was mapped out in front of him. It was a communications tower. Its roots dug into the earth, connected to an underground grid which stretched for miles and miles, but that wasn't what Ren needed. He spiraled upward, up and up, tendrils clamoring over each other, sizzling toward Crei's polluted sky.

Ren skidded to a stop in front of a ladder attached to the wall. He jumped onto the first rung and heaved his body up each step, heedless of Asher and Millicent calling behind him.

He wasn't strong enough to hoist the heavy metal cover off the access hole, but it was cracked and large chunks were missing. The holes were large enough for Ren to squeeze through. His clothes caught on jagged edges, but he wiggled until he pushed through the tunnel to the planet's surface.

He gagged, even through the fabric of his shirt. He shielded his eyes from the sun crackling through the smog, seeming to light it on fire, and creating waves of heat that shimmered in the distance. He pulled free and stood on the ground with orange ash and gravel and dust beneath the heels of his boots. He stood at the foot of the tower, a black hunk of metal rising from the surface, stark against the sky. But as he stood there, craning his neck skyward, he was also in the tower, streaking to the top and into the console, which was soaked in the noise of the planet.

Sound moved through him in waves, crashing over him like foam and spray in the lake. It was overwhelming at first, as though he had inhaled water—wrong and painful. But after a moment, he was able to filter the information, layer upon layer, siphoning out the relevant. He sorted through thousands of communications in a second. They burst through him, into his blood, into his bones, and then were propelled into the world. He was a conduit of information, of power, of light, of plans and messages.

He didn't realize Asher and Millicent had joined him until Asher's hand ghosted over his shoulder and Millicent's fingers brushed his. And then she was present with him, there in the tower. Her own star signature was a touch, a brush, against his, familiar from all their time in the *Star Stream* together.

And while Ren sorted and devoured information and was consumed by the funnel of communications, she rifled and hovered. He stacked, and she shoved; his organization fluttered around them like paper.

"What are you doing?"

"Looking."

"You're not helping."

She ignored him, flitting around him like a gnat. She burst through another set of information, disrupting Ren's process, but when she did, Ren caught a sound.

He turned his head, saw Crei awash in blue, and listened.

"What do you hear?" Millicent demanded.

Ren shushed her.

Vos's voice rang in his ears, familiar and discomfiting. He dug through the static and the encryption—Vos was more careful here than he'd been on Erden—until he found the words. "Regroup on the west abandoned line. Beneath the holy ruins…"

Ren didn't hear the rest of the message. He was cut off, then forcibly shoved out of the system. Millicent pushed and sparked, ejecting him. Gasping, gagging, his head pounding with pain, Ren fell to his knees with his fingers curling in the rough dirt.

"Ren! Ren, what happened?"

Ren clutched a hand over his mouth as he shivered with sweat and his stomach heaved. He bent over, elbows scraping along the ground.

Asher followed him down. "What's going on?"

"Millicent," he gasped. "She pushed me out. We found a message and she…" Bile rose in Ren's mouth, and his stomach clenched.

Above him, Millicent swayed, eyes glowing, face blank.

"Ren? Are you okay?"

Ren pulled his shirt from his face and spat. Stars, he felt awful, as if a sudden illness had overtaken his body. His star curled trembling in his chest.

Millicent had done this to him before. On Mykonos, when she was under Abiathar's power, when she was more star than human, before Asher was able to break her free. She had the ability to force Ren from the systems. Was she able to pull him in as well? Was she the other one Liam had alluded to in their shared dream? The one who dragged him under water, into the ship, during his dreams?

Ren blinked. Their plan hadn't worked. She hadn't disconnected when she left the ship, as Ren had. There was too much tech on Crei, and now Millicent was home, where she had learned to control her star.

"Oh, no," he said.

Millicent's gaze snapped to him, eyes blazing blue, and then she shuddered. She shook; her long hair tossed every which way. She stopped and stood still.

Asher moved toward her.

"Don't touch her," Ren said. "She'll hurt you."

Asher absently touched his shoulder. "Millicent," Asher said softly, "what do you call—"

Millicent turned on her heel and ran. From one moment to the next she went from standing like a statue to sprinting over the barren surface of the planet.

Ren jumped to his feet and sped across the dead landscape, darting through half-broken buildings and flat, barren red land. She was faster; her trick had left Ren weak and stumbling as she leapt over obstacles with her dark hair flying behind her. Ren sucked in the metallic air, coughing and sputtering. The bite was horrible. It burned his throat and chest. He gagged again and bent over with his hands on his knees as he spat out the taste.

Asher passed him; his chest heaved, but his stride was fast and even.

"Come on, Ren. Even if we don't catch her, we have to get out of this air."

Ren nodded, wondering how Asher had been so far behind, and sprinted again. Tears streamed down his cheeks, and he bit down on his lip to keep his mouth closed.

Millicent was far ahead of them now, a figure on the landscape with the pink and orange sky behind her as well as the sprawling remains of several buildings. She skidded to a halt on a gravel patch and bent down.

Ren squinted, and saw the lid at her feet. She pulled it open and disappeared into the ground.

"She went down," Ren yelled.

It was becoming difficult to see through his watering eyes, but Ren felt Asher's presence ahead of him, close by.

"I saw. Let's go."

Together they popped the lid open. Ren slid in first, bypassing the built-in ladder and falling the short distance to the bottom. He landed on his feet, but fell backward as his boot slid on broken stones.

Asher came behind him, pulling the cover closed from his position on the ladder and encasing them in darkness.

Ren sat, legs and feet aching, eyes and nose dripping. He couldn't catch his breath. He rubbed his chest and coughed. He spat again and wiped his face with the hem of his shirt. "You okay?" he croaked.

Asher was nearby. Ren heard the crunch of his footsteps and the short, staccato sound of his breathing. "Fine." His voice was raspy. "I would be better with light."

Ren closed his eyes and reached out with his power, looking for any tech. He found some and pushed into it, fixing what he needed, and, in a few seconds, the lights hummed on. The tunnel lit up and he peeked to find a long line of embedded rope lights in the ceiling following the length of the tunnel.

"It's an abandoned transport tunnel," Asher said.

Ren stood. He brushed off the dirt, wiped his face again, and glanced at Asher. He looked as bad as Ren felt. His eyes were bloodshot, and his blond hair looked brown and streaked from the dirt. Tear tracks stained his cheeks.

Asher looked at Ren; his expression seemed concerned. His stomach full of sparks, Ren bit his lip as Asher swept his gaze along Ren's frame. Finding him uninjured, Asher's unease disappeared, and the flat affect he had worn since Erden slid into place.

Ren's heart sank. He swallowed and turned his attention to the tunnel. It had obviously been abandoned for a long time. The tech was old and dusty, corroded in a few places, and the interior was just as bad. Boulders and rocks littered the tracks, water had gathered in puddles in a few places, and they heard squeaks of local creatures. Even with the glow of the lights above them, the gloom was thick, but the at least the air was clean. Air recyclers were on somewhere.

"She went this way," Ren said, tripping his way down the dark tunnel. He stumbled over a large rock and caught himself on the carved wall.

Asher caught his bicep and steadied him. He panted, his breathing staccato. "How do you know?"

"I can feel her star."

"We should find a way back to Rowan," Asher said, but he didn't stop feeling his way down the tunnel. "There has to be a connection to a running track."

"And leave Millicent to run to Vos? Who knows what she's thinking. She could tell him where I am and who I'm with. She could be confused. I don't know."

"She's slipped, Ren. You know that. She's worse off than Nadie was."

"Yeah, and I felt guilty enough leaving Nadie. I don't want Millicent to be that way too."

"You can't save everyone, Ren. You never could."

Ren jerked his arm away from Asher's grasp. "You don't have to tell me that."

"Apparently, I do."

"Then leave, Ash. Leave and find a way back. I'll join you later if I can."

"I'm not leaving you."

"Why? There's no reason for you to stay. You've made that clear."

Asher made a hurt noise. "You're a cog, you know that?" he said, voice thick and strange. "I have every reason."

Ren huffed. He ducked under a leaning and broken support, shuddering as he imagined what might happen if the pillar gave way completely. The farther they journeyed, the more Ren understood the reasons for abandoning this particular tunnel. A cave-in was imminent, judging by the sagging supports and the debris littering the ground.

"We pick the worst times to argue," Ren said, following a curve in the tracks.

"I'm not arguing."

Ren rolled his eyes. "No, you're being yourself."

"Ren," Asher said, voice low, "did you ever think about how we were able to leave Delphi?"

Ren's throat went tight. "I thought about it a lot, and I decided that if you didn't want to tell me, then I didn't want to know."

"You're a powerful being who the Phoenix Corps wanted under their control. I was considered AWOL."

"Was considered?" Ren asked. Then he stopped, the realization sudden. "You gave them you." He turned to look at Asher, really look at him. "Why? Why would you do that?"

"Why have I done anything since the prison cell?"

Ren's heart ached. "I don't—"

"You!" Asher threw his arms out to the side. "You. Okay. Telling VanMeerten about your nightmares got you back home. Following you and Jakob in the snowstorm was to ensure your safety. Revealing myself to Zag was to give you time to escape. And yes, I gave them me."

Ren crossed the space between them and grabbed Asher in a fierce hug. He wrapped his arms around Asher's shoulders, and Asher clutched him back, clenched his fists in the fabric of Ren's jacket.

"You shouldn't have done that. Your year was almost up, and you gave them more time."

Asher nodded curtly. "Yes. Among other things."

"What other things? What else did they want? Ash?" Ren stepped back and grabbed Asher's hand. "What else?"

He didn't get a chance to answer. The high whine of charging weapons interrupted them, and Ren cursed himself for missing the ping of tech so nearby. He turned to find a group of soldiers leveling weapons at them; the red slash of the Baron's standard was on their shoulders.

Reeling from the revelation, Ren swallowed down the lump in his throat. "Well, we found him," he said, holding up his hands.

Asher sighed.

"Take me to Vos." Ren demanded, sticking out his chin.

"Why should we?"

Ren let his eyes glow blue. "He'll want to talk with me."

"Holy stars," one of them whispered. "Two in one day."

Ren shared a glance with Asher before he was pushed forward; the end of the stunner was a blunt force between his shoulder blades.

"Get going."

They walked. One of the guards took point, and Ren and Asher followed with the others trailing behind them. For once, Ren wasn't afraid. This was what he wanted. He had Asher at his side. He could disable the weapons if needed. And he was going to finally talk to Vos.

They took a turn into an offshoot of the track, a narrower arched hallway, which widened into a larger space. It looked as though it was once a control center and was filled with screens and maps of the tunnels. On the map, Ren noted they were much closer to the tower where the *Star Stream* was docked than he had realized. Ren slowed, noting the pattern of the map and their position, before receiving a poke in the back to keep going. They went through another doorway.

The platform had been cleared, though a few turnstiles remained. There was a stone raised area and on it sat a shabby throne.

Vos sat there, legs crossed, hunched over. He rested one elbow on his raised knee; his chin was in his hand. His black hair was shorn close to his head, different than at the citadel, but it was him. He wore an outfit similar to the ones Ren had seen on the people of Crei—long sleeves and pants and boots, simple and dark, though a red slash adorned his shoulder—a mark of his standard. He seemed bored, with a blank expression on his thin face, but his sharp gaze landed on Ren and Asher. While he didn't seem surprised, a slow smile spread across his lips.

Standing at the base of the throne was Millicent, surrounded by troops with weapons trained on her; she didn't appear to be in any distress.

"Millie," Ren called. She lifted her head, eyes glowing, long hair falling in her face. "Come here."

She tilted her head; the movement was oddly slow. She paused, then she tiptoed away from the circle of soldiers, joining Ren's side unhindered.

Vos clapped. The noise startled Ren and echoed in the underground cavern.

"That was almost as impressive as Abiathar, and you didn't even need to tap into a star to do it. But between you and me, your ability is a little more extraordinary than mere suggestion."

Asher stiffened beside Ren. He took a step forward, shielding Ren with his body. But Ren didn't need protection, not from this man.

"Where is my brother?" Ren called.

Vos laughed. "Straight to the point. I like you." He jumped down from the raised dais, and his black boots scuffed on the stone. He didn't come closer, but leaned back on his elbows. "You're the one who escaped and foiled my designs for Mykonos. I really should kill you. You've set me back quite a bit, but I have other plans."

"I'm not interested in your plans," Ren said. "I want to know where my brother is. He disappeared in one of your raids on our village."

Vos shrugged. "He could be anywhere. I'm certainly not the only one interested in your kind." He leveled a gaze at Asher. "But you know that, don't you?"

"I don't know what you're talking about," Asher said, but his heart wasn't in it.

Vos laughed at the obvious lie. "So you didn't send a message to the Phoenix Corps? About half an hour ago? It left from the same console that your friend here used to scan for my beacon."

Asher frowned. He didn't answer; his lips were thin.

"You didn't," Ren whispered, turning to study Asher's face. "Did you?"

Asher's jaw clenched so tight Ren swore he heard his teeth grind together. "I told you. They wanted me among other things."

Ren took a step to the side, *betrayed*. And he stared at Asher with disbelief. "You used me."

Asher's façade dropped, and he paled, looking stricken. "No. No, it was for your freedom. Me and Vos for you. That's the deal."

"I'm not going peacefully," Vos said, with a wave of his hand. "But it doesn't matter. I'll have two technopaths to cover me while we escape."

Shocked, Ren took another step and wobbled. Asher reached out to steady him, and Ren knocked his hand away.

"No." Ren said to Vos. "I'm not going with you."

"Oh, I think you will," Vos said. "Think about it, Ren. That's your name, right? Ren?"

Ren nodded. He heard the question, but his thoughts were a blur. Asher had *crossed* him, as Nadie said. Asher had betrayed him.

Now it was his turn. In this future, the one Nadie had seen, Ren would cross Asher as well, but Ren bucked against it.

He wouldn't.

He wouldn't.

"What you have to decide, Ren, is if you want to join with me and have your freedom to fight against the Corps or stay here and be captured again. You grew up on Erden. You grew up with choices. You have dust ingrained in your bones. You may be a star, but you are of dirt. You will never be anything but an oddity to the drifters and to the Corps. Do you want that? To be under the control of a military which would see your village, your family, burn?"

Ren's chest heaved. His mouth went dry. "No."

"No. No one would. Come with me," Vos said, holding out his hand. "Come with me. Escape, and together, we can show the drifts what you're really made of."

Ren swallowed.

Millicent turned to him. Her fingers brushed his hand; her touch was searing. "I've watched you," she said, voice soft, seductive. "I've watched you struggle with what you are. You can't be star and flesh. You can't be both. It will destroy you. You will burn up from the inside until your skin is ash and your bones brittle."

"I… I…"

"Embrace what you are. They can't protect you from yourself. Let go."

Ren shuddered. "It was you," he whispered. "You pulled me into the ship. You influenced me, made me do all those things in my dreams. You made me almost hurt the crew."

"I helped you unlock your power. I helped you shed your restrictive shell."

Ren swallowed. "You're a star."

"Yes, and you are too. Come with us. Be happy. Be what you were made to be."

Ren took a step, swayed toward Millicent's outstretched hand. "I... I don't know."

"Ren, don't," Asher said. "They aren't telling you everything. It's a trick."

"I've watched you," Millicent said again. "In the ship, you are free. In the wires, in the circuits, you are happy."

I watched you. Ezzy had told him that too. She had watched him, in the fields, in the village, but he wasn't happy there. He remembered longing for a better life, for more.

"We don't have much time before the Corps invades our little sanctuary. The choice is yours, but make it quickly."

Millicent crossed the room with her back turned to Ren and Asher. She took Vos's hand, twining their fingers.

"I am made of stardust. I don't belong in the ground."

"No, you don't, little star." Vos smiled at her and then lifted his gaze to Ren, questioning. "Come on, Ren. Leave this birdman to his flock. You belong with us."

Ren shuddered. Vos was right. If he stayed, he'd fall under VanMeerten's control again. There would be check-ins and panic attacks and the threat of Perilous Space. If he left, he might have a chance to find Liam. He would be free to make choices.

"Ren, don't be a duster idiot. His freedom comes with a price. He's going to use you to kill people, to destroy the drifts. Are you willing to pay that? Do you think he'll let you leave if you want to? What about

Liam?" Asher pleaded. He didn't reach out; he was hindered by the soldiers standing between them, but he begged.

Ren looked around. Vos's people surrounded Asher; their weapons were trained on him.

"Liam's not here," Ren said. His voice choked. Tears welled in the corner of his eyes. He blinked, and they spilled. "I can't do this." His hands shook, and he flexed them. "You won't hurt him." He said, addressing Vos, gesturing toward Asher. "You'll let him go."

Vos bowed at the waist. "Of course. You have my word."

"Ren." Asher's voice broke on his name.

Ren took a step.

"I'm sorry I pushed you away," Asher said, words spilling out. "I didn't want to leave you, but I knew I'd have to in order to keep you free. I thought it would be easier for both of us, but I was stupid, okay? I was the idiot. *Don't go.*"

Ren wavered. He couldn't move. He couldn't decide. It was too much. But no, he'd chosen his family when he left Erden. He'd chosen Rowan and Ollie and Penelope and Lucas and *Asher*.

Asher had protected him the entire time. He didn't want to leave him. He scrubbed his hands over his eyes, then wrapped them around his stomach, holding himself together. His body trembled. His pulse raced. He felt as if he would quake apart.

He couldn't leave. He couldn't stay.

The ground rumbled beneath his feet.

"We're out of time, lads." Vos nodded toward his small group of soldiers. "He's coming with us, choice or not. Grab him."

They swarmed Ren, pinning his arms to his sides. They jerked his hands behind his back to bind them. No. No! He chose Asher. Ren fought. He squirmed and kicked, clawed and scratched. Asher shouted, pushing his way toward Ren, but there were too many bodies between them.

Above them, the ceiling cracked. Pebbles rained down. Large rocks fell, landing near where Asher and Ren struggled. The tunnel shook, and, with a blast, the rock opened to the sky.

Ren reached for his power, allowed it to flood him, and he drowned in it. The tech which surrounded him pinged in his senses. He flashed into the weapons of Vos's soldiers and into their comms, and pushed. Blue sparks gathered like fireflies caught in a wind, crackling like lightning. A thick tension hung in the air, a gathering storm of potential. Ren drew everything in; static and strength coursed through him, until he was full of energy and light and *power*. His star was a second heartbeat, alive with promise, and it consumed him.

It burst from him with a yell—an explosion of blue fire, sizzling down Ren's arms—and the men around him fell away, blown like leaves in a whirlwind.

The tunnel shuddered with the uniform stamp of feet and the whir of transports now hovering above them in the toxic air. Pieces of the tunnel fell in. Corpsmen swamped the area, filling the vast space with more bodies and tech and sound. Vos's troops, the ones still standing, fired back.

And in the middle of it all, Ren lit up like a star—fire and electricity pulsed out like the slap of waves on the shore and with the fury of a hurricane.

Vos and Millicent were gone. They disappeared from Ren's periphery. Millicent's signature faded as they ran, abandoning their people to the chaos.

Ren didn't care. He focused like a laser on those around him. Everyone was an enemy. Everyone was a threat. Everyone should cower. They were nothing in the face of a living star, and they would burn in his presence, they would fall to their knees as cinders.

Watch out. He's a technopath.
Get the weapon.
Ren, get down!

The chatter washed over him, joined the cacophony of sound and taste and touch as Ren fused with all the tech around him. He set comms to static and let loose a scream of white noise. Lights popped, raining sparks. Weapons disassembled. Transports fell to the ground. The ceiling caved.

Chaos reigned, and Ren was king.

A sharp crack pierced through the static and the power. Ren was snapped back into his body. He swayed on his feet. His eyes were half-lidded, as he stared at the destruction he'd wrought. Bodies, wreckage, and tech lay around him in the blast zone, but the hum of the tech was absent. He was disconnected from it all. Strangely, he didn't reconnect with his body as he usually did, as if there was another way for his body to not to feel like his own.

Zag stood a few feet away with an ancient weapon in his hand; smoke swirled from its barrel. Ren watched the wreath of gray as it dissipated, feeling as if he could follow, disappear into the ether like a ghost.

Asher stared at him with wide green eyes and an open mouth. He looked ridiculous. Ren wanted to laugh, but he couldn't because he had no air. He swallowed and gagged at the hot metallic taste on his tongue.

Ren swayed again. Fiery pain bloomed from his side. It spread; sizzling agony swept through his nerves, engulfed him, lit him up in a way he'd never experienced. It wasn't blue, like his power, but orange and red like flames. With a trembling hand, Ren touched the wound and raised blood-stained fingers.

"Oh," he said.

Then his legs gave out, and he fell like rubble.

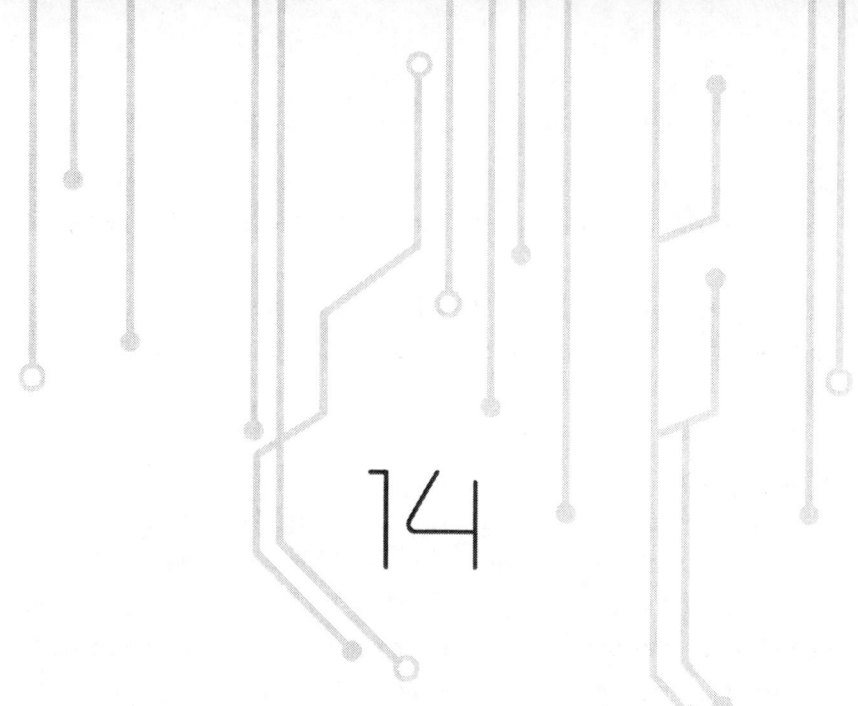

14

The ground beneath Ren was hard and cold. The colors leached away, leaving the world grey as he stared at the cracked sky.

"Ren," Asher was at his side, cradling his face in shaking hands. "Cogs, Ren. What did they do?" Asher pushed down on Ren's wound and it sparked another fire, but it was weak, sputtered out, and left Ren cold. "What the hell did he shoot you with?"

"Ash," Ren said, voice thick. "What?"

"Don't talk. Don't talk." Asher was frantic, barking at people, yelling—but his hands didn't leave Ren's body. Ren couldn't feel Asher's touch anymore. He missed it with an ache almost as sharp as the wound.

He was freezing. And then he laughed. Nadie. Asher had crossed him. But Ren would cross while in Asher's arms.

"What's so funny?" Asher asked. His voice was steady in the encroaching dark, but there was underlying fear—always fear.

"Nadie," Ren choked. "Crossing."

Realization, panic, and guilt flickered over Asher's expression, until it landed on determination.

"To the ship," he whispered. "To the ship. Hey! I need a transport. I need…"

Ren's eyes fluttered shut, and he drifted. The sharp taps on his cheeks and the urgent voice weren't important, and they were far away… so far away.

Noises. Voices. Movement.

Ren groaned when he was lifted; his body shuddered of its own accord. The pain was enough to rouse him. He stared up at the underside of Asher's jaw, where blond stubble caught the low light of wherever they were. They moved too fast, and the scenery blurred. Ren closed his eyes again; the jumble of sensation was too much.

"You stay with me. Okay? You can't get out of fighting with me by dying."

Ren smiled, then went limp again.

What happened? Ash, what happened!

Help me get him to the ship.

Stars! Ollie! Ollie, open the bay doors! And get Pen!

Ren stirred when they crossed the threshold into the ship; the *Star Stream* welcomed him, enveloped him in the warmth of its embrace. He tried to move, to alert Asher, but his body wouldn't respond. His power swelled in his chest, reminding him he was more than human, more than flesh.

Can you save him?

I don't know what… is that a bullet?

What the stars happened? Where were you two?

Put him there. Out of the way. I'll do what I can, but he's lost so much blood.

Are you okay, Ash? Are you hurt?

No. No, I'm… fine. Save him, please.

Hand me that! Where did they get a bullet for stars' sake?

This was their only option to stop him.

Why did they need to stop him? Ash?

Ren's hand fell off Penelope's table when she jostled him. His fingers grazed the hull. He didn't hesitate. He fled the pain and the turmoil. He fled his unresponsive body. He fled the phantom sensations of needles and hands.

He's still bleeding.

I'm doing the best I can. I don't know…

He fled toward safety. He fled into the ship. Ren dissipated into the ether, into the circuits, into the wires. There, he was happy. There, he was safe.

He's gone.

⏻

Ren watched from the vid feeds. He stared down at the figure on the cot, hooked up to machines, pale and small under blankets.

Someone sat next to the bed… someone… someone Ren knew. Asher. Asher sat next to the bed and held Ren's limp hand clasped in his own, mumbling words that didn't make sense. His blond head was bowed; his lips were pressed to his knuckles.

"I'm so sorry. What have I done? What have I done?"

Ren switched feeds, crossed the room, found another angle. He sat watching. Time ticked by, calculable down to the millisecond, not measured in moments or feelings, which were inconsequential to him now. All that mattered was the ship and the systems, operations and electricity and data.

"I have to leave. Pen is going to watch over you. And Rowan. And Lucas. Ollie, too, if he can stand to. He's upset."

The lights flickered. A short in the mechanism, but Ren didn't rush to fix it. Why did Asher need to leave? He shouldn't leave. Ren didn't want him to leave.

A woman—Rowan, her name was Rowan—walked into the room. She lightly touched Asher's shoulder. "They're here for you."

Asher gently placed Ren's hand back on the table and tucked the blanket tighter over the body.

"Watch him."

"You know he's going to come looking for you when he wakes up. It'll be the first thing he'll want to do."

"I don't know about that. I betrayed him."

"You were protecting him. He'll understand."

Power surged in the bay door mechanism; the lock stuck. People waited outside, dressed in uniforms, ornate birds on their shoulders—Phoenix Corps. Ren hesitated for half a second before fixing the glitch and allowing them entrance.

Rowan grabbed Asher in a hug, and they embraced tightly.

"We could run," she whispered. "They think he's dead. They wouldn't follow. And if they did they'd never find us."

"They would. And they'd figure out he's still alive and they would take him. And they'd hurt you and the crew."

She nodded, her chin digging into his shoulder. "Take care, little brother."

"You, too."

They parted.

Asher left.

Following him, Ren jumped to another feed and watched the bent figure walk down the corridor and into the bay. The group of soldiers waited for him. They surrounded him and escorted him out of the ship.

We're departing for Mykonos.

Aye, captain.

Stars and space.

We've got work.

Minutes. Seconds. Hours.

New coordinates.

Another drift.

A dock.

Space and stars.

Credits.

Coordinates. Route set.

A malfunction. Fixed.

A message.

Seconds. Hours. Minutes.

Wake up, brother! Wake up.

Ren gasped when he woke. His back arched off the metal; his mouth and eyes were open. His muscles pulled taut for a long moment before he flopped back to the table, exhausted. He breathed, lungs aching, body shivering from the influx of adrenaline and from the frigid air. He weakly raised his head.

The ship was dark. And Ren was alone.

the BROKEN MOON series conclusion
ZENITH DREAM

WHEN REN WAKES UP FROM his life-threatening injury, he finds himself on the *Star Stream* without Asher. He is informed that Asher has left with the Phoenix Corps and that the Corps believes Ren to be dead. Despite the opportunity to disappear, Ren is determined to fix his mistakes. He convinces the crew to join him for one last mission—find Asher, free Liam, and escape from the Corps' reach. But a war is brewing between the Corps and an army of star hosts, and, despite his wish to flee, Ren is drawn into the conflict. With his friends by his side, Ren must make a choice, and it will affect the future of his found family and the cluster forever.

Acknowledgments

THERE ARE SO MANY PEOPLE to thank for the existence of this second piece of the Broken Moon trilogy. First, I must thank the amazing team at Interlude Press for the support, patience, and opportunity to write this book.

I'd also like to thank my family. My husband, Keith, who takes on more than his fair share of chores and kiddo responsibilities so that I may have time to write and edit. I'd like to recognize my biggest fan—my brother, Rob, who bought way too many copies of *The Star Host* to hand out to his friends.

One of the hardest parts of writing a novel is writing in a vacuum without instant feedback. So I need to thank my team of friends who pushed me to keep writing and also listened to me rant, plot, and whine as needed. Thanks to Kristinn, Ruth, Katie, and my entire twitter feed.

Thanks to my coworkers at my day job who allowed me to practice my author signature on their copies.

And I'd like to thank Malaprops bookstore for being an amazing independent bookstore in my community and for their dedication to diverse books. Thank you for treating me like a celebrity when I came to speak to a small crowd about my debut.

And always thank you to my amazing friends from The W&M Sci-Fi and Fantasy Club.

Lastly, 2016 was rough for the sci-fi community. We lost several icons who had major impact on sci-fi as a genre, but also had an impact on me personally. They influenced my work and my life, and I am forever grateful for their movies, their music, their tv shows, and their dedication to sci-fi. Thank you, David Bowie, Ron Glass, Kenny Baker, Anton Yelchin, and of course, Carrie Fisher. To a young girl who wanted to be a princess and wield a blaster, Carrie's portrayal of Princess Leia was everything. I'll never forget the way she inspired me as a woman in sci-fi, but also as a writer, an unapologetic voice, and as an advocate for mental health. Though she is gone, her legacy will live on to inspire girls and women to reach for the stars and to accept themselves as they are.

ABOUT THE AUTHOR

F.T. LUKENS IS AN AUTHOR of Young Adult fiction who got her start by placing second out of ten thousand entries in a fan community writing contest. A sci-fi enthusiast, F.T. loves *Star Trek* and *Firefly* and is a longtime member of her college's science-fiction club. She holds degrees in Psychology and English Literature and has a love of cheesy television shows, superhero movies, and writing. F.T. lives in North Carolina with her husband, three kids, and three cats.

Her first novel in the Broken Moon series, *The Star Host*, was published by Duet Books in 2016.

One **story** can change **everything**.

an imprint of interlude press

@duet**books**

Twitter | Tumblr

For a reader's guide to **Ghosts & Ashes** *and book club prompts, please visit duetbooks.com.*

also from duet

The Star Host by F.T. Lukens

Ren grew up listening to his mother tell stories about the Star Hosts—mythical people possessed by the power of the stars. Captured by a nefarious Baron, Ren discovers he may be something out of his mother's stories. He befriends Asher, a member of the Phoenix Corps. Together, they must master Ren's growing power and try to save their friends while navigating the growing attraction between them.

ISBN (print) 978-1-941530-72-6 | (eBook) 978-1-941530-73-3

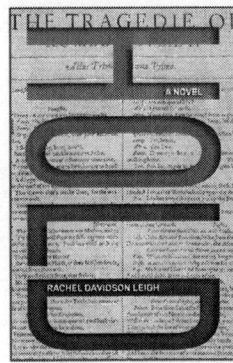

Hold by Rachel Davidson Leigh

After Luke Aday loses his sister, his best friends welcome him back to school with open arms, but it isn't the same. When he meets charismatic new student, Eddie Sankawulo, something life-changing happens: In a moment of frustration, Luke runs into an empty classroom, hurls his backpack against the wall—and the backpack never lands. Luke Aday has just discovered that he can stop time.

ISBN (print) 978-1-945053-09-2 | (eBook) 978-1-945053-10-8

Not Your Sidekick by C.B. Lee

Welcome to Andover, where superpowers are common—but not for Jessica Tran. Despite her heroic lineage, Jess is resigned to a life without superpowers when an internship for Andover's resident super villain allows her to work alongside her longtime crush Abby and helps her unravel a plot larger than heroes and villains altogether.

ISBN (print) 978-1-945053-03-0 | (eBook) 978-1-945053-04-7

CPSIA information can be obtained
at www.ICGtesting.com
Printed in the USA
LVOW08s1134020717
540115LV00002B/363/P